THE CHARMER
THE LEBLANC BROTHERS
LAYLA HAGEN

CONTENTS

CHAPTER ONE

JULIAN

"Uncle Julian, do you still have friends at the candy factory?" my adorable little niece, Bella, asked me. We were all gathered at our parents' and grandparents' mansion in the Garden District. Now that Christmas was over, everyone was preparing for the Carnival celebration culminating in Mardi Gras.

"Of course," I assured Bella.

She scrunched her little face in a frown. Even though she was already eight, I kept forgetting that she wasn't a baby or a toddler anymore. She was closer to being a teenager. I shuddered at the thought.

"I miss their candies."

Chad, one of my brothers who was sitting two chairs away, spoke to his daughter. "Cricket, you eat plenty of candy."

"But you always say that during the Carnival season I can eat as many as I want."

I was going to make sure she got a delivery of everything she liked, so I leaned into her, whispering conspiratorially, "I've got you. You can count on me, Bella."

She gave me a toothy grin.

I adored this little girl as if she were my own. My brother Chad had been a single dad for many years. His ex-wife had scarcely involved herself in Bella's life, which allowed my niece to spend a lot of time with the family.

"Is everything going according to plan for our float?" Mom asked. She was sitting next to Dad. Grandma Isabeau and Grandpa David were on the other side of the table along with Grandma Celine and Grandpa Felix. Yeah, this was a huge and crazy household. They all lived together and somehow made it work.

Our grandparents were very close and had been for decades even though they'd been rivals at some point in the past. They'd owned competitive businesses and had been dead set against my parents getting together at first, but it all worked out in the end, and the New Orleans conglomerate was stronger than ever because of it.

"There was a hiccup along the way, but my team took care of it," I replied.

"What happened?" Isabeau sat straighter in her chair.

"Is this because of the flooding that happened last month?" Mom asked. "I heard it affected the warehouses."

"That's exactly the issue, but don't worry, I'm on top of it. Everything will be ready in time for the parade."

The parade was an annual tradition, and our families had been involved for generations. The Carnival season was my favorite. It started at Epiphany in January and lasted until Fat Tuesday—Mardi Gras—which marked the end of Lent, the forty-day fasting season between Ash Wednesday and Easter. Basically, it was a big-ass party that went on for weeks, or months, depending when Easter was on any given year. There were numerous parades during this time, some smaller than others. Our own float—the motorized kind—was huge.

"Good," Celine said, putting her hand theatrically on her chest. "I couldn't show my face in town if our sponsored float wasn't perfect."

"I wouldn't dare show my face in this house if it wasn't," I assured her with a wink.

I rose to stand, ready to end the evening, "All right, everyone. It was good catching up, but I'm heading to the bar tonight," I said.

The house was quieter than usual tonight, but after all, it was just me, Chad, and Bella visiting. When all six of my brothers were here, plus Chad's fiancée, it was so loud that we could barely hear one another. But I liked the chaos and spending time with the family.

"Thank you for taking care of everything Carnival related," Isabeau added.

"Sure, my pleasure. You already have so much to deal with, Grandma. I can handle it."

She bristled a little at the word *Grandma*.

Because my parents had kids young, my grandparents had insisted that they wanted us to call them by their names. They only mellowed when Bella came along and called them Nana or a variation of it. They were still a bit iffy about us grandkids actually calling them grandparents, but I liked to tease them.

After bidding goodbye to everyone, I headed straight to my car. The drive from the Garden District to the French Quarter didn't take long. Fortunately, I had a good parking spot behind the bar, because the city was packed.

I got out of the car and knew we had a full house tonight by the sounds coming from inside. Even with the windows and doors closed, the noise found its way out. But on a typical Saturday night, the French Quarter was always busy. And things were only going to get crazier as the Carnival season approached.

The Orleans Conglomerate was a huge company and was made up of multiple branches: restaurants, bars, bakeries, music venues, you name it. The Broussard and LeBlanc families covered a lot of ground. I was running the bars. Each of my brothers ran different businesses, and even so, we still managed to get involved in plenty of other things, like the float business.

Isabeau acted like I was doing her a big favor, because she and Celine had been responsible for the float before they retired. But it wasn't inconveniencing me at all. I was an expert at delegating, which was the main reason why I'd been able to raise profits and open five more bars. My instincts were sharp, and I always hired people I trusted, which was key. Most times I could leave them to their own devices and rarely needed to follow up. But this float business had been more annoying than I'd anticipated.

The owner of the company who was previously doing all the decorations for our float had gotten wind of my last email. She'd sent me some very unprofessional emails in return complaining about my decision. Honestly, I couldn't believe the nerve of this woman and quickly forwarded her responses to my assistant. I didn't have time for anything like that. The woman just needed to accept it and get over it. It wasn't as if we were in breach of contract or anything.

"Julian, thank God you're here," one of my bartenders said as I stepped inside. The Lucky Spot was my favorite bar. I had an office here, too, and worked from it more often than from the headquarters of the conglomerate, which was on Royal Street.

I fucking loved coming here, and not just on weekends. I often dropped by during the week, too, after the workday was over. It was on Dumaine Street, right in the middle of the hustle and bustle. I liked the change of pace and the energy of the bar.

"Hit me up. What's wrong?"

"Some of our delivery guys didn't show up tonight."

Not uncommon, especially this time of year. So many suppliers overbooked themselves.

"Send some of the boys shopping right away." Any solution was better than none. "Do you know what we're out of?"

"Yeah, I've got a list."

"Perfect. Then give it to them."

I looked around at the customers packing the bar. They all had a drink in their hand and were chatting away or dancing. I'd never tire of the energy in this area. I traveled the world, but absolutely nothing compared to the French Quarter on a weekend.

I looked at my staff and zeroed in on Alexa, one of our younger servers. She looked flushed. No, on second glance, her eyes were red. Maybe she had allergies? I walked over to her.

"Alexa, you feeling okay?" I asked.

She looked up at me and answered, "Um, well, I'm coming down with something, I think. I thought I was getting better, but ever since I started the shift, my nose keeps running."

"Go home."

She jerked her head back. "But my shift just started."

"You're only going to get worse if you work when you're sick. Go home."

The corners of her mouth turned downward. "But I'm..." She shook her head.

"You'll still get paid for the shift. Tips too," I assured her. I took care of my employees.

Her mouth fell open. "Really?"

"Did HR not tell you about how we do things around here?"

She shrugged. "They might have mentioned something, but in my experience, things like that are too good to be true."

"Not at the Orleans Conglomerate. Go home. I'm here tonight anyway and can easily help out."

"Thanks, Julian. You're really a great boss."

"Music to my ears. Now come on, leave before you infect the whole place and we get a bad rep." I didn't particularly give a shit about a bad rep, but she needed to get home ASAP.

As I headed behind the counter, I took out my phone, intending to send an email to our drink suppliers to move the delivery time earlier in the afternoon.

Oh, for fuck's sake. I had another email from our former supplier for the float. The woman just wouldn't stop.

Title: Face-to-face meeting.

I snorted. The last thing I had time for was a disgruntled business owner. This was the third email she'd sent. My opinion of her had worsened with every single one of them. This was simply not how business was done. I'd been tempted in the beginning to tell my assistant to hire them back for next year but then quickly changed my mind. I didn't care for her unprofessionalism.

But curiosity won, and instead of deleting the email, I opened it.

Mr. Leblanc,

It is highly unprofessional of you to dissolve our contract without even bothering to meet me face-to-face, business owner to business owner. And frankly, using your assistant and lawyers to placate me is beneath the LeBlanc & Broussard name. This is the address of the shop if you find yourself in the vicinity.

Georgie

I stared at the email. Was she serious? Who did she think she was? Did she think I was running some mom-and-pop shop that I could just hop on by at the drop of a hat? If I met personally with everyone who had an issue, I'd never get any work done.

I deleted the message. She'd give up eventually. I emailed our drink supplier after that.

Georgie. What was that short for? Georgina? I imagined an elderly woman hiding behind her computer and writing angry emails. It wasn't my fault their warehouse had been flooded. Granted, it wasn't hers either. The only fault she had was making a bad contract that allowed me to pull out of it in case something like this came up.

Whatever.

They probably had insurance that would cover all the damage. Or they should have, anyway. It wasn't my responsibility if another business owner had their shit together or not. "Every man for himself" was my motto. I was just protecting my family's interests and legacy.

What the fuck am I doing? Am I starting to have a guilty conscience?

"We thought we might find you here."

The familiar voice knocked me out of my thoughts. My youngest brothers, Anthony and Beckett, were here. They often dropped by on Saturday evenings.

"Is it me, or is this place even more crowded than usual?" Beckett asked. "Carnival season hasn't even officially started."

"Sazerac?" I asked unnecessarily. That was another tradition of sorts in NOLA.

"You know it," Anthony said.

I shouldn't have favorites among my brothers, but these two were definitely at the top of the list.

Since I was the oldest and they were the youngest, there was quite a huge age difference between us. Nowadays, it didn't matter, but back when we were kids, it was another story altogether. I'd been fiercely protective of both of them. Then, once they were old enough to be up to no good, I taught them everything they needed to know, much to our brother Xander's chagrin. I often joked that he was adopted, because he was so different from the rest of us. Always exacting, always double-checking every detail. He was a grump.

"Is Zachary coming too?" I asked Beckett.

"Nah, he has got a date tonight. Speaking of which, I spotted my *next* date in the crowd."

"Beckett! Not in my bar."

"Dude! Your employees are off-limits, not your customers. That was the deal."

"You're right." I whistled as I put the cocktails on the counter in front of my brothers. "Your Sazeracs are ready."

As they chugged them down, I remembered Bella's request for sweets—and sent another email. I was determined to never disappoint my niece. She was very levelheaded—well, at least as levelheaded as an eight-year-old could be—and she rarely requested extravagant things. Although, she very well could, considering her family was one of the richest and most powerful in the city.

Chapter Two

Georgie

"All right, I'm done with this one," Zelda, my assistant and friend, said.

I got up from my seat, rolling my shoulders and moving my hips a bit too. I'd gotten stiff from sitting too long.

"That looks perfect," I told her, admiring the mask she'd just finished.

She yawned. Looking behind her, I noticed that everyone looked spent. I had a team of three, including Zelda, and they'd been working overtime ever since the damn flood.

Books & Beads sold—as the name suggested—books, beads, and everything anyone could want for Carnival.

"All right, you know what, girls? Everyone go home. I'll close up here."

Zelda looked at me. "Are you sure? You're tired too. You were here before everyone else."

True. But the work was endless, and if I didn't make it happen, no one would. There was no way I could ask them to come at six o'clock in the morning like I did when they were already so overworked.

"I'm fine." I stretched my arms over my head, plastering a smile on my face. "Everyone, thank you so much for going above and beyond. I promise I'll make things work. We'll get back on our feet."

Zelda gave me an uneasy smile while the rest of the team fidgeted in their spots.

I sighed. No one truly believed that. I wasn't sure I did either.

"We'll see you on Monday." Zelda narrowed her eyes. "Are you going to be here tomorrow as well?"

I pressed my lips together and then gave her a guilty smile. "Of course. The shop is open."

"But you'll be working on more masks, too, won't you?"

"Yeah."

"Look, I'll come, too, and—"

"Absolutely not," I interrupted her. "Come on, all of you, go. You deserve Sunday off. Things will calm down after Mardi Gras."

That was an understatement. Things might calm down permanently after Mardi Gras if I didn't manage to get some customers quickly.

I followed the team and, for no reason at all, started smiling. I loved my shop.

We had a little workshop in the back, although we did have a bigger operation near the warehouse. But at the moment, we were working on our exclusive handmade masks right here. People went wild for them last year.

The rest of the team filtered out while Zelda hesitated in the doorway. "Georgie," she said, "I'll come tomorrow."

"Please don't. Look, you're young. It's Saturday night. Go wild in the Quarter. But not *too* wild, so stay safe."

She laughed. "I'm young? I'm the same age as you."

I often forgot that I was twenty-eight. I'd been working at the shop since I was thirteen. In many ways, I felt like I was middle-aged already, especially now. The flood definitely added ten years to my life.

"There's no need. I'll work on the masks from the front so I can also tend to customers."

"If the shop is swamped, give me a shout and I'll come here, okay?"

"Thanks, Zelda."

I gave her a quick hug. She was a great friend.

After she left, I locked the door, turned the sign to Closed, and sighed. I'd been running back and forth today between tending to the shop and painting the masks, which was why everyone else had done far more masks than I had. The truth was, I would be swamped tomorrow because the Carnival season was approaching. But my team needed to rest.

I'd intended to hire some part-timers like I did every year, but the flood near killed us, and I just didn't have the funds to even think about extra help.

I loved, loved, *loved* Books & Beads. It was on Burgundy Street, where rent was acceptable and foot traffic was still great. It had been in my family for two generations. I came from a long line of strong Southern women. My nana had been a single mom and opened the shop all on her own. Then my mom took it over. She'd also been a single mom, and I'd practically grown up here in the store. Once I was thirteen, I was an unofficial part-time employee. After I finished my homework, I worked here right up to closing time. Then Mom and I would go back home to finish up on other chores. Once I turned sixteen, she hired me officially, paycheck and all. I'd felt like I was rich.

I studied business at Loyola College because I'd been determined to run this place successfully. Up until this flood, I'd done so well. I had insurance to cover much of the damage, so thankfully the repair work was moving quickly. But the main problem was that the contracts we used were old, from my grandmother's time.

She'd been far too lenient, allowing customers a loophole in case of natural disasters. Even if we could still deliver on time, they could cancel the contract without penalty.

My team and I had worked tirelessly since that fateful night two weeks ago, but our big, longtime family customers still dropped us. The one that hurt most was the LeBlanc deal because we were currently making all the costumes and decorations for their float. I'd used the insurance money to fix everything the flood had damaged—which I'd told Julian LeBlanc repeatedly. It seemed he just didn't care, and now I was sitting on all that inventory.

I clenched my jaw at the thought of that coward. He wouldn't even discuss this with me. I was sure if we met, he could see our progress and reconsider. But no, he was an ass. He'd just let his lawyers and their legal jargon handle it, and in my book, that was cowardly.

But I was determined to stay positive. Things would work out one way or another.

I looked around the shop with a smile. It was cozy and quaint and authentic to the time. Not much had changed since Grandma set it up. and that's what made us so popular.

The wooden shelves were older than I was. We'd updated the ones displaying the beads and other accessories a few years ago, mainly because I'd found others that better showcased our merchandise. We were one of a kind, even in the Quarter. People trusted us. We had a great reputation. Still a family-owned company, and we had prominent customers. Well, at least we used to.

Now, because Julian LeBlanc had canceled with us, our other big customers had followed his lead.

Sighing, I went to one of the bookshelves, grabbed my favorite book, and sat in Nana's armchair. The leather was worn but still intact. It smelled like jasmine—her favorite fragrance—and it comforted me.

She'd been a midwife as well, and she often said that she smelled like babies. I hadn't been around many to confirm that, but in my memory, she'd smelled heavenly.

As soon as I started reading, my entire body relaxed. This was hands down my favorite way of spending Saturday night: with a good book and wine. I got up and opened the cabinet, taking a small bottle of red from under the counter, where I kept snacks too. After uncapping it, I poured myself a glass.

Resituating myself, I took a sip. *Yum.* This was *perfect.* Mom once joked that I was twenty-eight going on forty-eight, but that was fine by me. On days like this, I truly missed my mom. She'd moved out to the bayou after retiring, and I didn't want to stress her out with the goings-on here. She'd asked how things were after the flood, but I assured her I could manage.

I finished my glass after reading only ten pages but decided not to pour a second one, since I hadn't eaten much today and didn't want to get drunk or even tipsy. I loved the French Quarter to bits, but on Saturday nights, one had to have their wits about them. Especially since I had to cross most of it to get to St. Louis to take the bus. I lived in the Gentilly neighborhood, renting the world's tiniest home. The bus ride took thirty minutes, but I didn't mind my commute because it gave me time to wind down.

Time to go home, Georgie, before the wine gets to your head.

I got up from my armchair, then washed and put away my glass. After straightening things up, I went to grab my bag. Before leaving, I checked the back door—and a good thing I did, because it wasn't locked. Then I went back to the front. I always left out the front door, as the back alley was a bit too dark for my taste.

Stepping out of Books & Beads, I took in a deep breath. The January air was cold and fresh. Jazz music and a cacophony of voices resounded through the streets. What an evening! I loved that I got to walk a bit through the Quarter every night, just to take it all in.

What if I make a pit stop before heading home? The wine was giving me dangerous ideas—and a lot of courage.

So, instead of going to the bus station, my feet took me another direction altogether. I knew Julian LeBlanc had several bars here in the Quarter—I'd stalked him a bit, thinking I'd give him a piece of my mind, but promptly chickened out. Apparently, he was often at the bar on Dumaine. I could take a look and see if he was there. Maybe I would even find an opportunity to talk to him.

I stopped short as droves of partygoers moved around me, realizing I hadn't even bothered to check my appearance. Ugh, I probably looked like something the cat dragged in. I was wearing jeans and a light sweater, and my blonde hair was piled up in a messy bun. I usually used black eyeliner because it made my blue eyes pop, but I hadn't managed to apply any today, as I didn't have time.

Oh, whatever. I wasn't going there to impress "the" Julian LeBlanc. I simply wanted to understand why he'd canceled our contract without a second thought when we'd promised we could deliver everything he needed for the float on time. But there was no swaying him—or his lawyer, at least.

I carefully waded through the Quarter, avoiding Bourbon Street. Not just because it was crazy on Saturday evenings, but because my ex-boyfriend, Kyle Deveraux, owned a large club over there. He was one person I hoped I never saw again.

Hard as I tried, I couldn't remember why I'd started dating him in the first place. He was different from the guys I usually went out with. Kyle was from an old, established NOLA family, and he never let me forget it. I made myself a promise after we broke up that it was the last time I'd date a powerful man.

I shook my head, determined to forget about Kyle. I'd always been good at recognizing the good in my life, so no need to dwell on the bumps in the road.

Instead of getting lost in my thoughts, I entertained myself by looking around. I loved the Quarter. I couldn't wait to live here one day. Right now, it was out of my budget, but it was on my vision board. I liked the architecture and how steeped in culture this area was. Most of all, I liked that everything here was old. I preferred old buildings to new ones. They had a soul of their own and a story.

Granted, lots of the stories told of the French Quarter homes were a bit creepy. Though I was born and raised here, I'd never seen a ghost or anything remotely similar. That didn't mean I didn't believe in them, though. All good Southern girls did. At least that's what my mom always said.

I was surprised by all the Carnival-themed decorations they had up already. I couldn't remember ever seeing them up so early. That was good in my opinion, as it should get people in the celebratory mood, and that meant possibly more business for Books & Beads.

The smell of beignets reached me from a passerby. I was starting to get even more dangerous ideas. After I spoke to Julian, I could head to Café Du Monde and indulge in a beignet before catching my bus. And I could also pass by my favorite Italian deli and buy a muffaletta sandwich. That would make an excellent dinner. I was a lousy cook, and I had nothing waiting for me at home.

I quickened my pace, and a minute later, I turned down Dumaine.

The bar was in one of those houses I loved—red facade and colorful shutters. It was chock-full, and the second I stepped inside, I could see its appeal.

Oh, sweet Lord. It was crawling with even more people than I'd expected. The French Quarter had no shortage of evening establishments, but there was something different about this one. It was huge but cozy at the same time. The lighting was inviting, but not so dim that you couldn't see where you were stepping. And the music was truly amazing. They had a live jazz band in one corner that didn't take up much space, and they played wonderfully. I was tempted to enjoy it for a bit, but I'd come here for a reason. I needed to find to Julian LeBlanc.

I headed to the bar, intending to sweet-talk one of the bartenders into introducing me to him. I assumed the man was in the back, working on the books or something. But I quickly realized this might take longer than I thought, as there were tons of customers lining up for drinks, and I didn't want to push my way forward.

I glanced at each bartender, and my gaze fell on one exceptionally good-looking man to the left of the bar. He was exquisitely handsome, with vibrant blue eyes, dark hair, a muscled body, and tattoos on his forearms.

Well, well, well. At least I have something to feast my eyes on while I wait.

He was chatting with two guys who resembled him a lot.

"Julian, I need another one of your Sazeracs," one of them said.

I mentally gasped. *The hot guy is Julian?* That just couldn't be. I knew I should've googled him to get an idea of who I was looking for.

"I'm honored," Julian replied.

"Hey, dude, it's my turn. I ordered my drink before him," a pissed-off customer said.

Julian looked directly at him. "I'll get yours next, and this one is on the house. How about that?"

"Well, I like that," the guy said. "You're okay, dude."

Julian smiled, averting what could've been a touchy situation.

So, Julian *did* have people skills. He simply didn't want to deal with me. And why was he so hot?

Oh, stop focusing on how hot he is, Georgie. That doesn't change anything. I kept my eyes firmly on him as I advanced in line. He moved his hands with dexterity, which told me he bartended often. When I heard that Julian LeBlanc spent time in the bar, I assumed he was somewhere in the back or just enjoying the music, not actually working. That earned him points in my book.

No, damn it, Georgie. Zero points. Zero!

I didn't want to antagonize him, though, so I needed to find a good approach. I needed him to actually talk to me long enough so I could plead my case.

My turn arrived a few minutes later.

"What can I get you?" he asked.

"Nothing, thank you. I need to speak with you. I'm Georgie." I swallowed hard. "From Books & Beads."

He narrowed his eyes. "Doesn't ring a bell, but I can get you a drink on the house."

Doesn't ring a bell?

"I emailed you a few times about the float decorations you canceled."

His eyes turned instantly cold, the smile he'd had for other customers falling. I knew it had been too good to be true. It had all been for show. Pity, because it had been mesmerizing.

"I need to talk to you about your order," I persisted.

He shook his head. "I have a full house tonight. I can't afford to waste any time discussing what's already happened. The order has been canceled. If you would excuse me, there are paying customers behind you."

"No problem. I'll just wait until the place clears out, and we'll talk then."

"The place won't clear out. It's a Saturday evening," he said slowly.

Did he think I was stupid?

"I can wait until there's a lull or something." I was determined not to back down.

"There is nothing to talk about."

The two guys he'd been chatting with before zeroed in on me.

"What's wrong?" one of them asked.

"Nothing, Anthony. I'm handling this." He turned back to me. "Our lawyers already explained that we're within our full rights to cancel our order."

"But why do that when we can get everything you need for the float in time? We told you that from the beginning." My voice cracked. Lord, I was nervous. "We've been preparing your float for generations, and we're the best at it. We know what you want."

"Well, we found another vendor quickly enough."

I winced. *Vendor!* That felt so cold. We were more than that. My grandmother had a relationship with his grandparents all these years. How dare he just blow us off like that! I was getting pissed and knew I needed to keep myself in check.

"Look, it's nothing personal," he went on.

Was it my imagination, or was he looking at my lips? My entire body felt hot, which was insane. I was supposed to be mad, determined, but it was as if my brain and my body were disconnected.

"The LeBlanc float was our biggest customer. This is ruining my business."

Why the hell did I have to tell him that? I didn't need his pity.

"I'm sorry to hear that, but business is business."

I swallowed hard.

"Your contract allowed us to—"

"Oh, you know as well as I do that that contract was drawn up by my own grandmother, not by a lawyer." My voice caught. "She was a good person. She wanted her clients to be happy. She never imagined someone would take advantage of it."

Julian was silent for a brief moment. That last part wasn't fair, and really, I knew about the clause, or lack thereof.

"This is very unprofessional behavior," he replied finally.

I saw red.

"Really? You think so? You think *I'm* the unprofessional one? You're the one hiding behind your lawyers."

"What the hell does that mean? I'm the CEO," he said. "I don't have time to deal with everyone I'm doing business with. That's why I have lawyers."

"Damn, that's harsh," the guy named Anthony said.

I swallowed hard. "Right, well, I can see we're not getting anywhere tonight."

"My decision is final," Julian insisted, and I could feel my world crumble a little. I'd hoped to make things better tonight, but I went and made them far worse. I could've convinced him to hire us again, even if just for next year, but what had I done instead? Completely antagonized him—the exact thing I'd told myself not to do.

"Lady, will you move out of the way? I'm waiting to order," a guy behind me said.

"Yeah, sure. Sorry. My bad," I said, stepping away.

I was definitely heading to Café du Monde.

CHAPTER THREE

JULIAN

I always prided myself on being very decisive. I never hesitated or changed my mind on things, and that had served me well in business. I'd rarely felt guilty regarding my decisions, but apparently there was a first time for everything. When I woke up the next morning, I started replaying the conversation in my mind that I'd had with my assistant about the float.

It all came back to me easily as I sipped my coffee while looking down the street from my balcony. I lived in the French Quarter, only two streets away from the bar and office. It was so quiet in the morning that it was almost bizarre, considering how crazy it got at night.

Around Christmas, my assistant told me that the company producing everything for the float we were sponsoring had been flooded.

"They assured us they're still on track to deliver, but we have a clause that can get us out."

I'd simply told her, "Make sure we'll get everything we need on time. But looking for another supplier sounds better."

That was it. I didn't ask her for details. I didn't follow up. That's how I operated. I simply gave instructions to my employees and trusted that they'd follow through.

I'd gotten the first angry email from Georgie on Christmas Day, which was what had alerted me that my assistant had switched suppliers. I'd been so annoyed that it ruined my Christmas, and my family picked up on it too. I'd never seen anyone react so unprofessionally.

But her words from last night filtered back to me. *"You know as well as I do that that contract was drawn up by my own grandmother, not by a lawyer."* Was that true, or was it just an attempt to manipulate me?

Fuck it. I didn't know one thing about her company. I'd assumed it was a big conglomerate, like everything was these days. And I'd figured it was a standard clause in their contracts, not something a despondent business owner came up with two generations ago.

Oh, for fuck's sake, Julian! Forget about it. The woman was just trying to get to you.

And yet... she'd seemed seriously desperate. I didn't like that. I always struck good deals, but I didn't take advantage of people. I didn't trample all over them.

Georgie was a spitfire. The way she'd challenged me had been *hot.* Her blonde hair, blue eyes, and tight sweater definitely got my attention. But I was disappointed by how unprofessional she was. Otherwise, she was just my type.

For fuck's sake. It didn't matter how attractive she was, or that I woke up this morning still thinking about her lips and had a hard-on that wouldn't quit. It was absolutely a no-go.

I took in a deep breath to cool off—to no avail. My mind was working furiously, trying to remember where Georgie's store was. I'd deleted her email, but I simply couldn't push this to the back of my mind. So I was going to deal with it.

Stepping back inside my living room, I grabbed the phone and called my assistant. I never disturbed her on weekends unless there was an emergency. This wasn't exactly one, but it felt like it.

"Oh my God, Julian. What's wrong?" she answered breathlessly.

"Relax. No emergency," I assured her.

"Oh, okay. You scared me."

"What's the name of the company making everything for the float?"

"Southern Carnival. It's one of the biggest producers in the South."

"No, the one we used before."

She sighed. "You got some angry emails again? I'm truly sorry. I tried to block her email, but the woman won't back down. But I can deal with her. I can put our lawyers—"

"No, just tell me the name."

"Let me check." After a few seconds, she said, "She's got a store in the Quarter, Books & Beads. The address is..."

I committed the address to memory and thanked her.

After hanging up, I looked up the business hours. They were open today. The photo that appeared in the Google search shocked me. It looked like a quaint little mom-and-pop store.

Good God, this is who we've been using for decades? That didn't seem right.

They opened in half an hour, which just gave me just enough time to get dressed and have another coffee.

One thing I enjoyed most about living in the Quarter was that I was within walking distance of practically everything I needed. This place was the center of my existence. But then again, most of my family had businesses in the Quarter too. My grandmothers had a fragrance shop on Dumaine. My mom ran a gallery two streets away. Our flagship restaurant, LeBlanc & Broussard, was on Royal Street. We owned many establishments throughout the whole city, but there was definitely a higher concentration of them in the Quarter.

On the way, I noticed a few groups of tourists, which indicated that the Carnival season had unofficially started already. Once the celebrations were in full swing, the streets would be packed at all times.

Books & Beads was on Burgundy Street, which was deserted at this hour. There was a coffee shop and a small pastry shop right next to her store. At first I thought it was closed because it was dark inside, but then I noticed someone moving around. It was Georgie. Damn it, she was even more attractive than I remembered. Even though the light was very dim, her curves were beckoning me.

I stepped inside, drawing a big breath. I only had one goal today: not to flirt with her. Flirting was like second nature to me. I loved women and loved to interact with them. Of course, I was completely professional with my employees—but Georgie wasn't one.

Bells chimed as I entered—they were hanging over the door.

"Good morning," Georgie said. Her voice was warm and welcoming, completely different from last night. Then she turned around and saw me, and her smile instantly disappeared. "Oh, it's you." *That* was the voice I'd expected. "What are you doing here?"

I stopped in my tracks, glancing around. The place looked very old but welcoming.

"In your email yesterday, you told me to stop by if I wanted to further discuss the issue at hand."

"So you *did* read it to the end. I wasn't sure. I thought you'd just deleted it like all the others. You made it clear last night that there was nothing to discuss." Her voice was even sharper than yesterday.

I walked up to the counter. She was arranging a stack of beads behind it.

"Listen, I'll put all my cards on the table. I don't micromanage my team."

"What's that supposed to mean?" Her blue eyes were stunning—not like the sky but more of an aquamarine.

"It means that when one of my employees tells me there is a problem and they have a solution, I simply tell them to solve it. I don't ask how they do it. I trust that they'll take care of it. I wasn't aware of the details of this case."

She gave me a smile, but it was sardonic. "That must be nice."

I frowned. "What?"

"Having other people handling everything for you."

"You run this alone?" I asked, glancing around the store.

"I have a small team, but I do know absolutely everything that goes on around here."

"My assistant simply chose the option that would make sure we got everything on time."

"But that's just it," she huffed. "I told your team that we were already rebuilding your order. We were halfway done, actually."

That sucked. It meant she was sitting on those costs and inventory.

"I assume that my team simply considered changing suppliers to be a safer option."

Georgie laughed, looking down. Her blonde hair had been tied up yesterday, but now it was loose. It almost reached her elbows, and it was so thick and luscious that I wanted to find an excuse to get closer to see it better.

"You know, we've been working on that float for over sixty years. Ever since my grandmother signed a contract with your grandparents."

"I didn't know that," I admitted, "nor have I ever looked at the contract."

"Right. It's all just another task for you. Something that isn't even in your purview, right?"

"Exactly." Not that I liked how that sounded. I was involved and treated people right, but I was ready to agree that I dropped the ball on this and it never should've happened.

Keeping her head down, she told me, "But here's the thing. This is my life's work. Once word got around that you dropped us, others followed suit, and now..."

She didn't need to finish that sentence. She was in deep financial trouble. Sure, the insurance would've covered whatever was damaged by the flood, but if she'd already started working on replacing what was lost, she was in the red.

"Georgie, I have a proposition for you."

She snapped her head up, looking at me. Fuck yes, there was hope in her eyes! She was even more gorgeous than before. I wanted to get close to her, but that was not an option. This was strictly business, nothing more.

"Starting with the next Carnival season, you're in charge of our float again."

Her face instantly exploded in a smile.

Fucking hell, that smile would light up the entire damn Quarter.

"Oh my God, that would help so, so much."

"You have my word. I'll have my assistant get back to you next week with all the details. It's far too late to do anything about this year, unfortunately."

"It's helpful to know that I can count on you for the next season." She bit her lower lip. "I'll make do with this one. Tourists are going to start arriving in droves anyway, and we're ready for business." She pointed around the shop.

I couldn't imagine anyone being able to make a living out of selling books, beads, masks, and whatever else she had hanging around here, but I didn't say that out loud. I didn't like to flaunt my status, although sometimes I did it without realizing.

She moved her hips from one side and then the other, and then did a... was that a pirouette? Yes, it was. The change in her demeanor was incredible.

"Oh, I can't wait to tell everyone else on Monday. They've been expecting me to tell them that we'll close our doors after this season ends."

Fuck, was the situation that dire?

"How many clients dropped you?" I asked cautiously.

Her smile fell again. "Five of the biggest ones, so we have a lot of extra float material this year. If you know anyone who needs it, you can send them our way."

I fucking would, except I didn't know anyone—again, not caring about details and all that.

"But a win is a win," she continued. "And who knows, maybe the rest of our clients will change their minds as well."

If they were anything like me, they probably didn't even know they'd changed suppliers. But I didn't want to ruin her mood.

"Thanks, Julian. I really, really appreciate it." She bit her bottom lip again.

I looked away, exhaling sharply. I needed to get away from this woman or I was going to become very unprofessional. Georgie was too damn attractive not to flirt with.

"Are you taking part in the parades?" I asked her.

"Are you kidding? Of course."

"I have a tradition. I call it Sazerac Day. When the first parade passes my bar, I give free Sazeracs to everyone." That typically happened very early in the Carnival season. This year, the celebrations would last two months, which was when Mardi Gras was.

"That's got to be bad for business," she said. "I wouldn't have expected it from you."

I grinned. "Believe it or not, I'm not all about numbers all the time. I like to have fun. It's next Monday, so drop by."

What am I doing?

Oh, fuck it. I never was one to overthink, and I wasn't going to start now. I wanted to see Georgie again, and yes, I was still feeling guilty as shit for basically screwing up her business.

"I won't say no to a free Sazerac. When does everything start?" she asked.

"No fixed schedule, but text me your phone number, and I'll text you when everything's ready to go."

"That's not how it works." She put a hand on her chest, widening her eyes theatrically. "I take Carnivals very seriously. If I'm taking part in a parade, I want to be dressed accordingly."

That made me laugh. "Didn't realize that you actually want to be part of the parade. I'm just watching."

"I like to dress up for watching too. You can find my shop number listed online."

"Seriously?" I exclaimed.

"Yeah. I like to be available for any and all inquiries—not that I get too many. Different approach, huh?" she said with a laugh.

"Definitely." I looked around again. "So, your grandmother opened this place?"

"Yes, over sixty years ago. She did it all on her own." Her voice was dripping with pride. "She'd just had my mom, and no one would hire her, so she set up her own business. In the beginning, she started by selling books from her own collection. As she made money, she started buying more books and then beads. One thing led to another, and she kept adding to her inventory." She was getting more animated now. I liked that she cared so much about her grandmother. She was unlike any woman I'd ever met. "Then she got into the float business. My mom practically grew up here. Then history sort of repeated itself when Mom had me. The three of us spent a lot of time here."

"And now you run the shop without them."

The light in her eyes dimmed a bit. "My nana passed away many years ago, but I still feel her presence every day I'm here." She pointed at a worn leather armchair. "That's been here since her time. I like to sit there and read every evening. Mom retired a while ago and moved out to Baton Rouge. But that's fine, honestly. She's worked since she was a teenager. Now she's enjoying life with her chickens and her goat."

"You know, it's funny, but my grandfathers took up fishing very seriously after they retired. My grandmothers insisted that they still wanted to have an occupation, so they opened a fragrance shop."

"Really? I didn't know that. Where is it?"

"On Dumaine."

"Oh, I think I've passed it a few times. I wanted to go in, but the prices scared me away."

"If you tell my grandmothers you're the one doing our float, they'll give you a discount. They look for any excuse to give discounts to people. I don't know why they don't just lower the prices." I chuckled.

She smiled at me, and I could see her guard lower a bit. I didn't know why it was important to me, but I was determined to leave the shop on good terms.

Screw it, not just that. I had to be honest with myself. I wanted Georgie to like me.

"What did your grandmothers say when you told them you were changing suppliers?"

"I didn't tell them," I admitted. "It didn't even occur to me."

"I see."

"So... you'll stop by next week?"

"Are you just inviting me because you still feel guilty?" Georgie asked. There was a twinkle in her eyes.

"You can bet on it."

"Good. You should feel guilty."

I threw my head back, laughing loudly. I liked her sass. "I don't think I've ever met a business partner who talks to me the way you do."

She put her hands on her hips, rolling back her shoulders. That pushed her chest forward, and I took in an eyeful. Big mistake. I wasn't going to be able to forget the sight anytime soon.

Glancing up, I noticed she was red in the cheeks. Of course I'd been fucking obvious.

"I'm glad to shake things up," she whispered.

"You know what? Because I feel so guilty, I'll give you two Sazeracs on the house."

She narrowed her eyes. Damn, she was so delicious. "Any reason you're trying to get me drunk?"

I held up my hands. "No hidden agenda here."

"On one condition: you drink two with me."

That made me laugh again. Damn, I hadn't laughed so much on a Sunday morning in a long while—and it wasn't because I was a grump like my brother Xander. It had just been a while since I had such a good company.

"That's a promise," I said.

"Are you going to be in full costume?"

"Absolutely not."

She smirked. "Hmm. That almost feels wrong. I'd like to see you in one."

I was flirting with a dangerous idea. Later in the Carnival season, I was throwing an exclusive party in the Marriott on the day of the parade. Having Georgie there would be my highlight. But I'd just met this woman—I couldn't up and invite her to the presidential suite at the Marriott. It would sound fucking stalkerish. Inviting her to come to the bar on Sazerac Day was enough.

"What are you going to wear?" I asked her.

"That's going to be a surprise. For both of us. I haven't even decided yet. I always play it by ear." She waved her arms around. "But I have plenty of inspiration here. We'll see if you recognize me at all."

"I'd recognize you from a mile away, Georgie. Even blindfolded—"

Her mouth formed an O, and I stopped midsentence. *So much for not flirting.*

I cleared my throat. "Let's just say, you're memorable."

"Huh. I guess I should tell more of your business partners that if they ambush you at the bar and give you a hard time, you might soften and give them what they want."

Despite my resolution, I leaned in, almost to her ear, and said, "No, Georgie, trust me. No one would achieve that. It's you and only you." When I straightened up, she was completely red in the face. "I'll see you on Tuesday," I said.

"Yes," she whispered.

I couldn't fucking wait.

Chapter Four

Georgie

I absolutely loved Carnival season. Then again, considering my line of work, it would be a surprise if I didn't. The city came alive at this time of the year, and as I'd predicted, our handmade masks were a hit with tourists. And the beads, too, as I kept them reasonably priced.

I was manning the shop from opening until the evening, and Zelda was in charge of everything going on in the back. I'd given them the good news first thing on Monday morning. Getting our biggest client back for next season had done wonders for everyone's mood.

I couldn't get Julian LeBlanc out of my mind, though. Who could blame me? His blue eyes were simply unreal.

He'd followed through with his promise. I'd gotten an email from his assistant early on Monday and had already set everything in place. I was using a new contract template—one put together with an actual lawyer a few years back. It was far less lenient than the one Nana had set up and wouldn't release our clients so easily. But I hadn't heard from Julian since, so I'd almost forgotten about his invitation for Sazerac.

Until the following Monday.

The first day of parades was always madness in the Quarter. So much so that I closed the store in the afternoon, as the streets would be too crowded with floats and celebrations for anyone to shop.

At one o'clock, I received a text from an unknown number.

Unknown number: Free Sazeracs will start at 2:00 PM.
Signed Julian LeBlanc.

Ha! He didn't forget. I was definitely not going to say no to a free Sazerac on the first day of parades.

My heart was beating fast for no reason at all as I texted back.

Wait a second, was heat creeping up my cheeks? This wasn't right.

But I was excited about going, so I was going to enjoy it—every moment.

Georgie: I'll be there, wearing a mask.

I felt extra sassy for that. Since I'd planned to join the celebrations today anyway, I had my outfit with me.

I'd gone with black tights and a dress in the traditional Mardi Gras colors. It was glittery and festive, and I absolutely loved it. I put on a jacket, too, because I didn't want to catch a cold. There was one time of year that I couldn't get sick, and it was now.

I got ready in the back of the store, humming to myself.

"Georgie, I'm going. Need anything?" Zelda asked a while later.

"No. Where are you going to be?" I asked her. Everyone was celebrating today.

"Bourbon, probably." She winced. "I'm sorry."

I looked directly at her. "Zelda, you don't have to apologize for going to Bourbon Street. Hell, you can even go into his club if you want."

She shook her head adamantly. "Oh, no, no. I'm never stepping foot in there again. I'm not giving that asshole one cent for drinks or anything else."

It felt good to know she was in my corner. I wondered if I was going to see my ex today, and that made me shudder. I really couldn't be so unlucky. He liked the celebrations, too, but to quote him, "It's mostly to rub shoulders with the right people." I couldn't see him lining up for free Sazeracs.

Forget about Kyle, Georgie. He's firmly in the past. He can't hurt you anymore.

And yet the damage he'd done had left lasting marks. I hadn't even realized it at first. I'd simply been too dazed by the breakup.

One day, I'd gone to his club and waited for him by the couches, as usual.

Then a gorgeous woman approached, sitting next to me.

"I'm with Kyle now, so you're not welcome here anymore," she stated matter-of-factly.

I thought it was a practical joke, so I started to laugh.

"I'm going to have to ask you to leave," she went on.

I gawked at her. "Are you serious? Did he put you up to this?"

"He did ask me to give you the message, yes. He figured it would be easier this way."

I looked her straight in the eyes. "You're joking."

I felt as if someone had slapped me. We'd been going out for six months at that point. Granted, we were going through a rough patch, but that was the most humiliating thing I'd ever gone through.

"I'll ask security to escort you out if you don't leave on your own."

I'd run out of there before she could see me burst into tears. And I never went back.

In the months that followed, I'd been too heartbroken to even consider dating. The first time someone asked me out after the breakup, my initial instinct had been to simply run away. That hadn't changed yet.

One day this huge hole in my heart would mend, I was certain. I just didn't know when that day would come.

I put my mask on even before I left Books & Beads. My costume was a bit over the top, but I'd always been a bit weird and owned up to it. The day was gorgeous, the sun shining brightly, warming up my face. The Quarter was alive, chants from revelers resounding on the streets.

Jazz bands played throughout the area, and a lot of bars had their doors open, letting the music fill the streets.

The crowds grew bigger and bigger as I approached the bar, although the parade hadn't reached Dumaine yet. Smiling from ear to ear, I stepped inside. There were several other people in costumes, but none of them were quite as loony as mine.

The place was even more packed than the last time I'd been here. It was really cool of Julian to offer free drinks. I shuddered to think how much it had to cost him.

I didn't need to wait too long to get to the bar. I was fully expecting to see Julian at the counter, and my stomach rolled with disappointment when he wasn't.

Oh, Georgie, what's gotten into you? Shake it off. I was hoping to spot those iridescent blue eyes at some point, though.

I waited until one of the bartenders was free and got his attention. He looked at me and smiled, then said, "Sazerac, right?"

"Yep."

"Is this your first one?"

I grinned. "Yes!"

"Okay."

"Wait, is that how you check that no one drinks more than one?"

He laughed. "Most people try to stick to that, anyway."

I found that hard to believe, but hey, if it worked for them, who was I to question it?

I looked at him intently as he prepared it, so mesmerized by the dexterity with which he moved that I didn't realize someone was watching me.

"Told you I'd find you."

My body lit up instantly. I turned around and sighed. Oh yeah, those iridescent blue eyes were trained on me, molten hot. When he stared at my mouth, the temperature of my body elevated. Instead of chastising myself, I declared victory. At least I knew my body was still capable of feeling something in the presence of a gorgeous man.

"What gave me away?"

"The mask, your energy. I don't know. I told you you're special." He tilted closer and whispered, "And that I'd recognize you anywhere."

"I made it easy for you, didn't I?"

"You dressed like that for me?"

Would you look at that? Even my ears were on fire now.

I cleared my throat and put the mask in the bag I had slung over my shoulder. "Sorry to disappoint. I always like to dress for the parades. I take every chance I get."

Straightening up, he gave me a dazzling smile before glancing at the bartender. "I'll have a Sazerac with Georgie."

"Here you go."

After clinking glasses, I took a sip. "*Yum.* This is amazing."

I loved the cocktail. The mix of rye whiskey, absinthe, and lemon was perfect.

He grinned. "We serve the best Sazerac in town."

I rolled my eyes, though I wasn't sure he could see them. "Julian, every bar in this city claims to have the best Sazerac."

"Yes, but we've won awards," he said with a wink.

"Well, it definitely deserves it."

Even though there were a few inches between us, my entire body was still sizzling.

"Hey, you started drinking without me," another voice said.

Julian turned to the newcomer, his face instantly lighting up. "Zachary, hey! Grab a drink and join us. Georgie, this is my brother, Zachary."

I smiled at him. "Hi, Zachary."

He looked me up and down before saying, "Damn, I approve. Someone who knows how to dress for Carnival."

"Always," I said.

"Georgie owns Books & Beads," Julian shared. "She's actually the one in charge of decorating our float. We ran into a bit of an issue this year—my mistake—but she'll be back in charge next year."

I nearly dropped my glass, shocked that he'd called it *his* mistake.

Zachary shook my hand. "Pleased to meet you. Whatever happened this year, I'm sorry. I'll kick his ass. Thanks for making us the best damn float decorations in town for all these years."

I didn't know if it was the Sazerac already going to my head or these guys paying me compliments, but I was ecstatic.

"Thank you, Zachary. I like you."

Julian trained his gaze on me. "And you based that decision on what?"

Zachary snorted. "The fact that I'm amazing, dude. Cheers."

He grabbed his glass of Sazerac from the counter and clinked it to mine and then Julian's.

"Perfect, as usual," he exclaimed after taking a sip. "I'm going to make the rounds. I've spotted some friends."

After he left, I asked Julian, "Is your whole family around here?"

"No. It's too crazy for most of them. We're having our traditional brunch at LeBlanc & Broussard during the Carnival season." I was thinking how much I loved that restaurant when he added, "I can't wait to see my niece."

"One of your brothers has kids?"

"Yes. Chad, the second oldest of us. He divorced Bella's mom a while ago, and we all kind of pitched in to help. All of us brothers spend a lot of time with Bella. But now that he's engaged, we see less of her. I miss the little munchkin."

Oh goodness. Be still, my beating heart. I took a few more sips of my drink.

"Easy there. Pace yourself," Julian said.

I giggled. "Yeah, whoops. I'm... Huh. I went a bit too fast."

"Want me to tell the bartender to prep the second one?"

I licked my lips. "No, I need to pace myself, like you said."

"Sure. Let me know when you're ready. So, how is business going? Were the handmade masks a hit?"

I opened my mouth to answer, then froze. *No, he can't possibly be here.* And yet there was no mistaking that profile. The blond hair cropped short, the high cheekbones, the suit.

Kyle Deveraux was standing here in the flesh.

"Georgie, are you okay?" Julian put a hand on my arm, holding me still.

Oh my God, I'd been swaying. I suddenly felt faint.

"Do you want to sit down? Are you feeling sick?" he asked.

"No, I just saw someone I'd hoped never to see again."

"Who?"

"My ex-boyfriend."

Julian followed my gaze. "Who is it?"

"The blond guy with a killer profile and shitty personality."

"Kyle Deveraux?" He sounded incredulous.

"You know him?" *Crap.* They probably ran in the same circles.

"Yes. Not my favorite person either," Julian said through gritted teeth.

I glanced down at my hands, grasping the glass even tighter, and then took a huge gulp, emptying it.

"I think I'm ready for that second Sazerac now."

Julian eyed me intently. I felt all kinds of hot under his scrutiny.

"Georgie..."

"Ha. No, mister. No warning me. Trust me, I need liquid courage."

"Julian, we need you here. There's been a mishap," one of the bartenders said.

"Georgie, are you okay?" Julian asked me softly.

"Yeah, sure."

"I won't be long. I promise." Those eyes seemed even more surreal after the Sazerac.

"Take your time. I can't monopolize you for the whole celebration."

But suddenly that sounded like exactly what I needed. I felt safe with Julian even though I barely knew him.

"Second round for Georgie," he told the bartender without taking his eyes off me. Then he winked, and I swear my underwear felt tighter around my delicate parts.

The bartender looked at me in surprise, which was saying something for a bartender in the French Quarter. He glanced at my empty glass and simply nodded. "Right away."

I turned to face the bar, putting both elbows on the counter. I hoped to God Kyle wouldn't see me. I usually loved chatting with people at parades, but right now, I simply wanted to make myself small and invisible.

Of course, I had no such luck. Seconds later, I heard his familiar voice beside me.

"Of course I'd run into you here," Kyle said.

Taking in a deep breath, I steeled myself and turned around to face him. "Hello, Kyle."

He looked down at me and snorted, shaking his head.

"What?" I asked, tilting my head and putting one hand on my hip. I hoped my body language conveyed that I didn't give two shits about him and that his presence didn't affect me at all.

"I can't believe you're wearing that."

"It's what I like. It's Carnival season, and I enjoy it."

"You can enjoy it and still have some taste," he said.

I scoffed. "Oh, Kyle, you and I are so done. I have no intention of taking any more abuse from you."

He stared at me. "What the fuck are you talking about?"

"You always like to make me feel like I'm beneath you."

"Make no mistake, you are. The things I heard from people when we were going out were insane. Starting with how you dressed to work at your little shop."

I was slowly dying inside. Why did his words still affect me?

"Here's your Sazerac," the bartender said. He eyed Kyle. "Problem?"

"Mind your own business," Kyle told him.

"We're good." I tried to smile at the bartender, but I was certain it was more of a grimace.

Turning back to Kyle, I asked, "What are you even doing here? I thought you considered all the other establishments in the French Quarter way beneath yours. Oh, by the way, this is much better than the Deveraux Club."

He bristled. The one thing he couldn't stand was anyone telling him he wasn't the best at everything.

"I've got to check out the competition. And you liking this place more only tells me that mine is the superior one. Your taste is questionable."

I took a huge gulp of the Sazerac and then flashed him a smile. "Then so is yours, considering you went out with me for half a year."

His eyes turned cold, and I knew he was about to dish out some more crap, but that was okay. I had my Sazerac, and I planned to make good use of it.

CHAPTER FIVE

JULIAN

Some shit always happened during important celebrations. It was an unspoken rule. This year, a freezer crapped out. That meant no ice and warm drinks, and no one needed that.

I'd sent the busboys to buy bags of ice, and they'd just returned. They'd have to run to the store every hour so we'd have fresh ice.

"Everything is under control," I concluded, watching them put the ice in small buckets to take to the front.

"Julian?" Andrew called to me. He was my head bartender today. "Can you come here for a second?"

"Sure." If we had another emergency, I was going to lose my legendary calm. Or I was going to call Zachary. I was good with emergencies, but he was excellent at multitasking.

"Listen, someone's accosting that lady friend of yours. I'm not liking the way he's talking to her."

Fucking Deveraux.

"Thanks for letting me know."

I walked from the back room straight to the bar. Georgie was in the same spot I'd left her, talking to Kyle.

I took in her body language, and I fucking hated it. Her shoulders were hunched forward. Her head was tilted downward. She'd come in here so happy, and now she looked completely different.

I knew Kyle Deveraux too well. We'd gone to the same school, and now we were running similar businesses.

He was a jackass, plain and simple.

I headed straight to them. The second I overheard the conversation, I saw red.

"Why are you even here?" he asked. "These aren't your type of events. You like to be out on the street with the rest of the peasants."

What the actual fuck?

I walked up to Georgie, standing right next to her.

"I invited her here." On instinct, I added, "I couldn't have my girl miss out on the first celebration of the season." Georgie nearly stumbled into the bar, but I put an arm around her waist, keeping her in place. "Still got some of the Sazerac? Give me a swig. I need it." I took her glass and winked at her, only drinking a small sip.

She looked at me questioningly, and I purposefully brought my ear close to her mouth as she whispered, "What are you doing?"

I couldn't fill her in without Kyle catching on. Not that I actually knew what I was doing. Playing it by ear was my specialty, after all.

I pressed my fingers deeper into her waist. I gave her back the glass and brought my mouth level with hers. "Just follow my lead."

At first, I only intended to make it look as if we were very comfortable being so close to each other, but the smell of her perfume messed with my senses. It went straight to my head, and suddenly kissing her seemed like the best idea in the world.

It would certainly throw this moron off his game and make him leave with his tail between his legs. In fact, I was running out of excuses not to kiss her. I'd wanted to do it ever since I'd gone to her store.

So I went for it, pressing my lips to hers slowly at first... but then she opened up for me. I groaned against her mouth. *Fuck me!* I pushed my tongue in, slowly savoring her. She tasted like Sazerac, of course.

Clearly, Georgie wanted this kiss as much as I did. I explored her without restraint, barely registering that my employees were watching, along with a lot of customers. I didn't care. This moment was fucking everything. It fired up my body, and now all I wanted was to keep kissing her. Scratch that—I wanted to touch her too. I *needed* to lift her onto the counter, part her legs, and explore her until she shuddered in my arms.

The sound of a glass breaking and a wave of liquid flooding my shoes brought me back to the present moment.

"Oh my God, I'm so sorry," Georgie said.

"Don't worry, babe. I made you lose your head. I'll take that as a compliment." I kissed her forehead for good measure before turning around.

That moron was still here. He looked between the two of us and snorted. "Right. This is a thing."

"Yes, it fucking is. So go bother someone else. Not my woman." I felt Georgie shudder even though I wasn't touching her anymore.

"Suit yourself," he said, then stomped away.

"Fucking finally!" I exclaimed. I turned around to look at Georgie, but she was already crouching on her haunches, gathering glass with her bare hands. "Georgie, stop. I'll get a broom."

"I'm really sorry for this." Her voice was shaking slightly.

I lowered myself catching each wrist with my hands. "For what? The kiss? Because I'm not."

She finally looked up at me, biting her lower lip. Her pupils were dilated. Her body language told me she didn't regret it one bit. In fact, she might even want another one, but she sighed. "I'm sorry. I can't process it. This was... He always throws me off my game."

"I thought we'd return the favor. That's why I kissed you." *Among other reasons, like I've wanted to kiss you since the last time I saw you.*

She grinned. "It was a good one."

"Let's get up. I don't want you to get cut."

One of the guys was already coming our way with a broom and dustpan. Rising to our feet, we stepped out of his way to allow him to clean up.

"I'm really sorry you had to witness that," she murmured.

"Georgie, stop apologizing. It's not your fault."

"I disagree. My silly ex came into your bar and started making a scene."

"Kyle likes to attract attention to himself. Doesn't matter if it's good or bad."

Her eyes widened. "You know him well."

"More than I'd like to. Want another Sazerac? You didn't get to drink much of the second one."

Some of that vibrant energy had slipped back into her eyes, but she wasn't nearly as ecstatic as she'd been when she first came into the bar. I fucking hated that moron for bringing her to this state.

"I think I've had enough alcohol for the day. I had some food, but I'm not sure if it was enough."

I leaned in close. "Wanna here a secret? We've got beignets."

Her eyes widened. "What? Oh my God, where? Why didn't you say that?"

I laughed. Yeah, that did it. The light was back in her eyes. She was starting to forget about that idiot. I had half a mind to have him escorted out of the bar, but that would cause a huge scene that we didn't need.

"We keep them a secret and sort of push them on people who can't hold their liquor too well."

Georgie was laughing in earnest now. "I see. You think I'm drunk."

I grinned. "Nope. I just want to spoil you."

"Well, I never say no to beignets. Does anybody in New Orleans? It's mandatory to love them."

The smile she flashed me made me want to go to Café Du Monde and buy her beignets every damn day. "You'll have to come in the back with me for that. We haven't brought them out yet."

"Sneaky beignets. I like this more and more."

I put my arm around her shoulders, bringing her close as I led her to the back.

"Just in case he's watching," I explained, and she instantly tensed.

"Good thinking."

That was absolutely not the only reason. I simply wanted an excuse to touch her.

Right before we stepped into the back room, I looked behind me, surveying the crowd. Sure enough, that fucker was checking us out. Fantastic.

I led her to the smaller storage room where we'd put the beignets.

"Did you buy them from Café Du Monde?" she asked.

"Of course! They're everyone's favorites—including mine. Some of my brothers swear there are better places in town for beignets, but I'm old-school."

"So am I." She immediately grabbed one and bit into it, closing her eyes. That impulse to kiss her again was back, and I was barely keeping it at bay. There was no reason for it right now, and yet I wanted to.

Georgie only opened her eyes once she finished. "That was exactly what I needed, and I didn't even know it."

"Is there ever a bad time to eat beignets?"

"You and I have a lot more in common than I thought," she whispered.

"I think so too." I checked the time. "The parade should reach us in about ten minutes, so if you want another beignet, grab it now, because otherwise..."

She reached for one before I even finished my sentence. This woman was something else.

As she chewed, I played with a dangerous idea. "Don't go out on the street to watch the parade."

"Why not?"

"I have a better spot to watch it from."

It was so easy to make this woman light up. How had that moron managed to snuff out this joy?

"I'm game."

"There's a balcony upstairs. Since it's on the second floor, you'll feel like you're part of the parade."

"But isn't it already booked?"

"No, it's not open to the public. It would be just you and me, Georgie." Despite my best intentions, I leaned in closer.

"Okay," she whispered. "I've never actually watched it from a balcony in the Quarter. The lady living above Books & Beads isn't keen on having guests, and all the other viewing places are always so packed."

"Then let's hurry. We'll see the parade coming in."

Georgie literally shoved the rest of the beignet into her mouth, looking like a squirrel with her cheeks about ready to explode. She covered her mouth with her hands and giggled.

Placing my hands on her shoulders, I turned her around and guided her forward. The spiral staircase leading to the upper floor was in the supply room. It was extremely narrow, and I avoided it at all costs if I had anything to drink.

"This is perfect," she said when we reached the top. The sound of trumpets and jazz music and people cheering was already deafening.

When we stepped onto the balcony, we saw the parade coming from the end of the street.

"I love the view. This is why everyone is paying big money to watch the celebration from balconies."

I zeroed in on her lips.

"Do I have something on my mouth?" she asked.

"Powdered sugar."

Georgie only had a little bit of sugar in one corner, but that wasn't why I was looking. The truth was, I simply couldn't stop myself. She rubbed at her mouth quickly, and when she lowered her hand, her lips were red. They were full and sexy with the look of just being kissed. The impulse to do just that was growing stronger by the second. But I knew I had to get myself under control because I didn't want to make her uncomfortable. Running into her asshole ex did that already.

She turned around as the parade came closer, clutching the railing with both hands and looking down at the street. I was usually downstairs with my team, putting out fires at this time of the day, but no way in hell was I going to leave Georgie's side. Watching the parade with her was a different experience altogether.

She was dancing lightly to the sound of the music. "I found one downside. I can't catch beads from here."

"Beads?" I asked incredulously. "I would think that's the one thing you don't need."

"I don't *need* them," she said. "But I like the tradition."

"I'll find you some beads," I promised.

She glanced at me for a brief second, and I had the impression that she was checking out my mouth too. My cock twitched at the thought. *Aw hell!* I was usually in more control, but right now I needed something I never thought I would.

I hoped my reasonable side would prevail or I was going to kiss this woman right here against the railing.

She swallowed hard. I leaned in slightly, but then she turned around abruptly, looking down at the street. This was a smaller parade, but it encapsulated everything I loved about this season in New Orleans. The energy was damn infectious. Everyone was enjoying themselves to the maximum, celebrating life and being part of this incredible culture.

"I like that costume so much."

She pointed at a woman who was wearing what looked like a full body tattoo, though I was certain she had to have some clothes on because it was cold. Which reminded me...

"Georgie, are you cold? I can bring you a blanket from inside."

"Oh, no. I've had Sazerac and beignets, so my body temperature is higher than it should be, but in a good way. Does that make sense?" She kept dancing.

I chuckled. "No, but that's okay. Just enjoy yourself."

I was watching her more than the parade. She was so at ease in her own skin, and it just drew me to her. Georgie was a confident woman who also happened to be super sexy. I was having a hard time finding reasons to stay away.

As one of the bigger floats came by, she said, "Oh, I can't believe that's going to make it down the street."

"I know." It was questionable, but somehow they always made it through.

One of the reasons motorized floats weren't allowed in the French Quarter anymore was the streets were too narrow. This one was cutting it close, but that gave me an idea. Some of the dancers would literally pass by our balcony throwing beads like there was no tomorrow. Georgie was too excited to even notice, dancing and pointing out which costume she liked most. But I had a plan. I found one of them throwing out beads, and as they passed the balcony, I grabbed a fistful.

Georgie wasn't paying me any attention, dancing even wilder than before. Damn, the woman could move. She didn't see what I was doing, so I put a hand on her waist, moving along with her. She startled slightly but then leaned into my touch. *Hell yes.* I held my other hand up in front of her.

"Here are your beads, my lady. I never break a promise."

She gasped. "Julian, oh my God."

I put them all around her neck as she kept dancing.

"You've got excellent rhythm," I whispered in her ear.

"You're not so bad either."

"Not so bad, huh? Was that supposed to be a compliment?" I teased.

"I don't want you to get a big head. I mean, you're a fantastic kisser. If I compliment your dancing skills, too, where would that get me?"

"Tell me more about my kissing skills. What did you like?"

She was far more relaxed than she'd been right after we'd kissed. That was good. Maybe her initial discomfort had simply been because that moron was still hovering around.

"I don't know. Everything. You've got a way about you." She giggled. "Oh, man, I think that Sazerac is working."

I laughed. "I think so too."

She covered her mouth and half turned to look at me. "Sorry, that was far too much information."

"I liked every bit of it," I assured her.

We made eye contact for a few seconds, but then she glanced away. We didn't talk at all for the rest of the parade, just danced and enjoyed the moment. Our chemistry was palpable. Georgie was very different from the women I'd previously dated. Her sincerity drew me in just as much as her curves.

"I've never had so much fun at a parade," I informed her as the celebration wound down.

She turned around. "That cannot possibly be true. You've probably attended a million of them."

"I have," I said, "but sharing it with you was a different experience altogether. I don't think I've seen anyone enjoy it as much as you do."

"Um, hello? Did you see all the people down there? They were having a lot of fun."

"But I've always watched it from the sidelines. This was different. I love that you celebrate it with no restraints."

She smiled sheepishly. "Well, I might go overboard. I didn't see anyone in the bar wearing a glittery dress."

"It looks fucking amazing on you."

She snapped her head up, lips parted.

"And *you* are amazing," I continued. "I hope you didn't let one word that moron said get to you."

Her demeanor instantly changed. *Fuck, why did I have to bring him up?*

"I try not to, but it's hard. Mom raised me to never care about what others say. She had to endure a lot worse, considering my dad left when I was little. It was a hard time for her."

"I'm sure," I murmured.

"But I'm not made out of stone. Kyle did throw a few punches to my self-esteem, but you fixed it all with your beignets and beads. And just being you."

"Don't forget the kissing."

She nodded. "And the kissing, yes. That was a highlight."

It was on the tip of my tongue to say that I could repeat it any fucking time. She only had to give me a sign and I'd kiss her senseless.

"I think I should be going."

"No, don't. Stay." I wasn't sure what I had planned, but I knew I didn't want her to leave.

She licked her lips. "Your crew might need you downstairs eventually."

"They probably do. I lost track of time."

That was an understatement. I'd been gone for far longer than intended, yet I didn't regret it one bit.

"Hey, bro, what the fuck? We've been looking for you forever. We thought you bailed on your own party," Beckett called up to me from the street. "Oh, hi," he said, looking at Georgie. "You look familiar."

Anthony was with him, too, sporting a knowing smile on his face.

"Everyone, this is Georgie. Georgie, these are my brothers, Beckett and Anthony," I said.

I unconsciously put a hand on her shoulder, and my brothers zeroed in on that the gesture. I knew without a doubt that I was never going to hear the end of this.

"I'll be down in a minute," I assured them.

"I should get going," she repeated.

As much as I hated her leaving, I had to get back to work. *Darn.*

"I'll walk you to your store."

"That's crazy," she scoffed. "You've got a full house here, and your brothers are waiting."

I cleared my throat. "I don't want that fucker getting anywhere near you."

That was true, but it was also an excuse. I simply wanted more time with her.

She licked her lips, looking sideways. She was fucking beautiful. Those eyes and full lashes drew me in and held me captive.

"I'm sure he's already gone. Thanks a lot for everything."

"Julian!" The call came from down the spiral staircase. It belonged to one of my bartenders.

"See?" she said with a smirk. "You'd better join everyone before they think I've kidnapped you or something."

I wiggled my eyebrows, leaning in. "I wouldn't mind if you kidnapped me, Georgie. Not at all."

Chapter Six

Julian

During the Carnival season, it was traditional for my family to brunch together at LeBlanc & Broussard. The restaurant was packed as usual, but we had a space reserved just for us. This was our flagship restaurant on Royal Street. It was on the ground floor of a three-story building. Upstairs were the main offices.

"Dad, this is the best pecan pie," Bella exclaimed. She was sitting at the head of the long table, munching on a slice. She'd had other food, too, but my niece loved her pies.

I was sitting a few seats away from Bella, Chad, and Scarlett. Since the two of them got together, my brother needed my help a lot less. Before that, he would often call me out of nowhere to ask if I could watch Bella for a bit while he had to run an errand. Nine times out of ten, I said yes because spending time with my niece was one of my favorite things. I missed our time together as I wasn't seeing her too often now.

"How was Sazerac Day at the bar?" Isabeau asked. She was a few seats down the other end of the table.

I was flanked by Beckett, Anthony, Xander, and Zachary. I leaned forward over the table so I could make eye contact with my grandmother.

"It was a success, as usual. People enjoyed it."

"Not that he would actually know. He spent most of it on the balcony with a very attractive young lady," Anthony said.

I straightened up, staring at him. *What the hell has gotten into him? Why would he put me on the spot like that?* He knew I didn't like talking about my private life. None of us did, for that matter.

"Do you have something to share with us?" Celine asked.

"We're all ears too," Zachary said. "We tried to ask him what was going on, but he wouldn't say a word."

When they were kids, I could intimidate them into not giving me shit. But that had stopped working about a decade and a half ago.

I was stunned when I realized that the entire family was watching me. My parents were leaning with their elbows over the table, eyes trained on me.

"It was a favor to a friend."

"We'll need more than that." That came from Zachary.

Fucking hell. I'd expected more from him.

"I don't see why it's any of our business," Xander cut in.

I could always count on my exacting brother to be impartial. Still, no one looked away, anticipating my answer.

"Are you going to have a girlfriend, Uncle Julian, like Dad? That's awesome."

I turned to look directly at my niece. The hope in her eyes gutted me. I didn't like to disappoint her, but I had to nip this in the bud immediately.

"No, Bella. No girlfriend for me."

There was a collective grunt from the table.

"Then why were you there alone with her?" Zachary asked. "Unless these two are embellishing it. I didn't actually see you up there on the balcony."

"They're not." I realized I could give them a version of the truth. "Georgie is the one who decorated our floats over the last few years. This year, there was a mishap, and I canceled our agreement."

"Darling boy, that's not right," Celine said. "We made that deal with her grandmother a long time ago. She was such a good soul."

"I've fixed my mistake. Frankly, I didn't really pay attention to what was going on, and my assistant had made some changes. Anyway, she'll be producing everything for the float again next year. I invited her to Sazerac Day as a show of goodwill." I chose my next words very carefully. "While she was at the bar, she ran into someone who was giving her a hard time."

"A bully?" Bella piped up. "Bullies are the worst."

"Something like that." What an accurate description, though I hated that Bella had encountered someone who'd given her a hard time. "She needed to get away, and I offered for her to watch the parade from the balcony."

Mom beamed from ear to ear. "I'm so proud of you, son. That was the gentlemanly thing to do. Now, can everyone move on from this conversation?"

"I have some questions," Isabeau said, ignoring Mom. "What do you mean, there was a mishap and you had to cancel it? Because of the flood?"

"Yes. My team decided to go with another supplier to avoid the risk of anything going wrong."

Isabeau put a hand on her heart. "Oh, no, no, no. I'd told Stella all those years ago that the clause she had was no good, that it gave people an easy way out. She was just too kindhearted. But at the time, the poor woman was desperate for clients, and no one would take on a new supplier without it. I promised her I'd never make use of it."

I could see my grandma was feeling bad about this. *Shit.*

"As I said, I've rectified my mistake, and Georgie is happy."

Isabeau was still staring at me. "But that means other clients must have dropped her, too, right?"

I nodded. "Correct."

"Were they able to get any of them back?" Celine asked. She seemed shaken too. I was starting to wonder if their connection to Georgie's grandmother was more than buyer and supplier. Maybe she'd been a friend as well.

"No, she hasn't," I admitted. Georgie hadn't told me everything about her business, but I knew that was pretty much the case.

The two of them looked at each other but didn't add anything else. Their silence was making me uncomfortable.

Even after the conversation moved on, my mind was still on Georgie and her business. I felt responsible and had this overwhelming urge to help her get back her clients. If they were old NOLA families like mine, I probably had connections to them. I often attended events where I socialized with them all.

Fucking hell, Julian. You're simply looking for an excuse to see her again.

As we all helped ourselves to another round of dessert, I found my grandmothers sitting next to me instead of my brothers when I returned.

"What's going on?" I asked them.

"We're very worried about this news, dear. About Books & Beads," Isabeau said. "Stella was such a good woman. She was a midwife, actually, and helped me when I gave birth to your father. It was a very difficult birth. We were lucky to both be alive, and it was all thanks to her. It all happened so fast, and there was no time to call for a doctor. She was on her own and knew just what to do. After that, I promised her that I'd help her no matter what. A few years later, she opened her business making beads and everything else people needed for costumes and floats, as well as selling some bags and things. I haven't been in Books & Beads for ages, but it was a very lovely, quaint shop."

"It still is."

"She knew we had our own float even then. One year, she asked me if she could help. One thing led to another, and I became her very first client."

My eyes widened as the guilt piled on. "I didn't know that."

"Then I kept introducing her to friends of ours, and word caught on," Isabeau went on.

"I actually started working with her, too, long before our families merged," Celine said. "I would so hate for her work to be all for naught. She truly was a lovely woman, God rest her soul." She did her usual sign of the cross. "I met her daughter once too. Is she still at the shop?"

"No, she retired. Stella's granddaughter is running it."

"Georgie, right?" Isabeau asked. Her memory was impeccable, as usual.

"Exactly."

She turned to Celine. "We should visit the girl one day. Ask her if there's anything we can do to help."

"I'm on it," I assured her. I did this, and I needed to fix it.

"Meaning?"

I narrowed my eyes. My grandmothers never questioned me, but considering my blunder, it was fair. Thankfully, my plan had already crystallized in my mind.

"I'll ask Georgie to come with me to several events throughout the Carnival season. I get invitations to dozens of them. I bet I run into her old clients there and don't even know it."

"That is a lovely idea," Isabeau said.

Yes, it was. Now, I only had to convince Georgie of it.

"We should visit the girl anyway," Celine added.

"Yes, we should," Isabeau replied.

Mom was looking at them with a wry smile, shaking her head. She was mostly silent during our family get-togethers. I asked her why once, and she said that my grandmothers had enough to say for everyone and that she preferred to stay quiet.

Mom was a calming presence in this very energetic family.

"Uncle Julian," Bella said, "will you go with me to the buffet again?"

Chad gave me a warning look. I knew what that meant.

I nodded at her. "Sure, but let's go over to the fruit section. I'm dying for some strawberries."

She scrunched her nose. "I'm not. Who needs strawberries when you've got pie and chocolate?"

That was the thing about buffets. When there were sweets available, why indeed go for fruit? But I knew how to persuade Bella. It was a talent of mine.

As we headed that direction, I explained, "I'm trying to eat healthier. Want to help me pick out some fruits?"

"Sure!"

I loaded some grapes on my plate, throwing two into my mouth. "They're delicious."

Bella's eyes lit up. "Can I have some too?"

"Sure."

I felt fucking victorious. Ever since she started eating solid food as a baby, I'd been the one who convinced her to try new things, like broccoli.

As we loaded our plates with several types of fruit, I told her, "I miss coming over to watch movies with you."

She looked at me from the corner of her eye. "I miss you, too, Uncle Julian. Maybe we can tell Dad."

"I will." He and Scarlett could definitely have more date nights. I was more than willing to step in.

"Do you know what movies you want to watch?" I asked her.

"I've had *Goblet of Fire* on my list for some time."

I barely bit back laughter. I liked to spoil my niece, but I didn't like to go against my brother's rules. She was his daughter, after all.

"Bella, your dad said you're too young for it."

She looked crestfallen. "But you know Dad. He's always so cautious."

"What he says goes, baby girl."

"I'm not a baby," Bella mumbled.

God, she's growing up so fast.

I'd seen *Goblet of Fire*, and it was definitely not for someone as young as Bella. That shit got really dark really fast for a kids' movie.

Chad had his eyes trained on Bella's plate when we returned to the table. He looked at me in surprise. The smile I gave him might have been a bit too smug, but I couldn't help it.

As I sat down and overheard my grandmothers still talking about Books & Beads, my mind immediately returned to Georgie. I wanted to speak with her right away. I had a few events in mind where she could run into all the right people. I could pave the way for her.

The businessman in me knew there was a much easier way to accomplish this, however. I could write emails and call the right people. Her contracts would be reinstated very quickly because I was very convincing.

But I wanted to see Georgie again, and now I had the perfect excuse.

CHAPTER SEVEN
GEORGIE

"This has been the most incredible sales day," Zelda said as we balanced the books. She looked at the ledger as if she couldn't believe it herself.

"I told you everything would work out." We'd sold a record number of beads today, and our handmade masks were such a hit that I'd actually asked the team to make a few more.

She laughed. "No one has your energy, Georgie. I swear you keep this place alive all on your own."

"If not me, then who?"

"You think we'll have more customers this evening too?"

It was already five o'clock in the afternoon. Most tourists were pretty spent after running around all day, but at this time of year, things worked differently.

"I'm pretty sure we will," I said.

"I can go buy us a po'boy."

My stomach instantly started to rumble. "Oh, yes, please. Extra mayo for me. And pickles."

"One of these days, Ms. Judy will forsake us as clients. She always tells me, 'You're the only one who wants mayo and pickles.'"

"I can't eat it without them." It was the way my nana used to make po'boys. It was her own special recipe.

"All right, then. I'm going right now. I'm starving too."

"Ask the girls if they want something. And here, let me give you some money." I grabbed my bag, digging out my credit card and giving it to Zelda, "I'll buy for everyone. We've all worked so hard today."

She looked at me strangely. "Georgie, you don't have to, but thank you. Oh, and most of the team has already left. You told them to, re-member?"

I smacked my forehead. "I'm so hungry that I forgot."

"All the reason for me to hurry with that po'boy." Zelda winked and then darted out the front door.

I didn't know what I would do without her. She was truly a godsend.

Since I had a spare moment, I checked my phone. It had beeped a while ago, but I'd had my hands full with customers. I always tried to work with each person, asking them what parade it was for or if they were buying it for another occasion and if they already had an outfit so I could match it for them. I enjoyed advising every single client.

My stomach somersaulted when I noticed a message from Julian.

Julian: Hey Georgie, I've had an idea about how I could make up for you losing some business this year. Give me a ring when you have time to talk.

What is he talking about? Why would he even have to make up for it? He'd already reinstated his contract, after all.

And why was I smiling from ear to ear? Maybe because that after-noon on the balcony had been one of the best days of my life. It held a special place in my heart. Not only because it was a first for me to watch a parade that way, but also because Julian was my hero for standing up to my ex.

And the kiss! Holy smokes!

I'd worn the beads he caught for me every single day since. Yep, I was a bit loony, but I totally embraced it. Most customers thought it was part of my costume for the shop. Zelda had side-eyed them a few times, probably wondering why I was wearing beads we didn't make, but she didn't ask anything.

Since I had a bit of time, I decided to call him.

"Hi, Georgie."

Mmmm... that deep, rumbly voice was delicious on the phone. It coursed through me, making me shiver.

"Hi! I just saw your message."

"I figured you've been busy. So, I've been thinking about what happened with your other customers. Can you tell me some of their names?"

"Sure." I rattled off the six key ones from the top of my head.

"I know four of those, and some will be at the events I'm attending throughout Carnival season."

I licked my lips. "Okay, I'm listening."

"I'd be honored if you'd join me."

"Where?" He couldn't be suggesting what I thought he was...

"To the events."

My eyes nearly popped out of my skull. "You can bring just anyone?"

"I'm always welcome to bring a plus-one."

My heart was beating fast. Was he feeling sorry for me? That seemed unlike Julian. He'd practically told me that he didn't have time to second-guess his decisions or ask for details when he said his assistant was the one who dropped us. But the fact that he was thinking about me and my problems and then came up with a solution... well, that seemed like the exact opposite.

"What's in it for you?" I decided to play it coy and tease him.

"You'd relieve me of a lot of guilt."

"Why exactly do you feel guilty? You reinstated our contract."

"I can't explain it. But I often act out of instinct and don't question it."

Wait, his instinct told him to help me? I needed to know more, but it sounded like he didn't have the answers either.

"So, where are we going first?" I asked him.

"A party in the Garden District. I'll send you all the details."

I bit the inside of my cheek as reality dawned on me. These events were very elegant and sophisticated, and I didn't have many fancy clothes—something Kyle had always pointed out. God, why didn't *I* break up with *him*? He never treated me very nicely. He'd make those comments sporadically and always laughed. Initially, I honestly thought he was just teasing... until I knew better.

"When is it?"

"This Thursday evening. I'll forward you the invitation."

My heart was beating so fast now that I could barely hear him.

"I'd be happy to join you. And thanks a lot, Julian." I caressed the beads I was wearing, smiling like a fool.

"Perfect. And when I see you, we'll chat a bit more about the rest of the events."

"What's the dress code?"

"Elegant."

My heart sank. Just as I'd thought. I had to come up with something because no way in hell was I going to embarrass him.

"Great." My voice was tight. "I'm just thinking about what to wear."

"If you want, you can send me pictures of outfits, and I can give my opinion."

For some reason, I imagined him wiggling his eyebrows as he said that. *Hmmm... is he flirting with me?* The idea didn't sound bad. The problem was that I didn't have more than one outfit.

"Won't be necessary, but thank you for the offer."

"Georgie, don't fret it. You're so damn beautiful that it doesn't even matter what you wear."

Oh, this truly was flirting.

I cleared my throat. "Can you send me the details?"

"Sure, I'll do that right away."

He sent me a message as soon as we hung up. He'd copied over the text of the invitation.

Julian:

Dear Mr. LeBlanc,

We're honored to invite you again to our annual Mardi Gras Ball. As you know, past events have been a hit.

I read the rest quickly, then googled the address and the event name and saw a few pictures from previous years. It was even more elegant than I'd assumed. It wasn't simply a party but truly a ball, complete with floor-length gowns and tuxes. I had absolutely nothing to wear, and I couldn't afford to splurge on a dress right now.

An idea percolated in my mind. Mom had been to a few balls when she was younger, and she had a dress I'd always loved. I'd worn it to a friend's wedding a few years ago, and it had been a hit.

I called her right away, since business was still pretty slow. There was usually a break like this between four and six o'clock, which was why I stayed at the store as late as possible during this season.

Mom answered after a few rings. "Hey, Georgie. Done with the day, sweetheart?"

"No, just having a lull."

"Right. I nearly forgot it's Carnival season."

I laughed. "Mom, how can you say that? There are plenty of celebrations around you."

"The animals keep me so busy that I forget what day it is half the time." I smiled at the happiness in her voice. I was glad that she was so at peace. "Need me to come over to help out?"

"No, no. That's not why I'm calling. Listen, could I borrow your red satin dress again?"

"Sure. What do you need it for?"

"Funny thing, I'm attending a ball in the Garden District."

Mom whistled. "That's so exciting. I'm happy for you. It's going to be an experience, for sure."

"I think so too."

"Who sent you the invitation?"

"Oh, nobody. I'm just a plus-one."

There was a pause before Mom added, "You got back with Kyle Deveraux?"

"God, no," I exclaimed. "Why would you think that?"

"Sorry. Forget I asked."

"It's fine. Remember we had those issues a while ago with the warehouse being flooded?"

"Yes."

"Well, I lost some clients because of it. I convinced one of them to work with us again next year, and he offered to put me in contact with some of the other clients."

"There was no other way for you to reach them?" Her voice was a bit strict.

"I contacted them, but I didn't get anywhere."

"So, who exactly is this client?"

"The LeBlanc family."

"Oh, I met the grandmothers years ago," Mom said. "They're good people."

"Why don't I remember them?"

"You were a toddler perched on my hip. Your nana was always very fond of them. She used to say that if it weren't for them, she wouldn't even have a business at all. So, when do you need the dress?"

"Thursday."

"Goodness. When can you drop by? Actually, you know what? I'll come into the city."

"That would be a lot of help." It took a while to drive out to her house and back, and I didn't like to leave the store for so long during this time.

"It would do me good to walk around the Quarter at this time of the year, see if I miss any of it."

I started to laugh. "You know you don't."

"Well, no, I don't." Mom absolutely loved her quiet life with her animals.

I was happy that she'd gotten exactly what she wanted. She lived in a very secluded area of the bayou that people weren't fond of, but she could afford to buy much bigger property, living there.

"All right, darling. I'll see you then."

Mom arrived at four o'clock on the dot on Thursday. I'd been giddy the whole day, thinking about this afternoon, but the second she entered the shop, I was even more so.

The place was bustling with customers, so I couldn't get to her right away. I was too busy explaining to an elderly lady which beads and mask would go best with her costume, and she seemed to like all of my ideas.

"I'll take the lot," she ended up saying.

"Excellent."

"It's the first time I've come down to New Orleans from DC. I plan to make the most of it as long as these old bones can keep me walking in the parade."

Oh, I liked her. She was feisty.

I smiled. "You'll have a lot of fun. Zelda will cash you out at the counter."

After she left, I went to Mom and briefly hugged her. "Thanks so much for coming over."

"Sure, no problem." She was holding the dress in a garment bag. "I've steamed it, and it's ready to wear."

"I still have to take care of a few customers."

"We've got plenty of time. Unless you want me to do your hair too?"

I nodded. "I brought my curling iron, and I'm going to need your help with it."

"Then chop, chop. We should've started half an hour ago. I'll relax a bit in the back, okay? I can catch up with whoever's there now and see how things are going."

My stomach somersaulted. *This* was why Mom offered to come here—she wanted to check up on how the business was doing.

Serves me right for downplaying the effect of the flood instead of telling her exactly what was going on.

My phone vibrated, and I immediately checked it.

Julian: Still up for being picked up at five?

Georgie: Yes. Mom is here helping me get ready.

Julian: I can't wait to see you.

My heart skipped a beat.

No pressure.

After Mom slipped into the back, I saw to the four other customers in the shop before joining her. She was chatting with Danielle and Eva, who were working on the masks.

Mom and I went to a separate room, where there were a few chairs and a mirror along the wall between boxes upon boxes of supplies.

"You've got everything you need here?" she asked.

"Yeah, I do."

"Then I'll do your hair first, and you can tell me all about this Julian LeBlanc."

"Okay?" I felt my face go red, and I laughed nervously as I sat down. I'd already plugged in the curling iron by the outlet near the mirror. "There's not much to say, really. I met him recently, and he simply offered to..."

"Take you to a ball? That's unusual."

"He *is* a bit unusual. But in the best way."

"Just be careful, okay?"

She started by applying my makeup. Mom was really good at this. She'd done my hair and makeup forever, starting with prom. I'd always loved how she brought out my best features.

"You had a rough time with Kyle," she continued. "I wouldn't like to see you jump into something else if you're not ready."

"Mom, it's nothing like that, I promise you."

"Well, all right, then. I don't want to spoil your fun. Just let me work my magic."

Forty minutes later, my makeup was perfect, as was my hair. My mom truly was a whiz. She'd pulled it into a very elegant half updo, my blonde curls very natural around my shoulders.

She took the dress out of the plastic cover and held it for me while I carefully slipped it on. It felt almost like water on my skin.

"This fabric is amazing. I can't believe it's lasted all these years."

"It looks much better on you than it used to on me."

I scoffed. "Mom, we have the same body type." It was why I could even wear it in the first place.

"But you wear it better, my girl. You're so beautiful." She tilted her head at me with a small smile.

"Thanks, Mom. I need to hurry. Julian should be here in a few minutes, and I still need to put on my shoes."

"I'll check if he's here."

Before I could stop her, she darted out the door.

I pulled the shoes out of the box and put them on, then took a few steps around the room to get accustomed to them. I didn't wear heels very often, and I would have to be extra careful outside in the Quarter—cobblestone and heels did not go together.

When I felt confident that I wouldn't fall flat on my face, I hurried to the front of the store. Sure enough, Mom and Julian were conversing behind the counter near my favorite armchair. Zelda was chatting with two customers but kept throwing glances at Mom and Julian. She sighed in relief when she noticed me. I winked at her to let her know I totally had this.

But when I approached Mom and Julian, I realized I totally didn't.

"So, if you've got any thoughts about my girl, know that I will keep an eye on you."

"Mom!" Jesus, I felt like I was going to go up in flames any second now. "Oh my God, you've been harassing Julian all this time?"

He turned, giving me a brilliant smile. "Yes, she has. And don't worry, I can take it."

I opened my mouth but didn't manage to get any words out. The man was wearing a tux, and my hormones went straight into overdrive.

Hello, dirty thoughts. We've got a long evening ahead of us.

Chapter Eight

Julian

Georgie looked shell-shocked. I was trying to keep my eyes focused on her face. The second I'd noticed her in that red dress, I could barely think straight. She was simply stunning. With great difficulty, I turned to look at her mom.

"As I promised, I'll take good care of Georgie."

"Thank you."

"Julian and I should go," Georgie cut in.

"Yes, please. Don't let me keep you," her mom said, then turned back to me. "Say hello to your grandmothers."

"I will. Actually, they'd love to see you. They've got a fragrance shop on Dumaine, in case you're in the Quarter for longer."

She glanced at me in surprise. "They do? But they must be well into their—"

"Don't tell them that," I cautioned. She gave me the first real smile of the day. "They're very proud that they're still running their shop. They have plenty of energy."

"You know what? I will pay them a visit," she said. "You two have fun. But not too much fun." She winked.

"Mom!" Georgie said. She sounded truly embarrassed, but there was no need. Her mom had been completely right about everything. It was as if she knew that my interest in her daughter went far beyond helping her get clients back.

I smiled at Georgie. "All right. I parked in the back."

"We can go out that way."

Georgie walked me through the shop. The rear of her store was much smaller than I'd imagined. Once we stepped out, I led her to the car.

"Are you okay?" I asked her. She was too quiet.

"Yes. Umm... I'm really sorry about Mom. I don't know why she acted like that. She's usually calm and warm."

"She *was* calm and warm. She just warned me not to hurt you. She wants to protect her daughter. I understand."

Georgie stopped in her tracks. "Oh, Julian, she actually said that? I'm s—"

"Don't apologize." I instinctively touched the side of her face. The contact felt so damn good. It wasn't nearly as good as kissing her, but it came pretty close. "I tried to explain what was going on, but she didn't seem to buy it."

Georgie laughed nervously. "I tried too. She came over to bring me this dress. It's hers. It's appropriate for the event, right?"

"You could wear nothing and I swear you'd be the best dressed woman there," I told her.

Her eyes widened. "Julian, the things you say."

I cleared my throat, but instead of changing the subject, I doubled down. "I mean it. You look fucking amazing. This dress is fire on you."

She gave me a brilliant smile as I opened the car door for her.

Even though there was traffic, we reached the Garden District in time. Finding a parking spot was another story, though.

I scoffed at all the Aston Martins and Ferraris. Everyone liked to show off at these things. As we drove past a yellow Ferrari, I felt Georgie stiffen.

"What's wrong?" I asked.

"Nothing."

"Georgie?"

She'd talked my ear off about all the ball traditions she'd read about, and now she'd suddenly gone quiet. And she was very, very pale.

"Are you feeling sick?"

"No. I just saw Kyle's car."

I groaned. "Fuck, I didn't think about that. Of course he's here."

"He's probably going to be at most of those events of yours."

"I do run into him a lot during this season," I admitted. "We don't have to go. I'm fine doing something else, just having a fun evening out."

Georgie looked at me, and a hint of a smile played on her face. "You're wearing a tux, and I'm wearing Mom's best dress."

"We can go to a fancy restaurant and have a delicious meal."

"But you RSVP'd that you're coming with a plus-one," she whispered.

"Fuck that RSVP. I don't give a shit about it. I just don't want you to feel uncomfortable in any way."

Georgie closed her eyes for a brief moment. When she opened them again, they held a strange determination.

"I don't want to hide. He and I live in the same city. I mean, we don't run in the same circles, but we're bound to bump into each other from time to time. I'm not a coward, and I have no reason to hide."

"Of course you don't. But that doesn't mean you have to face him tonight."

"I don't want us to leave, Julian."

"Are you certain?"

"Yes."

"All right, then. But you tell me the moment you're uncomfortable and we'll leave, okay? Let's find a parking spot."

As I moved down the street, I said, "You want to tell me what happened between the two of you? How long were you going out?"

"Only six months. He seemed so charming and kept telling me that it was a completely new thing for him to date someone who... well, was in another social circle."

"What a jackass! He actually said that?"

"Well, yes, and worse. It was bizarre, but I was always up to my neck in work, so I didn't have time to second-guess anything or think about his remarks too often. He'd always make snide comments like 'your little business' or 'that one-woman shop.'"

"How did you decide to dump his sorry ass?"

"That's even more pathetic. I didn't. His new girlfriend broke up with me."

It took all my self-control not to punch the wheel. "You can't be serious."

"Unfortunately, I am." She sighed. "I don't want to rehash the details."

"He's always been a little fucker. Believed himself to be better than anyone. He was insufferable in school and now in business as well. His chain of clubs is not nearly as big and profitable as his ego would like you to believe."

She seemed to perk up a bit at that. "Really? Because he wouldn't stop bragging about it."

"Sounds just like him."

I finally found a parking spot two streets away. We walked to the mansion at a very slow pace. "By the way, if that moron accosts you again, how about we continue what we started at the bar?"

She straightened up, glancing at me. "What do you mean?"

"Do I need to remind you about us kissing?"

She gasped but then smiled and looked away. Even so, I could see color creeping up her cheeks. And it wasn't just a reflection of the red fabric of her dress.

"The look on his face was priceless," I went on. "And I did tell him you're my girl. I'll keep doing that. I mean, it'll probably appear like that anyway, considering we're arriving together."

"I thought you said everyone's free to bring a plus-one even if it's just a business partner."

"In theory, yes. But most people don't do that. They just bring their wife or girlfriend or whatever."

"Julian," she said. "You didn't tell me that."

"It's not a big deal."

We resumed walking, and I held her by the waist as firmly as before. Since she didn't make any move to free herself, I assumed she truly did need the support. Then again, the sidewalk was a bit of a death trap even without high heels. There weren't potholes in it per se, but some of the tree roots had grown completely out of control, cracking the pavement.

"I'm not sure what you have in mind," she said after a few moments.

"Neither do I. Let's just play it by ear."

"I don't like lying."

"We don't have to. We'll tell people exactly what happened. We met after I unfairly dropped your services. You gave me a piece of your mind. I found you so damn irresistible that we ended up kissing."

I felt her entire body shiver. She parted her lips, then looked down at the sidewalk again.

"You just came up with this?" she murmured.

"Yes. I'm a very spur-of-the-moment guy. It drives my family nuts. Some of my employees too."

"I can't imagine why."

"But it does sound like a good plan, doesn't it?"

She glanced at me again. When she nodded, my whole chest expanded. "Yes, it does."

Hell yes.

For tonight, Georgie was mine to touch and hold close.

CHAPTER NINE

GEORGIE

I'd always loved the Garden District. I even had my favorite mansions. Then again, every born-and-bred New Orleans resident did. I'd rarely been inside one, though, so tonight I couldn't help but glance around in awe. This one was a Greek Revival style with majestic columns and a lot of marble on the facade.

Inside, though, it was even more impressive. I wasn't an art collector or connoisseur, but the paintings hanging on the walls had to be worth a fortune. There were fresh flowers in every corner of the room. It felt like a fairy tale.

"Let's drop off your coat." Julian pointed at an elderly gentleman dressed to the nines who was taking guests' wraps.

I unbuttoned mine, and then Julian started to take it off. The second his fingers brushed my bare shoulders, I shuddered. My mind immediately went to the kiss we'd shared at his bar. It had been so hot that I could almost still feel it on my lips. The man had some serious kissing skills.

"Are you cold?"

"Huh?"

He pointed at my skin. Ah, of course my goose bumps were showing.

"It's just how I react when the fabric brushes my skin." What kind of a lie was that? No one would believe it.

But Julian didn't question me. Instead, he tilted closer. "Ready for showtime?"

That made me laugh. "Sure!"

He gave me his arm, and I gladly took it. Walking on heels would never be my strong suit even on a flat surface.

"So, what exactly happens at these things?" I asked.

"Eating, drinking, and rubbing elbows with"—he quoted with one hand—"'the right people.' I think I've closed more business deals at events like these than in the office."

"Really?" I asked.

"Yeah. People are more open to discussing business after a drink. And I think they assume if someone was invited here, it's a sign that they've been vetted."

"Interesting," I murmured. "Your world is so different from mine."

"It's not very exciting, I assure you."

"Quite the contrary. I find this very exciting."

"Then why do you look like you're about to run away?" he asked in a teasing tone.

I stopped in the act of looking over my shoulder. "Is it that obvious?" I whispered.

"Yes."

"I'm sorry. I keep looking around for Kyle."

Julian stopped walking and turned around, staring straight at me. "Georgie, we can still leave."

I shook my head. "No, really. I want to make the best of this evening. It's a new experience for me. And *you* are excellent company."

"And why is that?"

"Hm, I can't explain it. It's just a feeling."

He grinned. "I'll take the compliment."

As we entered what I assumed was the main party area, I gasped almost audibly. "Goodness, this room."

It dripped with wealth. Everything was tasteful and grand. The crystal chandeliers, the golden ornaments along the walls, and the paintings were a dream.

There were multiple tables around the room, but not a lot of people were sitting down. Most were milling through the crowd.

"You said the Tableau family were your clients, right?" Julian asked.

"Yes. I've only ever met their employees, though. I don't know them."

"But I do. Let's go say hi."

My eyes widened. "Am I supposed to pitch them? God, I'm so far out of my comfort zone, it's not even funny."

Julian frowned. "Why?"

"I don't really do things like this. I'm not used to sealing deals. I've been working with all the contracts my grandmother and then my mom put in place."

"But if you don't get your old clients back, you'll have to start pitching to new ones anyway."

"True. And I can't really postpone it any longer."

"You're going to win them over."

"Any tips?" I asked.

"Be yourself. Actually, wait. Don't give them a hard time."

I started to laugh. "Funnily enough, I wasn't going to do that."

"So, I'm the only one who got to see that side of you? I'm honored."

"Not sure what got into me. I think I was just riled up from writing back and forth, and you were the first one who pulled out of the deal."

"Which was a mistake. I'll point that out to them. Now, let's hurry. They're grabbing drinks. I bet if you wait too long, someone else will monopolize their attention."

I nodded. "You're right. Let's go."

We headed toward a gorgeous couple who seemed to be in their fifties. The woman had dark brown hair styled in a sophisticated updo with pearls placed throughout it. Her husband looked very elegant in his tux. His beard was a mix of gray and white even though his hair was still dark.

"Bo, Calliope, so good to see you tonight," Julian said.

They looked at him with pleasant smiles.

"This is Georgie," he introduced us.

"Lovely to meet you, Mr. and Mrs. Tableau," I said.

"Any friend of Julian's can call us by name," Calliope informed me.

"And it's a very gorgeous name, Calliope."

"I keep telling her that"—Bo put an arm around her shoulders—"but she insists it's too old-fashioned."

"Oh, darling. It's not just old-fashioned. It's old. My mom always had a penchant for strange names. As you can see, I'm still not used to it even though I'm an old bird now." She smiled like this was a discussion they'd had plenty of times before. "So, Georgie, tell us a bit about yourself."

Holy shit, that was fast. I figured we'd make some more small talk first.

"I have a shop in the French Quarter. Books & Beads."

I looked at them intently, but neither seemed familiar with it. Fortunately, Julian caught my discomfort and stepped right in.

"Georgie is in charge of making all the decorations and costumes for the float my family is sponsoring." His voice was somehow even more seductive than usual even though it was all business. It simply dripped with authority. "Actually, I remember that she was also doing yours."

Calliope and Bo exchanged a glance before focusing on me.

"That might be possible. I'm sorry. We don't really handle such details," Bo said gently.

My heart kind of collapsed in on itself at the word *detail*.

It felt strange that my life's work was a detail to others. But I remembered what Julian said earlier about the guests being more relaxed when they were in this environment. *Here goes nothing.*

"Yes, I did the Tableau floats until this year."

"Oh? What happened this year?" Calliope asked.

I was shocked by how concerned she seemed. "There was a flood, and some of the items I'd already prepared were unusable." I chose my next words carefully so I wouldn't offend them. "I contacted your team to let them know I could still deliver everything, but they decided to be on the safe side and switch suppliers."

"Oh my goodness," Calliope gasped. "I'm so sorry. Bo?" She looked at her husband with sincere distress in her eyes.

"How long have you been doing the floats for us?" Bo asked. He was also frowning.

"My grandmother started the business sixty years ago. Your family was with her from the beginning."

"This is an outrage," Bo said rather loudly.

"Honey, we must fix this," Calliope urged. "We don't do things like that. We believe in traditions, and our float has always looked perfect."

"Georgie, I take it my team has your contact information," Bo went on.

"They do." My heart was beating erratically. Could it really be this easy?

"They will contact you on Monday, and our business relationship will be reinstated. And I will have a word with them about making such a change. It's probably too late for this year, and I'm terribly sorry for that. Our float is set to be in a parade in two days, but we'll absolutely be back on track next year."

"Why, thank you, that would be wonderful." I was so ecstatic that I could hug the two of them. However, I tried to remain calm and unassuming, because I didn't want them to know I was here for this very reason. "I didn't expect this. It's very kind of you."

"Of course. Don't even give it another thought, my dear," Calliope said. "Please forgive us. We don't deal with these things directly."

"Oh, that's perfectly fine, really. Things happen, and, uh..." Was I stammering? Goodness, I didn't want to embarrass myself in front of Julian.

Thankfully, he cut in and said, "Don't beat yourself up, Calliope. I made the very same mistake. But I've rectified it, and Georgie will be in charge of our float again next year."

"As you should," Bo said. "Traditions are in place for a reason. There's no need to change something that's been working for decades. That's just madness. It's what I tell people at the office too. They drive me crazy with their need for change. Always innovating, always looking for the shiny new thing."

"Not all change is bad, Bo," Julian countered.

"I wouldn't expect anything else from a youngster like you." He patted Julian's shoulder with a chuckle, then asked, "How are your grandmothers?"

"They're great."

"I talked to Isabeau a few weeks ago," Calliope said. "She promised to be at the lunch at the Boudreaux house in two weeks. I can't wait to catch up with her. Hopefully she'll convince Celine, too, and your grandfathers, of course."

When she started waving at someone behind us, Julian said, "It was nice catching up with the two of you."

"And you," Calliope said. "It was great meeting you, Georgie."

"And you also." I shook hands with both of them.

Once they were out of earshot, I turned to Julian. He had a triumphant look in his eyes.

"Did that just happen?" I whispered.

"Yes, it did."

"It was so easy. I didn't even have to sell myself."

"I had an inkling that they probably had no clue what was going on either. I think most of your clients don't. And I know these old families. They like traditions, nostalgia, and they're loyal to those who are to them. Let's celebrate. Want a drink?"

"Sazerac?" I asked him.

"Maybe later on. Everyone starts with champagne." He leaned in closer, whispering conspiratorially directly into my ear, "Not my favorite, but it's important to keep up with appearances. And I know I've already said it, but you look fucking fantastic."

Feeling his hot breath on my skin sent me into yet another tailspin. Then he put a hand on the small of my back and I nearly whimpered.

How could his touch make me react like this? It wasn't even inappropriate. Julian was just being... well, a flirt, but I was starting to think that was simply the way he was with all women.

But I wanted him to only flirt with me.

Chapter Ten

Georgie

"We wouldn't want to stand out, would we?" I asked.

He laughed. "Oh, there is a time to stand out. It's just not this one." Straightening up, he turned to the bartender. "We'll take two glasses of champagne."

The sculpted mahogany structure was the most elegant pop-up bar I'd ever seen. It clearly wasn't a permanent part of the ballroom, but it fit perfectly.

We got our drinks right away, and I clinked glasses with Julian.

"To a very successful pitch," he said.

I grinned at him. "Thanks for making this happen."

"Stick with me, Georgie."

"I'm usually a very optimistic person, but I didn't expect this. Thank you."

"Just promise me one thing."

"What's that?"

"That you will have an ironclad contract, okay? For everyone. Including my own team."

I nodded. "I'm already on top of that."

"Perfect."

"Oh, this champagne is terrific."

"I agree. Let's find some finger foods too."

"Will there be a buffet?" I asked.

"No. Usually they have a waiter circulating with starters, and then all the food is served at the table."

I took another sip of the best champagne I'd ever tasted. I shuddered thinking how much it had to cost, but it didn't matter. Tonight it was free, and I planned to enjoy every single drop.

We immediately ran into another waiter with a food tray, but that was no surprise. Glancing around, I realized there were a lot of them circulating about. Julian took two small plates and handed one to me. They had an assortment of fried shrimp and what looked like a slice of a very sophisticated po'boy with a toothpick holding it all together. I immediately went for the po'boy.

"Mm, I needed this," I said before we set our glasses on a nearby empty table. I practically swallowed it whole and then proceeded with the fried shrimp. It was exquisite as well.

After we were both done, a waiter appeared out of nowhere so he could take the empty plates. Julian and I grabbed our glasses again.

"All right, now that we've got something in our stomachs, bottoms up," he said.

I grinned. "I was just thinking about downing the rest of it."

He winked. "I thought so after our Sazerac experience."

"Oh, so that's the impression I left on you, huh?"

"It's a very good one. Trust me," he assured me.

We clinked glasses again, and then I drank with much bigger gulps than before. Obviously, I couldn't finish it all at once, but neither did Julian.

Once we paused to breathe, he said, "We're going to need some water too."

"You've read my mind again."

"I'll be right back."

"I'm going to look at some of the paintings." The nearest one depicted scenery that was clearly straight out of the bayou. The shadows, the light, and the colors of the water and trees were so good that they transported me right there. I swear I could even smell it. I closed my eyes, drawing in a deep breath.

"You've got to be kidding me."

My eyes flew open. Kyle was approaching me. He looked me up and down once. "What are you doing here?"

"I'm here with Julian," I said breezily.

He snorted. "These aren't your type of events."

"I'm making some changes." I felt even bolder than usual. Why did he think he could just come up and talk shit to me?

"I see you're wearing your one good outfit. Jesus, you're—"

"Don't you fucking dare finish that sentence," Julian said, and I startled. I hadn't even realized he was coming toward us. He put the glasses of water on another table and turned to Kyle.

"Or what?" Kyle challenged him. "Will the illustrious Julian LeBlanc get his hands dirty in the middle of an event like this?"

"Yes," Julian said. The way he carried himself made me think he wasn't bluffing. His hands were pulled into fists as he rolled his shoulders backward. He was holding his head high.

Kyle snorted. "You actually came here with her?"

To my astonishment, Julian instantly transformed. He glanced at me, and his body relaxed.

"Of course. I wanted her to meet everyone." Then he came over to me and pulled me to him in a way that could only be described as intimate. The side of my body, especially my left boob, was pressed against his chest. We were glued to each other. I could practically feel the reverberations of his heartbeat against my rib cage.

"Just so you know, if you plan on taking her to more social events, that's the one good outfit she has," Kyle sneered.

Julian's eyes instantly turned from warm to fucking pissed off.

I looked straight at Kyle. "Not sure why you think your insults hurt me in any way. They just annoy the shit out of me and out of Julian, so please fuck off."

Kyle jerked his head back. Since he hadn't even bothered to break up with me in person, he had no idea how I could be when I was angry. At Julian's bar, I'd been too surprised to react. But now I had my wits about me.

Julian let go of me and moved closer to Kyle. "We can take this outside right now. Right fucking now."

"You would like that, wouldn't you?" Kyle said.

"Half the people in this room will cheer for me bashing in your face," Julian said through gritted teeth. "You shouldn't even be here, considering you've swindled half this city."

Now it was Kyle's turn to look angry. His smug smile disappeared. "Don't speak on shit you know nothing about."

"But I *do* know," Julian said. "So I'm going to tell you one last time. Fuck off."

"Whatever. Suit yourself." Kyle snorted before walking away.

Julian stood rooted to his place, breathing in and out quickly. I took the glass of water to him.

"Need a refreshment?" I asked.

"Yes." His voice was a bit on edge.

"I'm really sorry about that."

"Georgie, don't start apologizing again. Not your fault he's a jackass."

"What do you mean about swindling?" I wasn't intending to put Julian on the spot, but I had to ask.

"A while ago, he asked a lot of people to invest in this bright new venture. He ended up losing all their money. At least, that's what he told them. I'm pretty sure he pocketed it. It was a Ponzi scheme. I knew that without even reading the fine print."

"So, how did he get away with it?" I asked.

"Connections work in mysterious ways. And don't forget, no one wants to admit being made a fool. Especially no one in this room."

"Julian," a male voice said, and then a man came over to us. "What's that I hear?" He looked straight at me. "After all these years, you've finally brought a lady to introduce to us."

Julian's demeanor changed. He straightened up and schooled his features. "Robert, how do you do?"

He shook hands with Robert and then turned to me. "This is my Georgie."

Robert beamed at me. "Georgie, you are a miracle. I couldn't believe it when Kyle told me that Julian LeBlanc was here with a date."

I stiffened. *What's going on?*

"What's your family name?" he asked.

"Melrose," I said.

"Hm, that doesn't ring a bell."

Julian put a hand on the middle of my back. "Georgie runs Books & Beads in the Quarter. She makes the best damn Carnival items in town."

He spoke as if he couldn't be prouder of me. It filled me with warmth.

"That's great," Robert said. "Listen, Julian, I haven't had time to look over your proposal or Kyle's. Are you going to be at the Landrys' event?"

"I wasn't planning to," Julian said, "but if you'll be there, I'll RSVP."

"It's going to give us a good opportunity to talk. It's not the brightest and best on the social calendar, but it's good for business. I look forward to seeing the two of you again there..." He looked at me as if he couldn't quite place me.

"Georgie," I finished for him.

"That's right. I promise to learn your name too." With that, he turned on his heel and walked away.

Julian actually reached for his tie and loosened it.

"Julian?" I asked tentatively. "What was that?"

He looked at his empty champagne glass on the table and said, "An unexpected complication."

He seemed to be determined to get rid of the tie.

"Want me to help you with that? I think you're just going to make a mess of it."

He flashed me that very charming smile. "Please do, girlfriend."

My stomach somersaulted at his words. He'd said them playfully, but I still wondered... what would it be like to truly be Julian LeBlanc's girlfriend? I couldn't even wrap my mind around that. My fingers were shaking a bit as I walked up to him.

"Want me to take it away or just make it loose enough that it won't bother you?"

"That's an option?" he asked, perplexed.

I laughed. "Yes, it is. Trust me, I've learned a lot of tricks from doing costumes."

"Then by all means."

I worked my magic on his collar. It wasn't that difficult, but being so close to him was somehow messing with my senses. I could smell the scent of his skin plus his cologne or aftershave. Although, the five-o'clock shadow he was sporting was a clear indication that he hadn't actually shaved today.

"There!"

He took in a deep breath. "That is so much better." Then he touched his tie. "I can't believe this thing is still on. Thought it was going to strangle me."

"Stop by Books & Beads any time you need help with it."

"Careful, Georgie. I might take you up on it."

The prospect thrilled me to no end. His tone was flirty, but I still detected a bit of unease.

"Sorry, I feel like I need to catch up with whatever is going on. What did that Robert guy do to put you so on edge?"

"He owns two buildings in the Quarter. I want to buy them and open two bars. Robert is playing hard to get. One other person is interested. Guess who."

Now I was finally putting two and two together. "Kyle."

"That's right. I'm not even sure why he's making a play for it. He's up to his eyeballs in debt. Who knows what he did with all the money he stole. But that's not my problem."

I fiddled with my thumbs. "So, at this Landry party, you and Robert would talk shop."

"It seems so. I've been chasing him for long enough that I was ready to throw in the towel."

"That doesn't sound like you at all."

Julian gave me a wry smile. "I pick my battles. If something costs me too much time, I move on. In my experience, time is the most precious currency."

"It seems like Robert will be expecting me at the next event."

"Yes, he will." Julian paused, then said very sincerely, "Honestly, I'd like you there. This evening is already a hundred percent more fun than usual."

I laughed, though without much humor. "Really? You had to help me with the Tableaus, and then Kyle accosted us. How is it fun?"

"You make everything a lot less boring. Besides, there will be some dancing later. And you're the best damn dancer I know."

His eyes dropped to my middle for a moment, and then he brought them back up. He didn't even particularly linger on any inappropriate place, but it was enough to fire me up.

"Think about it. It's not a big deal. If you aren't in the mood, I'll just tell Robert that you couldn't make it. None of his business anyway. But we could run into some more of your clients."

"Huh, you're bribing me to come with you."

He grinned. "Sort of. But it's also true. I haven't spotted anyone else you mentioned tonight, though some could still come."

I deflated at that.

"Besides, Robert is a snob. The Landry party is the best out of them all. Probably because it isn't as highbrow. But people know how to party. They bring a jazz band and—"

"I'm sold," I said.

"—have live music," he finished. "Wait, that's what sold you?"

"I like music, and I like dancing. And if it helps you, I'm going to be there, of course. I owe you."

"No, you don't."

"For the Tableaus and sticking it to Kyle."

"You don't owe me a thing." He came closer and leaned toward me. "So, while I appreciate your enthusiasm, think about it before agreeing."

"Okay, I will."

"What's that I hear?" a man said, approaching us. "My brother has a girlfriend and no one knew?"

Julian turned in the direction of the voice. "Xander." He grinned. "I didn't know you'd be here. You don't usually come to these things."

"Had to make an exception for business's sake," he said. Then his eyes fell on me.

"This is Georgie," Julian said.

"Georgie, the one with the float business?" Xander asked. I was surprised that he knew about me.

"Precisely."

Xander narrowed his eyes. "So, when exactly did this happen? What's going on?"

I looked at Julian, ready to follow his lead.

"We'll talk about it later. Too many people watching us right now."

Xander nodded. "And I also heard from Robert that you're going to the Landry event. Beckett's the one who usually attends it."

Julian snapped his fingers. "That's right, I forgot. I kept thinking, why didn't I show up there the past few years? But it's because Beckett went."

"Yeah, and he actually enjoys it."

"I'll talk him into getting me an invitation."

Xander grinned, and his entire face transformed. "Beckett won't let you live it down as quietly as I am. Why can't you tell me what's going on?"

"Because Georgie and I are going dancing." He looked at me, and I smiled, nodding. "They should start the music any minute now."

Xander groaned. "Yeah, I don't know why they insist on playing jazz everywhere."

"Because it's parade season. If not now, then when?" I asked.

"Don't mind my brother. He's a grump," Julian said.

"I'm just saying," Xander went on. "It's much harder to talk business when there's music."

"I'll give you a hint, brother. You could actually enjoy yourself." Julian patted Xander's shoulder. "Not everything revolves around business."

That wasn't strictly true, though, was it? It was why I came with him here in the first place. But as Xander opened his mouth, probably to argue back, music indeed started to play. But it wasn't particularly lively, and I instantly realized I'd had the wrong expectations. This wasn't parade jazz but something totally different.

I glanced around and asked, "Is there a dance floor?"

"Not an official one. Most people just dance around the band," Julian said.

I pressed my lips together. "But I don't see anyone dancing."

Even with his brother there, he stepped super close to me, grabbing my hand and kissing the back of it. "We won't let that stop us, will we?"

My entire body was on fire. I'd come here today to hopefully sign back some clients, but this evening was turning into something else entirely.

CHAPTER ELEVEN

JULIAN

I'd always played things by ear, but even for me, this was slightly insane.

I'd intended to bring Georgie here tonight so she could gain back some clients. When she pointed out that Kyle's car was outside, I figured we'd kill two birds with one stone—she'd get back more business, and that moron would know not to mess with her. I hadn't counted on the entire room getting the idea that Georgie and I were together.

So why was I encouraging it? Dancing with her was going to send a clear message. The truth was, I couldn't wait to hold her close again.

And that was my answer. That was why I was dancing with her. I needed an excuse to get closer.

I was holding her tight and glanced over my shoulder as I pulled her onto the dance floor. She was already moving to the beat.

"Your rhythm is incredible," I told her.

"This isn't quite my usual speed, but I like it. I'm not sure how to dance to it, though."

"I'll lead you."

Her eyes widened, but she nodded, sucking in a breath. It was all the invitation I needed.

"Kyle is watching."

I put a hand on her waist as I moved my hips. She immediately matched my rhythm. We were so damn close that it was impossible not to be aware of her curves pressing against me.

"You're full of surprises, aren't you, Julian?" Her voice seemed a bit on edge.

I brought my mouth to her ear so it would look to everyone else—especially her moron of an ex—like we were flirting. "And I've got so many more."

Correction: I wasn't just pretending to flirt. I was full-on flirting.

I straightened up quickly, just in time to notice her lick her lower lip. It was working.

She grinned. "I can't believe he's watching. Actually, a lot of people are."

Since we were the only ones on the dance floor, that was no surprise. "Good."

"That doesn't bother you?"

"I'm dancing with the most beautiful woman in the room tonight," I whispered. "Let them watch."

The music became faster, and so did our moves. It was incredible how in sync we were. I couldn't help but think that we'd be the same way in bed. I'd explore her body until she begged, and then I'd give her more pleasure than she could imagine.

She was getting bolder, and I enjoyed it. She'd been so wild and free on that balcony, watching the parade. Here, she'd withdrawn ever since she saw Kyle's car. But now she was starting to let loose.

Others joined us on the dance floor, but they weren't nearly as good as we were. I twirled her around once and then a second time.

"Julian!"

I realized a second too late that she was about to lose her balance. She glanced down at her heels and half laughed, half shrieked as she tilted forward.

I stepped up next to her, catching her in time so she didn't spill onto the floor, but it was obvious to anyone watching that she'd been about to.

She giggled into my chest.

"Are you hurt?" I asked.

"My ankle aches a bit."

I helped her stand straight. "Can you put your weight on it?"

"Yes, but it's tender."

"Let's get off this dance floor."

I held my arm securely around her waist and led her out of the room and into a smaller one that was opposite from the entrance.

There were a few chairs here and high bar tables. I remembered from last year that it was where people fled for business talk. But it was empty right now, which was a sign that food was about to be served. It didn't matter. First, I needed to make sure Georgie was okay.

"Sit here," I instructed when we reached the nearest chair. After she sat down, I kneeled in front of her. "Which leg is the tender one?"

She held it up.

"I'm going to put my hand on your ankle and press gently. If it hurts, tell me, okay?"

"Sure!" Her voice sounded strange.

I glanced up at her. "You're already in pain?"

She shook her head vehemently. "No. Not at all."

I touched her ankle. Damn, her skin was so smooth. I wondered if it was like that all the way up. Then I started to press gently.

"It's not hurting, but it is a bit uncomfortable."

I looked up at her. "I can take you to have this checked out."

Her eyes bulged. "That's unnecessary. It's really probably nothing."

"Let's stay here a few minutes so you can ice it." I'd noticed buckets with champagne bottles around the room. There had to be ice in them.

I stood up, heading to the nearest one, grabbing a napkin from one of the tables next to it. I filled it with ice, then returned to Georgie. She was looking at me with a huge smile and tilted her head.

"Julian, I could've gotten my own ice."

She hummed the second I pressed the napkin to her skin.

"Not when your ankle hurts, you won't. If it's indeed nothing, then the ice will make the pain go away. Otherwise, the ice won't do jack shit."

"How do you even know that?"

"Years ago, I took a first aid course. I sucked at it, but I do remember a few things."

"How come you took one? Never occurred to me to take one."

"Zachary wanted to do it, and I figured he could use someone with him, though it turned out he absolutely didn't. My little brother was a pro at it. He truly loved learning all that stuff. I bailed, but he stuck it out until the end."

"That's so cute that you took the course with your brother. Do you often do stuff with them?"

"All the time. Since I'm the oldest, I watched over them often. I used to give Mom grief about it, but I actually secretly enjoyed it."

"And you hang out with your family a lot these days too?"

"We get together as often as we can. There's always something happening at my parents' and grandparents' house."

"They live together?"

"Yes, in a huge mansion not far away from here, actually."

I was keeping a hand at the back of her ankle and the ice at the front where she was hurting. Almost involuntarily, I started to feather my hands over her leg. Seconds later, it turned to goose bumps.

Shit! This isn't helping at all. I was already fantasizing about moving my hand under that red dress. In fact, I was fantasizing about getting rid of the dress altogether.

I swallowed hard, looking down at her skin. It was so damn smooth, so inviting.

The room went completely silent.

"They stopped the music," Georgie said.

"They're probably serving food." I looked sideways through the cracked door. "Exactly, the waiters are—oh, for fuck's sake. Kyle is coming this way."

She groaned. "I'm not in the mood for him anymore."

A self-serving thought crossed my mind. "I know a way to get rid of him without having to utter one word."

"Do share!"

"You trust me?"

She nodded. "Yes, of course."

"Good, because I'm about to kiss you again."

I sealed my mouth over hers, and she instantly parted her lips for me. I sucked her lower lip into my mouth first before giving her my tongue. She moaned, and it nearly brought me to my knees. The way she responded to me was out of this world. I kissed and kissed her without ever intending to stop. I simply couldn't. She tasted too good. The way she gave herself to me only made me need her more. I put a hand at her back, bringing her closer so I could explore her even deeper.

I felt her body vibrate against mine. I wanted to relieve her of that tension right here, right now. To take her somewhere no one could see or hear us and make this woman come. Several times.

She was so fucking exquisite. I'd never enjoyed a kiss as much as I did this one. I took my time, slowing the rhythm, turning it into a lazy exploration. She shuddered, sighing against my mouth.

"Here you two are. Oh, for fuck's sake."

I jumped backward. Xander was standing in the doorway. He glanced between the two of us with a raised brow.

"That would explain why Kyle Deveraux looked pissed."

"The ice!" Georgie was looking down at her feet.

"Oh shit. I dropped the ice," I said.

She immediately lifted herself from the chair. "Ouch!"

"Georgie, just sit," I instructed. She didn't argue. I'd been so lost in the kiss that I'd completely forgotten about the ice. "Still need it on your ankle?"

"Yeah, it did seem to help." Her voice was uneven.

"You're hurt?" Xander asked. "I thought something was off on the dance floor."

"I don't think it's anything serious," Georgie told him, "but it's aching a bit. Should we go have dinner?" She looked at Xander. "Have they served it?"

"Yes, but I have another proposition. Why don't the three of us ditch this party?"

Usually I'd contradict my brother just for the fun of it, but there was merit to his words. When I glanced at Georgie, she was avoiding my gaze. Was she uncomfortable? No, she'd completely enjoyed the kiss.

"My brother is right, and you do need to keep this ankle iced."

"But what about chatting up people?"

"There's going to be plenty of time at the next event. And I truly didn't see anyone else from your list."

She frowned. "I figured maybe some of them had come later."

"Usually the guests arrive before the food is served." That came from Xander.

Georgie shrugged with a sigh. "Then I guess we can go. Though I'm not sure if I can put much weight on my ankle."

"I'll help you." I took her hand as she rose and took a tentative step.

"It doesn't really hurt, but it's a bit uncomfortable."

"I can wait for you out by the entrance," Xander said. "You've got a coat?" he asked Georgie.

"Yes. It's white with gold buttons."

"I'll get it for you."

"Thanks, Xander."

He pointed at me. "But I still demand an explanation for, well, everything."

"Of course you do," I said just as my brother left. Then I trained my gaze on Georgie. "Are you okay?"

"Sure. This is just so unexpected." She was laughing, but it wasn't wholehearted and fun. It was nervous.

"Georgie, what's wrong? Tell me."

"I guess this evening sort of spiraled out of control."

"Yeah, you could say that. But don't worry. We're winging it successfully." I grinned, and she returned it.

"You're right. Now, is there any way out of here without crossing the entire ballroom?"

"No, so let's give them something worth watching." I wanted to support her properly, so I put my arm around her back. "I've got you. If you can't continue, just let me know and we'll take a break or something, but I won't let you fall."

She glanced at me sideways. "I wasn't even worrying about that."

We walked at a normal pace through the ballroom. Everyone was too busy eating to pay attention to us except that fucker Deveraux.

"Kyle is watching us," I murmured.

"I'm so happy he saw the kiss."

I felt as if someone had punched me. Obviously, the kiss had been for show, but I'd enjoyed it. But by the sound of it, it was simply a means to an end for her. Which should have been fine. I'd suggested the whole damn ruse in the first place, after all. So why the fuck wasn't it sitting right with me?

I decided not to dissect it too much. It was very unlike me. The reason why I enjoyed life to the max was that I didn't sweat over the small things. Yet this didn't feel small at all. It felt monumental, and that was simply bizarre.

"My leg is much better. But I do want to change out of these heels before I break my neck."

"I'll get you home so you're comfortable," I assured her.

As promised, Xander was waiting with Georgie's coat outside the door. He held it for her, and she immediately slipped her arms inside it. Damn it, I'd wanted to do that.

Good grief, am I sixteen or what? Looking for an excuse to touch a woman. It was insane.

"Where did you park?" he asked me.

"Around the corner. Georgie, it's better if you stay here, and I'll bring the car around," I said as we walked out to the yard slowly.

"Julian...," Xander warned.

"Ah, I still owe you that explanation," I said.

"That's right."

"Georgie, you need to know two things about my brother. He doesn't pull punches, and he doesn't mind putting people on the spot."

Xander looked at Georgie apologetically. "Sorry, Georgie. Nothing against you, but I don't like hearing secondhand information about my family. Usually we're very up-front with one another."

I sighed, figuring it was best to just get it out in the open. "The reason you don't know anything is that Georgie and I were simply pretending to be a couple."

Xander jerked his head back. "What's that even supposed to mean?"

"I used to date Kyle Deveraux," Georgie said quickly, and I realized she wanted to take the lead on this.

"That jackass? No way," Xander said, and now it was my turn to be shocked. My brother was a grump, but he was usually polite. Clearly, Kyle's reputation had made the rounds even outside the Quarter.

"Anyway, on Sazerac Day, he cornered me at Julian's bar. Your brother came up with this brilliant idea to help me get him off my back."

"The balcony thing makes more sense now," Xander muttered.

Georgie narrowed her eyes but didn't say anything. "Today, I came here with Julian because we assumed we'd run into some of the other clients who dropped Books & Beads. I actually got the Tableau family back tonight. But with Kyle, one thing led to another—"

"And now half of New Orleans high society thinks you two are together. Got it. Good luck with that." Xander chuckled.

I laughed, but Georgie asked, "What do you mean? Julian, is this going to be trouble for you?"

I shook my head. "Don't worry about it."

"Yes, do worry about it," Xander said, "because you know whose ears this will reach very soon."

"The family's," I groaned.

"Yes. So if I were you, I'd call or drop by the house as quickly as possible. Not saying you *should* do that. But it's what I would do," Xander said. I could tell he was fighting laughter.

"Thanks for your input," I replied sardonically. "I'll think of something. Please keep Georgie company while I bring the car around."

"Sure. I can use the time to give you tips as well, Georgie."

I turned to him. "Tips about what?"

"You, obviously."

Georgie laughed. "It's fine, Julian. Don't worry. I think I can handle your brother."

The surprise on Xander's face was almost comical. She could definitely go toe to toe with him, and I hadn't met many people who could.

"I'll be right back," I assured her, touching her lower back. I lingered a beat too long, and Xander cocked a brow. I immediately dropped my hand, glaring at him.

Damn, I was jealous, leaving her here with my brother. But I'd have her all to myself for the rest of the evening.

And I couldn't wait.

CHAPTER TWELVE

GEORGIE

How had tonight gone so insane? I couldn't even believe the chain of events.

Once Julian was out of sight, Xander asked, "How's your ankle? Want us to move closer to that railing so you can hold on to it?"

"It's fine. I'm placing most of my weight on the other leg. So, what tips were you going to give me about your brother?"

Xander was silent for a few seconds, and I couldn't tell if he was about to be serious or joke. "Julian is extremely impulsive."

"I sort of realized that."

"Sometimes that gets him into trouble."

"You think this could backfire?" I asked.

"It would be far-fetched to say that. But... he's been talking to Robert, right?"

"Yes."

"I don't like that. Frankly, I hope Kyle snaps up that building so my brother doesn't have to deal with Robert or Kyle. No offense."

"None taken." I shook my head, looking down at my feet. "I'm not even sure how I started dating him."

"The guy is a snake. On the bright side, you got the Tableau business back."

I smiled. "They were so nice. I didn't even have to negotiate or anything. They just offered to sign me back on."

"The Tableaus are good people. My grandmothers were up in arms when they found out what had happened. Apparently, they were very fond of your grandmother."

My heart swelled at that. "Yes. Nana and Mom mentioned Isabeau and Celine a lot. I've never met them, though."

"I'm certain they'll introduce themselves to you when you least expect it. They said something to that effect, anyway. And when Julian shares the news with the family..."

I was starting to get a bit unnerved. "Is that really necessary?"

"Yes, or they'll hear it from someone else for sure. It's unheard of."

"What exactly?" I asked.

"For Julian to have a girlfriend. Or at least one people know about."

My ears heated. It was a good thing it was dark outside or Xander would see exactly how fast I could blush.

"Do me a favor," he said as Julian's car approached.

"Sure, anything."

"Keep an eye out for my brother. See that he doesn't get himself into trouble."

"I'll do my very best," I promised.

"I'll help you to the car."

My ankle really was starting to throb. I hoped to God it was going to be fine by tomorrow after some Advil. I couldn't afford a day off during Carnival season.

Xander brought me all the way to the car, then opened the door like a gentleman before helping me inside. "It was nice meeting you, Georgie."

"And you," I replied before he closed the door.

"Give me your address," Julian said as he started down the street. Even in the dim lighting from the old-fashioned streetlamps, the beauty of the homes took my breath away.

I took out my phone and tapped my address into the navigation system before placing it next to the wheel.

My stomach rumbled loudly.

"You hungry?" he asked.

"Yes. Those canapés were great but small."

"What are you in the mood for?"

"Something simple, like red beans and rice. But anything goes, really."

"I know a great take-out place here in the Garden District. Opposite direction, but it'll just be a short detour."

"Perfect." I took off my shoes, which did wonders for my ankle. "Hmm. I don't think it's my ankle that's the problem but the heels themselves. I already feel much better. I don't know how I'll put them back on to get into my house."

"You won't have to. I'll carry you."

I turned to him and laughed. "Right."

"I mean it. I'm strong." He flexed his bicep for emphasis.

"Oh, I wasn't doubting that." I'd felt those muscles up the way they deserved while he was kissing me. I sighed just remembering it. I'd been so completely undone, I'd even forgotten that we were kissing because Kyle was watching. I simply enjoyed everything this gorgeous man made me feel.

And now I was more confused than ever.

A few minutes later, Julian announced, "We're here. I'll jump out and buy us dinner. Any preference if they don't have red beans and rice?"

"Surprise me. Want me to come with you?"

"No. Your ankle needs rest."

I relaxed in the seat after he closed the door. I was still trying to process this evening, but I'd need more time on my own to do so. Being around Julian clouded my ability to think.

Danger. That's a straight-up red flag, a voice said at the back of my mind, but I dutifully ignored it.

I didn't have too much time to mull over my thoughts because Julian returned a couple minutes later.

"That was fast."

"I know. It's why they're so popular around here."

The air smelled delicious. I glanced down at the paper bag he handed me. "Wait, there's a ton of containers here. What did you buy?"

I started to reach inside, but he stopped me. "You can only look once we get to your house."

"Why?"

"Because the anticipation will make you savor it even more."

Heat gripped my body at his words.

For God's sake, Georgie, he did not mean that in a sexy way.

Or had he?

When it came to Julian LeBlanc, I couldn't be sure of anything.

During the drive, I tried to convince him to spill all the secrets, but I had no luck.

Once we reached my house, I began to put on my shoes, but Julian boomed, "Don't. I told you I'll carry you."

"I thought that was a joke."

"It's not, beautiful. So grab your shoes and that bag of food, and I'll take care of you."

I knew it was just a saying, but his words warmed my heart. He came over to my side of the car and opened the door.

I held the food in one hand and my heels in the other.

"Ready?" he asked.

"Absolutely not, but I'm still willing to do it."

That was the kind of influence this man had over me. I was starting to enjoy it.

He lifted me very easily by putting one hand behind my knees and the other on my back. It would probably be better if I could cling to him, but my hands were full. I had full confidence that he could carry me to the house without dropping me.

He walked carefully to the front door. "There's no way for you to get out your key, is there?"

"Not at all."

He put me down and took the shoes and paper bag from me. I reached into my small clutch and immediately found the key.

I unlocked the door quickly, pushing it open. "Welcome to my humble home."

He looked around curiously as we both stepped inside. "This place is very cozy."

"I know, right? I love it."

"But it's far from the Quarter. How do you even get there every day?"

"I take the bus. It's perfect, really. The station is by St. Louis Cathedral and drops me off around the corner."

Julian frowned. "That's not safe at night."

"I've never had any issues. You can put the food there." I pointed at the small table between the kitchen and the TV. My bedroom was separate, but the kitchen, dining, and living areas were one and the same.

"Where do you live?" I asked him.

It was funny to see him wearing his tux in my house. It didn't fit my life. Everything else around here was either secondhand or inherited. He looked polished and in perfect shape, and I was the girl from the opposite side of the tracks.

"In the Quarter."

I sighed wistfully. "It's my dream to live in the French Quarter one day. Having my own little house or even just an apartment there would be fantastic."

"I'm sure you'll make it happen," he replied.

He always said just the right thing.

"Can I open everything you bought? The anticipation is killing me," I said theatrically.

He grinned devilishly. "Good. That was my intention."

"Fair warning: my expectations are sky-high."

"I *will* deliver. I never overpromise. You should know that about me." He looked me straight in the eyes as he said it, and I had the uncanny feeling that he meant something completely different.

I took out the five containers and opened them one after another. Two of them contained rice with red beans, and it smelled absolutely divine. The third had shrimp étouffée.

"I haven't had this in a while."

"It's their specialty. I figured you might enjoy it, since you loved the shrimp at the event. Savored it like it was a delicacy." He grinned.

He'd watched me that closely? That was good to know.

"Well, it was." The fourth container had a gumbo. "Oh, I haven't had gumbo in a while either. It takes forever to cook it. Mom makes a superb one, but I don't see her often enough." The last one had king cake. "Oh, what a treat!"

"It's not Carnival season without king cake, is it?"

"Precisely. I don't know why more people don't understand that."

I brought over cutlery for each of us, and as we sat down, I became aware of how small my table was. My goodness, I felt like we'd bump into each other—involuntarily, of course—no matter how we moved. It was definitely close quarters.

"God, I didn't even realize I was so hungry," I said as I took the first mouthful. "It's really, really good. Why aren't you eating?"

He was looking at me intently. "Want to make sure you're fine with everything first. You're far more relaxed right now."

"Well, I got rid of the shoes from hell. My ankle is much better."

"I'm glad."

"And being home helps. It's my safe place."

"Kyle still makes you nervous," Julian concluded.

I shuddered at the sound of his name. "Yes, and I don't know why. He wasn't like this when I was dating him—this vicious, I mean. He always had a snide remark here or there, but lately he's just been nasty. Anyway, I would've paid good money to see his face when he saw us."

"Me too."

"Well, for all I know, he might be at the Landrys' party too."

"I didn't even think about that," Julian said. "Yeah, I bet he will. But you know what? I'll just go on my own then."

"No, I've thought about it," I went on carefully, taking another mouthful so I could mull over my words before continuing. "I want to go."

"Georgie, you were tense most of the evening."

"How do you even know that?"

He moved his hand, touching my naked upper back. "This was more tense, and it was visible."

My skin turned white-hot at the contact, but I relaxed into his touch. "Now that you mention it, it does feel like the tension just melted away. But I'm enjoying the prospect of another event. Good food and music..."

"Don't forget the business connections," he added.

What were we doing? Convincing each other that it was a good idea for us to pretend? The idea of kissing Julian again made me think that even running into Kyle was worth it.

"All right, then. If you're sure. But don't you have to check if you can get an invitation first?"

He tilted his head. "Don't mean to brag, but I'm a LeBlanc. I *will* get that invitation."

"Hmm... that sounds a lot like bragging."

He winked. "Sometimes I can't help myself. Besides, we should smooth out a few details if we're telling people that we're a *couple*."

He said the last word in a strange tone, like he'd never uttered it in his life. I was fighting laughter with all I had. I was successful only because I stuffed another forkful of food into my mouth.

"You first," I managed to say.

"So, there are six of us brothers. I'm the oldest, and then there's Chad. He runs the restaurant branch of the Orleans Conglomerate. Obviously, LeBlanc & Broussard is the flagship one, but there are many in the portfolio."

"And you're in charge of bars," I said after I swallowed.

"Exactly."

"How many do you have?"

"Twenty."

My eyes bulged. "That's impressive. All of them are in the Quarter?"

"No, but quite a few are. We have ten in the city and ten more throughout Louisiana. Then comes Xander. He's the CFO of the Orleans Conglomerate and doesn't focus on a specific branch. I'm not even sure how that happened. One day, he started going through numbers, we all realized he was very good at it, and that was it. Then there's Zachary."

"Is he like you?"

"In some ways, yes. He's very blasé about everything, but he's also the one you want in charge if there's an emergency. He's the head of the shipping part of the company."

"The Orleans Conglomerate does just about everything, hmm?"

"Yes, though the shipping part is rarely talked about. Probably because it's not as flashy as the rest. My youngest brothers, Beckett and Anthony, are running the rest of the branches between them—bakeries and music venues and so on."

"How are those different from bars?" I imagined something akin to Kyle's place on Bourbon.

"Some are jazz clubs. We also have two big music venues for concerts."

The LeBlanc family had to be fabulously wealthy. I hadn't put two and two together until now, possibly because Julian seemed so approachable. I mean, I knew they were legends in the community, but it was more than I could've imagined.

"And you took over from your parents or grandparents?"

"Both sets of grandparents and my dad ran it for a long time. Each branch of the family had quite a few businesses. Some were direct competitors, which was why they weren't very keen on my parents being together in the first place."

I nodded. "Family rivalry. I'm starting to dig this. It's so juicy."

"It really is," Julian went on. "And my grandparents can't stop repeating it. They add more details every time. I keep wondering if some are made up or not."

"My nana was like that too. She kept repeating stories, but they were a bit different each time. When I was small, I figured it was just that old people had a bad memory. Then I started to suspect that she might be embellishing them."

"Exactly!" Julian snapped his fingers as if he'd had a light-bulb moment.

"Your grandmothers seem to be very involved."

"They're the soul of the family. Very outgoing too."

"And your grandfathers aren't?"

"They mostly keep to themselves. They're either at the house or out on the bayou, fishing. My grandmothers mostly attend events together."

"Whatever works for them is good."

After we finished eating, we moved on to the dessert.

"I admit, this isn't my favorite king cake in the city," Julian said, "but it's good enough."

"Which is your favorite?"

"The one our bakeries make, of course." He winked.

"And you're still not bragging?" I challenged.

"Maybe I am a bit, but it really is the best."

"I like this one too."

King cake was pure happiness for me. Well, honestly, any kind of cake was.

"What's your favorite dessert?" Julian inquired.

"Bananas Foster. Yours?"

"Don't think I have one."

My jaw dropped. "I'm trying not to judge... but I am judging."

We both laughed, then focused on the cake.

Once we'd finished, I started to put all the containers in the paper bag, but Julian stopped me., "No, I'll do this. Let's get you on the couch."

"My ankle's fine. I can walk on my own, Julian."

"It's doing fine because you're not putting any weight on it. Don't move more than you should."

I put my hands on my hips. "I'll have to get around on my own anyway because I intend to shower. Or do you have a solution for that?"

His eyes flashed, and I sucked in a breath. Then his gaze went down to my lips.

Holy shit. I was starting to believe he'd had very specific thoughts about me in the shower.

The tension increased with every passing second. His nostrils flared, and he glanced at the floor. "Try to keep moving to a minimum."

He stood up, putting everything in the containers and then taking the cutlery to the sink and washing it. I was tempted to jump to my feet just to see what he would do, but when I put my foot on the floor and tried to push myself up, I realized he had a point. It felt tender when I put weight on it.

So I stayed put, drinking him in instead. It was perplexing to see him washing dishes in his tux. It wasn't fair, but I couldn't help comparing him to Kyle. He refused to do absolutely anything. Throughout his life, he always had employees to do all the chores. It was unnerving.

After Julian finished, he dried his hands and turned to me. He looked so damn hot, standing there at my kitchen sink. That tux truly was amazing on him.

Though it would look even better off.

"I'll be on my way now," he said. "Let me know if your foot is still tender tomorrow."

"It'll be fine. I'll wrap it or something."

"We have a family friend who's a doctor. He makes house visits if we ask him."

My eyes widened. "House visits? That's still a thing?"

"No, it's a favor for us."

"I'm sure that's not necessary."

He pinned me with his gaze. "You only go to the doctor when you've got no other option, huh?"

"Pretty much."

He walked up to me, putting a hand on the sofa back and the other on the table. "Georgie, promise me you'll give me an update tomorrow morning. Otherwise, I'll come here and check myself."

That was *very* appealing. How exactly would he check? Just look at my ankle, make me walk, or touch it thoroughly?

"I promise I'll text you."

"Good. I'll be in touch with details about the Landry party." He straightened up. "Need my help getting up from the couch?"

"Yes, please."

He carefully slid an arm around my waist. Well, that was nice—I'd thought he might just give me his hand, but this was far too delicious to even question it. When he hoisted me up, I pressed myself against his chest. Completely involuntarily, of course, but my body still tingled everywhere.

When he stepped back, I felt his absence.

"I had a lot of fun tonight despite everything," he said as he walked toward the door.

"So did I. And your dancing really is on point."

He winked at me. "And I didn't even get to bring out my best moves. But I promise I will next time."

Chapter Thirteen

Julian

The next morning, I called Beckett first thing when I arrived at the office. It was ten o'clock, but neither of us was an early bird. Even so, he needed about five rings. I was about to give up when he finally answered.

"Morning," he said lazily.

"To you too."

"Why do you sound so chipper?"

"Beckett, it's ten o'clock."

"Why do you say that as if it's like noon?"

I laughed. "Know what? You do you. It doesn't really matter."

"So, why are you calling this early?"

"Listen, you've got an invitation to the Landry party this season, right?"

"Yeah."

"You attending?" I asked.

"I RSVP'd already, so yes."

"I want to go in your stead."

"Why?"

"Because I have some unfinished business with Robert, and he'll be there."

"Sure, man. No problem."

"Did you RSVP just for yourself or with a plus-one?"

"There is no plus-one, you know that." A few seconds later, he said, "Wait, *you're* taking a plus-one?"

Xander was right. There was no way around this. I had to fill my brother in. I probably had to fill in the rest of the family, too, although I wasn't sure how to go about it. I usually had nothing to update them on.

"I'm taking Georgie."

"How did that happen? I need some details."

"Relax, brother. We're pretending to be a couple."

But the word simply felt wrong. I certainly wasn't pretending that I was enjoying her company—and her mouth and body.

"I think I misheard. You said pretending?"

"Yeah."

"Why the ever-loving fuck would you do that?"

"She needs to get Kyle Deveraux off her back. I acted on impulse. One thing led to another."

He burst out laughing. "I knew that would eventually get you in trouble."

"*You* are lecturing *me*?"

"Not at all. But I always figured that I'd be the one to get in trouble first."

"So did I," I admitted.

"Who else knows in the family?"

"Xander."

"How the hell does he know before me?" he asked incredulously.

"He was at the Tableaus' event yesterday. Can you get off my back?"

"No. This is the most fun you've been up to in a while."

"It wasn't fun. It was insane."

"Riiight." I could hear him grinning through the phone.

"So, can you forward me the Landry invitation?"

"Sure! Though now I'm actually tempted to ask for a separate one, just so I can come and give you shit in person. And talk to Georgie."

"Suit yourself. I don't mind."

He paused for a moment. "This thing with Robert is about his buildings in the Quarter?"

"Yeah."

"The one Deveraux wants too?"

"Exactly."

"Are you sure you're not doing this with Georgie because you're in a pissing contest with him?"

"Everyone is in a pissing contest with Kyle. Actually, he is in one with everyone. And no, this thing with Georgie..."

My voice faded because I couldn't explain it. I tried to remember what had motivated me back at the bar. She'd been so vulnerable that I'd wanted to help out no matter what.

"You're far too silent," I said.

"I have nothing else to add, and since you woke me up, I'd better start dressing anyway. Promised the grandmothers I'd drop by the house."

That gave me an idea. "Do you mind sharing the news?"

He was silent for a few seconds and then started to laugh. "You're using me to spread gossip?"

"Not exactly. But I figured they'll find out one way or another. Quite a few of their friends were at the event yesterday."

"Now I'm getting what you mean. Sure, you can count on me."

"Thanks, brother."

After hanging up, I realized Georgie hadn't sent me the update she'd promised, so I texted her.

Julian: How's your ankle?

She didn't reply, so I started my day. Half an hour later, I got impatient and sent her a second message.

Julian: If you don't reply, I will come banging down your door. I'm not even joking.

She replied almost instantly.

Georgie: Sorry, I forgot. I was with customers. I'm all good.

I stared at her message. *What the fuck? She's at the shop?* That wasn't right. Yesterday, she was struggling to walk and leaned on me with most of her weight. *Unbelievable.*

I was about to FaceTime her, but now I couldn't focus for shit. All I could think about was if Georgie was in pain or not. Damn it. If I asked her, she'd just placate me.

I had to see her. So, I did something I rarely did and canceled my last-minute Zoom meeting. I came up with a shit excuse, but it would do. This was so out of character for me that I couldn't even believe I was doing it.

The Quarter was far livelier in the morning now that it was Carnival season. I arrived at Books & Beads ten minutes later. To my astonishment, there were a lot of customers milling about inside. I spotted Georgie chatting with one. I watched her intently as she moved around. She seemed to be doing fine. But still, I couldn't believe that she'd twisted her ankle yesterday and was at work today. Who did that?

Someone who has to show up at the store every day to make a living, the rational part of me said.

I often forgot how different our lives were. Growing up, my brothers and I wanted for nothing. Fortunately, we all had good work ethics. But we never suffered or wondered where our next meal was coming from.

But even though I saw Georgie was doing fine, I wasn't satisfied. I wanted to talk to her, so I went inside the store. Because of the damn bells, she immediately looked in my direction. Her eyes went wide.

"Excuse me," she told the customer she was advising. "I'll be with you in a few minutes." She walked straight to me. I took a few steps to the right so I wasn't in the way of anyone who wanted to come in. "Julian, what's wrong? What are you doing here?"

I swallowed hard. Fucking hell, it sounded ridiculous, but I owned up to it. "I wanted to make sure you're okay."

She blinked. "But I messaged you."

"I wanted to see you."

She opened her mouth and closed it again, looking down at her feet. "Honestly, I didn't even need a bandage or anything. I took an Advil last night after my shower." Then she looked at me and smiled brightly, tilting her head. "Which, by the way, was very easy to do."

I'd been obsessing over her in the shower the entire night. Did she know that? Did she have any idea how her words impacted me?

"It's not even tender anymore," she continued. "It only hurts if I put all of my weight on this leg."

"Fucking hell, Georgie, why didn't you take the day off?"

She looked at me strangely. "Because I knew the place would be full of customers. The rest of the team is at the warehouse, and I couldn't afford to close the shop."

"Let me call our doctor. He can come here to the store."

"Really, Julian, I'm fine. It's probably going to take a few days until it's fully healed, but that's no big deal."

What she was saying made sense. Yet all I wanted was to take her out of here and make sure she stayed in bed until it was completely healed.

My bed.

"You're sure it's not tender anymore?"

"Want to check?"

"Don't tempt me, because I'll take you in the back and do just that."

Georgie parted her lips, darting out her tongue. She licked her lower lip, then put both hands on her hips. "Easy there, cowboy. What's everyone going to think?"

"I don't really care."

Her eyes went wide. She probably realized just how serious I was. It was crazy. Absolutely crazy. But I couldn't help myself.

"Julian, I really appreciate that you care, but I don't want you to worry about me. I'm fine, okay?"

I swallowed hard, straightening up. What was I doing? I had no right to barge in here. No right to make any demands. Damn it if I didn't want those rights, though.

"All right. By the way, I cleared up everything for the Landry party. Once my brother forwards me the email, I'll send it to you, too, so you know all the details. Let me know if you change your mind."

"I won't."

"You can until the last minute. I really don't mind."

"But then who will be there to make sure you don't get into too much trouble?"

"What?"

She giggled. "Whoops, I'm sorry. I don't think Xander wanted you to know."

"What exactly?"

"He said to keep an eye on you."

"I don't need anyone to... Never mind. I'll have a word with him."

She looked over her shoulder, and I realized I was keeping her from working.

"I'll go."

"Thanks. I do need to get back to my customers."

"Sure."

I felt my phone vibrate as I stood off in a corner. Beckett had sent me the invitation to the Landry party. I scrolled to find the date so I could tell Georgie.

What the actual fuck? That can't be right.

It was in a month, after Mardi Gras.

I immediately replied to my brother.

Julian: Is the date right?

Beckett: Yes.

I didn't want to wait a month to see her again. But then I had a brilliant idea. My party at the Marriott was coming up.

I waited for Georgie to finish with her customer and then got her attention.

She headed my way. "Something wrong?"

I cleared my throat. "The Landry party is in a month."

She dropped her shoulders. "Oh. I figured it was going to be sooner."

Why was she so disappointed? Because she couldn't chat up some of her past clients? Or because she wanted to spend time with me just as much as I did with her?

"I was actually looking forward to another event," she continued.

"I have a solution. Every year, I rent a suite at the Marriott so we can watch the motorized floats from the balcony. I'd love for you to attend."

She opened her mouth and licked her lower lip again. *How can she be so delicious?* Then her entire face lit up. "Wait, you still have invitations for that?"

"Georgie, it's my party. I'm inviting you."

Say yes. Say yes.

"Oh, you need me there. It would look weird if your girlfriend wasn't there, right?"

That hadn't even occurred to me, but it was as good as an excuse as any.

"Exactly. Besides, I'm certain you'll enjoy it."

"I'd love to come."

Her assistant called her name loudly. Georgie winced.

"I'll text you all the details."

I watched her walk away. Evidently, she was fine. Now that I'd seen her, I felt calmer, which made no sense whatsoever. But it didn't matter. I had no idea what possessed me to come here, but I was determined to get myself together by the time she and I went to the party.

But I instinctively knew I'd take care of her in any way I could.

CHAPTER FOURTEEN

GEORGIE

Holy hell.

I was still looking at Julian out of the corner of my eye even though Ms. Daisy needed all of my attention. Poor woman. It was her first Carnival, and she was totally lost, but she'd come to the right place.

I swear I held my breath right until he walked out of my shop. I still couldn't believe he'd come here.

"Darling, I think I should just take a mask and be done with it," she said.

"Oh no, Ms. Daisy. I promise you, you'll walk out of Books & Beads with the best costume at the whole parade."

She smiled. "That would make my day. My poor Dominic always wanted us to come for a parade, and we never managed. We both worked our whole lives. Now that he's passed, I figured I'd go for the both of us."

Her words hit me like a punch in the chest. Emotion clogged my throat.

"We'll make Dominic proud, I swear."

Even though I had a lot of other customers, I took good care of Ms. Daisy until she left the store with a huge grin. Then I turned to the others. It was madness today. I hadn't expected my store to already be so full in the morning, but I was grateful for every single customer.

Between the masks being such a hit and the Tableaus signing back on next year, I was very hopeful that things would work out.

Around lunchtime, I was completely done for, and my ankle was throbbing a bit. I had a bad habit of resting on one hip—the one with the bad ankle. Another Advil would probably help. But I hadn't eaten much, and my stomach was very sensitive.

I could run off to the deli three doors down. It would take me less than five minutes to grab something. I wouldn't lose any customers, or at least not too many.

Before I could change my mind, I put up my "Back in a Moment" sign and hurried out of the store. I locked up and practically darted toward the deli even though my ankle was throbbing more and more with each step.

Once inside, I could simply relax and draw in a deep breath. Ms. Sophie made, hands down, the best po'boys in the Quarter.

"Georgie, hey. I haven't seen you in a bit," she greeted me once I stepped inside.

"I know. Zelda keeps coming to buy our food, as we've been so busy. I'd love a po'boy."

"Sure thing, girl. Extra mayo and pickles, as usual?" She said *pickles* with the utmost disdain, but it was a mark of how much she cared about me that she still made it the way I wanted it.

"Yes, please." I gave her a sheepish smile.

She shook her head, muttering, "Butchering recipes," under her breath.

"Don't bother packaging it. I'll just eat it right away."

"Girl, that's not the way to eat lunch. Have a seat." She pointed at the bar stools along the wall.

"No, really. I have no time. I'm alone at the store today."

"Tsk, tsk, tsk. You work too much."

"Hmm, but so do you."

"Never mind what I do. Do what I say, not what I do."

Laughing, I paid for my po'boy and took a bite the second she handed it to me.

"Thanks, Sophie. I have to go."

She simply shook her head.

Once I stepped out of the deli, I nearly choked. There were two elderly women in front of my store.

Shit.

I hurried toward them, saying, "I'm here. I'm here. Don't leave."

Oh, how unprofessional was I? I had a half-eaten sandwich in my hand, and the wind blew my hair right into it, landing in all that extra mayo.

"I'm so sorry," I said, panting as I stopped in front of them and quickly unlocked the door. "What did you need? Please come in. I'll clean up right away."

God, I was so flustered. I'd always been bit of a klutz, but I'd never managed to make a mess of myself in front of clients.

One of them handed me a wet wipe.

"Thank you," I said with utmost gratitude, setting the po'boy on the counter. After rearranging my hair, I threw away the wipe.

"What can I help you with?"

"Honey, relax. We're Celine Broussard and Isabeau LeBlanc."

The famous grandmothers! Just as Xander warned.

"I'm really pleased to meet you. What brings you here?"

"We meant to stop by before but haven't had a moment," Isabeau said. "Anyway, we spoke to our friend Calliope this morning—"

"Darling, no need to drive her crazy with unnecessary details," Celine said. "We knew your grandmother."

"I know. She often told me stories about you," I replied.

Celine looked around. "I'm ashamed to say that I haven't been here very often, but I do remember some things. That armchair was your grandmother's, wasn't it?"

My heart somersaulted. "Yes, it was."

It felt so good to share memories of her with someone.

"She told me that she liked to read in it whenever she had a lull in customers," Isabeau went on.

"I do the same."

Isabeau glanced at the shelves. "You've got quite a collection here. You're very talented."

"Thanks. I learned the trade from my mom, and she learned it from Nana."

"I'm glad you're carrying on the tradition. Are you a midwife as well?" Celine asked.

"Oh no. Nana was the only one in the family."

"I guess it's not very fashionable to do that anymore, but she was very good," Isabeau said. "If it weren't for her, I don't think my son would've... Well, never mind. I don't want to think about that night."

She truly seemed shaken. Celine put an arm around her shoulders. "There, there. Get yourself together, my dear. It's been ages."

"Did you want to sit down? I have another chair behind the counter."

"Nonsense, girl," Isabeau said. "We're not that old."

I shook my head. "I wasn't implying that. I just want you to be comfortable."

"We are. You enjoy that po'boy. We know what it's like to scarf down food whenever there's a lull. I'm sure this one won't last long. People are probably just grabbing lunch."

"All right, if you're sure. I am hungry." I lifted my sandwich to take a bite.

"Is your ankle okay?" Isabeau asked, and my eyes widened.

"Darling, you can't scare the girl like this," Celine told her. Turning to me, she said, "We spoke to Beckett this morning. Then to Xander, who mentioned you hurt yourself. My friend Calliope also called me. Among other things, she mentioned that you fell while dancing with Julian. You two were the talk of the evening."

Suddenly, I was starting to feel ambushed. I wondered why exactly these two were here. Not just to remember my nana, I guessed.

"It's just throbbing more than I thought. Could you maybe not mention that to Julian?"

I realized my mistake when Isabeau's eyes went wide. "Why not?"

"I think he's worrying a bit too much about me."

"He is, is he?" Celine said with a cat-that-ate-the-canary smile. "Will you look at that?"

"I can call our family doctor," Isabeau said. "He's been with us forever. He'll drop by here if—"

"No, thank you." *Damn!* I didn't want to be impolite. Mom taught me never to interrupt people while speaking, but she looked so determined that I was half afraid she was going to call him before she finished talking. "Julian already offered, but it's not necessary."

Isabeau's jaw actually went slack. "Did he now? Oh, Adele raised him right. So, Calliope tells me that you're going to join him for the Landry party as well."

"That's right," I whispered, unsure what else to add.

Celine gave Isabeau a triumphant smile. "I think you'll enjoy that very much. It was always one of our favorites, too, even though a lot of people looked down on it."

The bells rang the next second. and a young guy came·in with his mom.

Isabeau looked over her shoulder and then nudged Celine. "We won't be keeping you. We just wanted to meet you. And we're very happy that Julian came to his senses."

Celine tsked. "We can't believe he dissolved the contract in the first place. Our deepest apologies."

I shook my head. "There's no need, really. We figured it all out."

"Yes, but see," Isabeau said, "when I signed that contract with your grandmother, I promised her that I'd look after her family."

For the second time today, my throat clogged up with emotion. "You did?"

"Yes. I told you, I owe her everything. I wanted to make sure she and her family were cared for."

I smiled softly. "She always did say that you've been her guardian angel."

"I tried." Isabeau reached into her purse. "Do you like lilac?"

"The flower? Sure. It's my favorite flower in spring."

"We've got a very special fragrance for you," Celine said as Isabeau put a small bottle on the counter.

I perked up. "That's one of your perfumes? Julian told me about your store. I'll drop by one day."

"You're welcome anytime. Can you tell us if you like it at all?"

I carefully took the small green bottle in one hand and uncapped it.

It was love at first sniff. I immediately caught the lilac aroma. It was soft and smelled like spring in a bottle. There were more scents mixed in, of course, but I'd never been too good at telling what was what.

I glanced up at them, putting the cap back on. "I absolutely love it. Thank you so much. Um, how much do I owe you?"

"Nonsense, girl. It's a gift," Celine said.

"But why?" I whispered.

"For your nana's sake," Isabeau said. Her eyes were a bit teary.

"All right, then. Thank you. But I want each of you to take a string of beads."

"We really don't—" Isabeau started just as a client stepped in.

"I won't take no for an answer."

That made both of them grin.

"I can see what Julian sees in you," Celine said.

The newcomer cleared her throat and asked if this was going to take much longer. Celine assured her that they were going to leave right away. At my insistence, they did each pick up a string of beads on their way out, though.

What a strange day. First, Julian came in all grumpy and determined and somehow off, and now his grandmothers had visited me. Those two seemed to know far too much about everything.

As Isabeau predicted, the lunch lull was over quickly, and I was overrun with customers again. I didn't get another break until four o'clock.

I was sitting in my armchair, about to grab a book, when I realized I had some unread messages from Julian. One of them, the first one, was extremely long, and upon reading it, I quickly realized it was the invitation to his party at the Marriott. I grinned when I read the last line—**Dress code: casual. Bring your best Mardi Gras outfit!**

Oooh, that's right up my alley.

Julian: I heard Isabeau and Celine paid you a visit. I hope they didn't scare you off. Give me a call when you have a chance. I need an update.

I glanced at the bottle of lilac I'd left on the counter all day and opened it again, dabbing a bit on my wrists. It was divine. After taking another sniff, I called Julian.

"I was starting to get worried," he said.

"Hmm. Were you planning on barging into my store again?"

"It wasn't that dramatic."

"That's debatable. So... Celine and Isabeau seemed to know a lot."

"I hope they didn't scare you off."

"They didn't, but now I'm curious. What exactly do you think they could've told me to scare me off?"

"When it comes to my grandmothers, you never know. They wouldn't do it on purpose, but it's second nature to them."

"They were very sweet. We spoke about my grandmother, and they even brought me a perfume. I'm not sure about all the notes, but they did mention it has lilac."

"Lilac?" Julian sounded incredulous, and then he started to laugh.

"What?"

"Oh, for fuck's sake."

"Julian, you're worrying me."

"Never mind."

"No, no. You can't leave me hanging like this."

He sighed. "They have this superstition that lilac has certain qualities. Celine made one for my mom when she was young, and she met Dad right after. That convinced her that it has some special power. They made a perfume with lilac for Scarlett, too, and they credit her and Chad being a couple to that."

"Wow." I didn't know what else to say.

"I'm sure they'll tell you all the details soon enough."

"You think I'll meet them again?"

"If there's one thing I know about my grandmothers, it's that if they introduce themselves to you, it means they want to know you."

My heart fluttered at the prospect. The two were so warm and comfortable, almost as if my own nana was here with me again. "I wouldn't mind. Listen, do they know about our arrangement?"

My cheeks were turning hot just at the mention of the word.

"I believe they do, especially if they spoke to Calliope. Beckett also talked to them."

"Your brother Beckett?"

"Yeah. I filled him in this morning, and then he was the one who informed them of everything that's going on."

I couldn't let this teasing opportunity pass. "You couldn't tell your own grandmothers, huh?"

"It's complicated" was all he said.

I needed to tease him some more. "By the way, the invitation doesn't say anything about dancing. Will there be any?"

"Usually not, but I can take you dancing somewhere else afterward."

My, my, was that an innuendo? My body certainly acted like it was.

"I'll hold you to that," I said.

"It'll give me the opportunity to show off my skills when no one is watching."

Well, innuendo or not, I was blushing again. What a surprise.

"Where exactly are you planning to take me dancing that will have no people?" I asked him.

He didn't answer right away, but I could hear the sound of his breath through the phone. It was quickening.

"I can find a private spot in every bar I own."

His voice was definitely lower and so damn sexy. I tried to ground myself by taking a sniff of my wrist, but the lilac somehow clouded my mind. I found myself even more susceptible to him.

"I need details. How exactly do you want to dance with me, and why isn't it for other eyes to see?"

"That, Georgie, is something I can't tell you. I've got to show you."

Oh, man. If he was here right now, I would definitely fake sprain my ankle so he could carry me again. Where? I wouldn't even care. As long as I had those strong arms wrapped around my body, I was game for anything.

Was the lilac giving me these strange ideas? Yup, I was definitely blaming it on my new perfume.

"You're selling me on this more and more."

After another pause, he said, "I can make good on that promise today, actually. I can pick you up after closing time and bring you back here to the bar."

My heart was beating so fast now that I felt lightheaded. Goodness, this had never happened to me before. *It's definitely the lilac.* "I'd love that, but I'm not sure my ankle is up to it."

"What?"

"I've been on my feet a lot, so I think it's best if I just rest tonight."

"Georgie—"

"No need for the doctor," I cut in, knowing what he was about to say. "Really. Nothing more than Advil."

"I don't like the sound of that. You shouldn't abuse Advil."

"Geez, you make me sound like a junkie."

"That's not what I meant."

"Julian, why are you insisting on this?"

He sighed. "I don't know. I can't help myself."

It sounded more like a confession that it was completely out of his control.

"I'm really grateful that you're keeping an eye out for me, but I'm good. I can take care of myself."

"Doesn't sound like it."

He could be *so* infuriating. "Are you always this insistent?"

"No. I make an exception for you because you're special."

"How so?"

"That's something else I can't explain."

Yep, I was getting lightheaded again. Maybe it wasn't the lilac. Maybe it was Julian. Or a combination of the two.

"For the party," I said, deciding to change topics, "should we figure out more details? In case anyone gets nosy about us?"

"Don't worry about it. No one will care enough to ask questions."

"Okay."

"But you do know more about me than I know about you," he said.

"That's not true. You've told me a lot about your family," I teased, "but not yourself. What do you like? What do you hate? Why did you even decide to take over the bar business? Why do you keep expanding it when you've got so many already? Sounds like a ton of work."

"I'm an ambitious person. I want to make my mark on the Orleans Conglomerate, which is not as easy as you'd think. My grandparents and sometimes even my dad put up a fight every time I want to open something new."

"Why?"

"They're afraid we might overwork ourselves. Besides, my brothers and I are pushing to expand past Louisiana into other hotspots like New York, London, and so on."

"That makes a lot of sense."

"Next time you see my grandmothers, tell them that."

"Ah, so, first Beckett and now me to do your dirty work. Is it my imagination, or can you not handle your grandmothers?"

Julian laughed. "No one can handle them, trust me. But over the years, I've learned that the secret to making headway with the grand-mothers is by taking baby steps."

"Right..." I paused a moment, thinking. "Sorry to sound like a broken record, but are you sure we shouldn't have a story or something? Or just generally know more details about each other?"

"I can't imagine anyone being intrusive enough to ask if you know those things about me."

He'd caught me there. I wanted to know, but I couldn't admit that to him. It would basically mean admitting that I'd been enjoying our pretend kisses and dancing too much.

"I'm not sure, Julian. People can be nosy."

"I'm very good at telling them to mind their own business."

Damn. I had to get creative if I wanted to know more about him.

"I'll think about some more questions for the party, then."

"And if you want to go dancing at any point before the party, let me know. I'm your man."

I'm your man. Why did that sound so appealing?

"I'll think about it," I said, "but this is a busy season, so..."

"No need to explain yourself. By the way, I'll send you a gift, specifically for the party."

I licked my lips. "What is it?"

"It's a surprise. You'll get it tomorrow morning."

My heartbeat was erratic. I didn't even know what to say.

"I can't wait to see you," he whispered.

"Me either."

After hanging up, I dropped my head on the back rest, taking in a deep breath.

Oh, Georgie, you told yourself you were never going to date a powerful man again.

But I wasn't dating Julian. I was simply pretending... and enjoying it.

Po-tay-to, po-tah-to. I was playing with fire again, and I knew it.

Chapter Fifteen

Georgie

The next morning, I arrived at the store forty minutes late. The bus had gotten a flat tire, and it took forever to fix it. Luckily, Zelda was opening today.

I wondered when Julian was going to send the gift or if he was going to bring it himself. I'd definitely love that. I was looking for any excuse to see him. I had a yearning for him that I couldn't explain.

To my intense disappointment, there were no customers inside the store.

I will never get used to this, the highs and lows. Why was yesterday so chock-full and today empty?

"Hey," Zelda said when I stepped in.

"Have we had any customers today?"

"There were two girls earlier. They bought a handful of beads and cheap masks. And you got a delivery."

Aha. Guess who had butterflies in her stomach? That's right, me.

She pointed at an elegant box at the side of the counter. It was non-descript.

"Thanks. Who brought it?"

"Someone working for Julian LeBlanc."

I grabbed the box and said, "I'll just go in the back."

"Sure."

She had a very sneaky smile. Could she tell from my face? Oh, who cared?

I didn't even make it out of the front room before opening it.

"Oh my," I sighed.

Inside was a truly exquisite mask. It was porcelain, which meant it cost a fortune—I'd never dared to use it for my own masks. It was clearly hand-painted with very delicate strokes.

I put it on and dashed into the bathroom, glancing in the mirror. I already knew what I was going to wear. It would match perfectly. I put it back in its box and immediately took out my phone, messaging Julian.

Georgie: I received the mask. It's truly exquisite.

Julian: I'm glad you like it. I bet it will take me no time at all to recognize you.

Georgie: Will everyone wear a mask?

Julian: Yes, me included.

Georgie: That's generous, giving everyone masks.

Julian: The invitation actually specified for everyone to bring their own mask, but I wanted something special for you.

Georgie: But then you know what it looks like.

Julian: No. I specifically instructed my assistant not to tell me any details.

Georgie: I'm not going to make it easy for you to recognize me.

Julian: Trust me, Georgie, I'd recognize you in a room with a million other women. You draw me in no matter what.

Holy shit, when did this game turn seductive?

Just like that, my heartbeat was way out of control as I made my way back to the front.

"You okay?" Zelda asked. "You're flushed all of a sudden."

"I'm good. Let's get ready to work."

"By the way, the girls and I will try to hunt down a spot to watch the motorized floats. Want to join us?"

I bit the inside of my cheek. "Sorry, I can't. I have other plans."

"No problem," Zelda said.

Would it make me look like a snob if I told her I was watching it from the Marriott suite? Probably. I could try explaining what was going on with Julian. But as I said the words in my mind, I realized how far-fetched they seemed, so I decided to keep the information to myself.

For the rest of the day, I kept thinking about my outfit for the party while tending to customers.

Julian had assured me that his party would be something like the gathering at the bar. Casual. But how casual could an event at the Marriott be?

Oh, I had to stop fretting. It was Carnival season, and I had the perfect outfit.

The day of the party, I was extremely proud of my attire. At four o'clock in the afternoon, I told Zelda I had to leave early. I'd thought about schlepping my costume with me to the store, but I preferred to change at home.

"Actually, you know what? I think you can close," I told her, and her relief was palpable.

"Oh, thank goodness because the girls told me that I should really get there soon if I want to have a shot in hell of reaching them. The place is packed already."

I grimaced. "Then go, go, go."

"Are you sure it's okay to close the store?"

My shoulders slumped. The truth was that this was a bit silly. We'd lose a few customers, but what the hell? I had a once-in-a-lifetime opportunity to see motorized floats from the balcony at the Marriott. I was a firm believer in hard work, but I could afford this luxury for myself and my girls. Since motorized floats weren't allowed in the French Quarter anymore, the parades on big boulevards like Canal Street were the only way to see them.

"Yes. Take the time off and celebrate."

She grinned. "Thanks, boss."

Getting out of the Quarter was absolute madness today, but I knew shortcuts, so I decided to walk. I wasn't going to take the bus from the cathedral today but rather jump on three stations farther down, beyond St. Charles Avenue.

The flaw in my plan was that I didn't count on a delay. The bus came fifteen minutes late, but then I was finally on my merry way home. Once I arrived, I dressed very quickly, putting on a short multicolored dress. It was another sparkly one, but in my opinion, if there was ever a time to bring out the sparkle, it was definitely during Carnival season. The colors complemented my beautiful mask too. I put it on just to see how I would look.

Oh yeah, I looked like a sexy vixen. Well, maybe not sexy, but enticing for sure.

I swallowed hard, lowering the mask, as I remembered Julian's messages. How he insisted he would recognize me even with the mask. Was he flirting or simply paying me a compliment? I didn't know. All those fake kisses felt too real. It was messing with my head.

Maybe I should have a chat with him just in case any kissing comes up and tell him he should keep it to a very decent, almost boring level.

"Ha, don't be silly," I told myself in the mirror. "If you're going to get fake kisses, they should at least be delicious."

There was no reason to hold back. Except... I was already looking forward to an opportunity for a fake kiss, which was crazy. That wasn't the point of this at all.

I had a feeling I'd completely lost the point, though. Why was I even attending this party? It wasn't really for networking. I was dressed like a Mardi Gras flag, and Julian told me that most people actually went there to see the floats and get drunk.

No, I had to be honest with myself. I'd said yes to his invitation because I wanted to see Julian. The floats, too, but mostly Julian.

As if on cue, my phone beeped.

Julian: When will you be here?

Georgie: I'm still at home, but I'm hurrying.

Julian: Don't worry. Plenty of time until the floats arrive.

I finally arrived at the Marriott forty-five minutes later. Traffic had been insane, but once I stepped inside the lobby, I completely forgot about it. It seemed like I was in another world altogether. One of luxury and peace where nothing ever went wrong. I could feel the calm seep into my bones.

The suite was on the fifth floor, and I immediately realized why Julian had indicated I use a specific elevator. There was a man inside who asked, "Going to Julian LeBlanc's party?"

I nodded.

"Come on in."

"This is a cool job. You escort people there all day long?"

"Yes. And you're lucky that it's just you in the elevator. Last group was so big, I thought the doors wouldn't close."

"A lot of people have arrived already?"

"Yeah. Everyone likes free booze," he said with a chuckle.

As the door slid open upon our arrival, he nodded. "Good luck."

"Which door is it?"

"You'll see it soon enough."

He was right. It was impossible to miss. Julian hadn't just rented out *a* suite but the *presidential* suite. I couldn't even imagine how much that cost.

I suddenly looked down at my dress. No, I wasn't going to question myself. I was a very confident woman. I didn't want to let Kyle get into my head, but apparently he had already. Nevertheless, I was determined to enjoy this evening.

I unbuttoned my coat as I arrived in front of the double doors. There were two women on either side, both wearing a black-and-white outfit.

"Hi, may we take your coat?"

"Sure."

One of them took it from me while the other held a tray with flutes. "Champagne?"

"Yes, please."

"You should put the mask on," she said seriously.

I gasped. "That's right. Can't believe I forgot."

I turned with my back to the room, quickly taking the mask out of my purse and putting it on. Then I twirled to face them.

"How do I look?" I asked.

"Fantastic. By the way, your dress is by far my favorite one tonight."

My face exploded into a grin. "Thanks. I wanted to watch the floats in style."

"As you should. I'd do it, too, but this party always has fantastic tips, so I try to sign up for it every year. Have fun!"

"And you."

With the mask on, I felt no shame checking out other people's outfits. Julian had been right. It *was* casual. Lots of jeans, lots of T-shirts that were a mix of gold, green, and purple. Though I also spotted a few other dresses that were just as glittery as mine.

Where's Julian? I glanced around the room once but didn't spot him.

I went to one of the windows, looking out. We were going to have an absolutely perfect view. I couldn't believe my luck. I was feeling even sorrier for my poor team, standing in lines for hours to catch a glimpse when I had this perfect view.

"Hello, gorgeous." Julian's unmistakable voice resounded from behind me. "I told you I'd find you. I noticed you as you came in."

CHAPTER SIXTEEN
GEORGIE

Was his voice even rougher and sexier than usual, or was the champagne already working its magic? That couldn't be—I'd only taken a few sips.

I glanced at him over my shoulder and pouted. "No Mardi Gras colors?"

"No. I always wear all black to stand out. You look exquisite. Even better than in my imagination."

I swallowed hard, looking all around us. We hadn't spoken about what we were going to do today. Were we faking being a couple? Had he spotted anyone who needed to think we were together? Was that why he'd leaned in so close and was so openly flirting?

Goodness, I need to chill. I took another sip of champagne to calm my nerves.

"Thank you for the mask."

"You're welcome. It looks great on you. Makes you even sexier." He grinned devilishly.

My heart pounded fast. I quickly looked around. There was no one within earshot, so the compliment had been for my benefit only. This was confusing.

"How's the party so far?" I asked him.

Why was I making small talk instead of asking him what I really wanted to?

"It's great. Everyone's loading up on food—which is in that corner, by the way." He pointed over his shoulder with his thumb.

I hadn't noticed that there was a buffet set up adjacent to the entrance.

"Want me to bring you anything?" I offered.

"I'll drop by later."

"Listen, Julian," I started.

He stepped closer again. "What do you need, my dear?"

"Are we...?" Oh, how could I phrase this without making it awkward? "Is there anyone here tonight who thinks we're together?"

"There are quite a lot of people from the last party. And there are plenty who know Deveraux. But that doesn't mean anything. I really don't care what others think."

"Hmmm... but better to be safe than sorry, right?"

"Georgie, don't overthink it."

That was easy for him to say. Faking that he was attracted to me came like second nature to him. But I didn't know how to play along without giving away the fact that I actually *was* attracted to him. A lot.

So, all this closeness, the playful touching, had been for the guests' benefit. But that compliment had been just for me, I was sure of it.

"Let's go to the buffet. I've got a surprise for you."

I raised an eyebrow. "Ooh, this evening is getting better and better."

He put his hand to my back, and I leaned even closer to him.

Oh yeah, I can see a lot of benefits to having to fake this tonight.

With the mask on, I was even more daring. I put a hand on his chest and felt him take a sharp intake of breath. Then he cleared his throat and covered my hand with his. I stilled for a second, fearing he might take it away. But he didn't.

Could I use this opportunity to feel him up more? No, he was keeping my hand in place on purpose.

Hmm, what's that about?

A second later, he stepped back, interlacing our hands and then leading me to the buffet. He pointed right to the center of it.

"Bananas Foster!" I exclaimed.

"Just for you."

I turned to look at him. His hand was at my back again. I put mine back on his chest. "For me? You mean, it wasn't on the menu?"

"No, but I added it last minute."

I shook my head. "That couldn't have been easy."

"I'll give you a hint. I'm the boss. But I did have to do some legwork. Luckily, one of my brothers owns restaurants, and the dessert chef agreed to make an exception."

My heart was pounding in my ears. It was a good thing we still had our hands on each other because I felt like I might lose my balance. This was definitely what swooning was.

This is for show. It has to be. Don't mix things up, Georgie.

Only, how could it be for show? He wasn't shouting about it at the top of his lungs. He was simply telling me... while holding me close to his chest.

Okay, so maybe it was a bit for show, but I still swooned.

I planned to enjoy this to the max. I had a sexy man putting his hands all over me, who'd bought my favorite dessert just because. What was there not to enjoy?

He did finally let go of me as we both got some food. At least three people approached him in the meantime, and I realized we weren't going to spend a lot of time together. I pouted as I put some gumbo on my plate. What had I been expecting? He was hosting the party, after all.

I simply took my plate and champagne glass and wandered back to the window. The crowds were getting bigger by the minute. Excitement ran through my body. I wondered if they were going to play music, but it wasn't really necessary; once you opened the window, it would filter in from the street. The atmosphere down there was infectious.

The music started about half an hour later. I could hear it even through the windows. I glanced around and asked loudly, "Anyone mind if I open a window?"

"Go ahead," Julian clearly said from across the room, then walked over to me.

I opened the windows, then stepped out onto the balcony. The floats were still pretty far away.

I knew Julian was behind me before he even spoke. "Want me to bring your coat?"

"I'll just be here for a bit."

"I know you. You'll stay here until the whole parade has passed."

I smiled sheepishly. "Guilty as charged."

"I can keep you warm, but I think your coat is a good idea anyway."

"Finally, I found you two."

Oh man, this can't be a real. I recognized the voice only because it was a bit too similar to Kyle's. Enough to give me the creeps.

I turned around to face Beau, his brother. Julian had turned around at the same time.

"Oh, for fuck's sake," Julian said.

"Yeah, that's right. You forgot to uninvite me, unlike Kyle."

Huh? I wanted to ask Julian what was going on, but not in front of Beau.

He looked between the two of us. "I can't believe this. Julian, you're going to burn a lot of bridges in the Quarter if you keep uninviting people because of your girlfriend."

Julian laughed. "There is nothing I wouldn't do for her."

Yep, I was swooning again. He sounded like he meant every word.

"And don't you dare lecture me on burning bridges," he continued. "Half the business owners in the Quarter have a bone to pick with you and Kyle."

Beau rolled his eyes, then looked at me with disdain. "Those are just rumors. Unlike you and this—"

"Don't you dare," I said. "God, you're just as bad as your brother."

"I did warn him that you weren't a good fit for him. I can't see how anyone with a respectable family name would—"

"Get out," Julian said. His tone was surprisingly calm, which would explain why Beau didn't take him seriously.

"Yeah, right."

Julian gestured for someone at the other end of the room, and then a bouncer came up to us. An actual bouncer.

Holy shit! I hadn't even seen the guy—and he wasn't hard to miss because he towered over absolutely everyone. Then it dawned on me that he was probably supposed to stay out of sight and only step in in case of trouble.

"Jay, please escort Mr. Beau Deveraux out of the suite."

"You've got to be shitting me—" Beau began, but Julian cut him off.

"For your own sake, don't make a scene. I will personally tell everyone to whom I know you and your brother owe money that I don't mind if they claim it right here."

Beau frowned. "You wouldn't dare."

"Get out or you'll find out." Something in Julian's demeanor told me he was completely serious.

Beau must have gotten the same memo, because he didn't push.

"There's no need to escort me anywhere," he said, angrily pulling at his jacket. "You're going to run the LeBlanc name into the ground acting

like this, going out with people like her, and... Christ." He looked at the
two of us again, then turned on his heel, hurrying to the exit.

"Anyone else giving you trouble?" Jay asked Julian.

"No, Jay, thanks. I'll let you know if I need anything else."

"Sure, sir."

After he left, I turned to Julian. Even though he was wearing a mask,
I could clearly see he was fuming. His nostrils were flaring. He kept his
eyes fixed on the entrance as if monitoring it to make sure Beau didn't
return.

"You uninvited Kyle?"

I saw his Adam's apple bob. "I'd planned to do it anyway, but it
slipped my mind. After I invited you, I told my assistant to boot him
out, but it didn't occur to me to tell her to do the same for anyone from
his family."

"Julian, why did you do it?"

He turned to me. I couldn't see his eyebrows because of the mask, but
the way his brow knitted could only mean he was frowning.

"What do you mean? Because Kyle makes you uncomfortable."

"I know, but he's part of your world, and this party is for them. You
didn't have to do it."

"Fuck yes, I did. Georgie, if someone makes you uncomfortable, I will
remove them. It's as simple as that."

Whatever was going on between me and Julian, he was growing on
me. And that was dangerous. *So* damn dangerous.

"Thank you," I murmured.

He looked down at my bare arms. "I'll bring your coat."

"Good idea." I couldn't believe no one else was out on the balcony
yet. The music was coming in quite loudly now. I closed my eyes, drawing in a deep breath. I felt even more connected with the music like this.

I started to move. Left, right, left right. I turned around once, too, and then opened my eyes. Ha, Julian was looking at me. I could feel it before I even saw him.

"How long have you been standing there?" I asked him.

"Not long. I just wanted to watch you. You look so happy."

"I have my favorite food, my favorite day ever, *and* my favorite guy."

His eyes flashed, and he stepped closer. "Is that so?"

I nodded. "Absolute favorite." I turned around quickly, shoving my arms inside the coat. I didn't want to button it up, though, because it would restrict my ability to move.

"Why?" he asked in my ear, and I knew exactly what he meant.

"He's different from anyone else I've ever met," I whispered to the wind, but he caught my words. I'd spoken from my soul, revealing a piece of me.

He didn't ask anything else, and I was beyond grateful. I wasn't ready to bare myself even more.

More people joined us on the balcony, but no one was moving.

"Why is no one dancing?"

"It doesn't matter, Georgie. Dance like no one's watching," he whispered in my ear. My skin turned to goose bumps. "Dance as if you're dancing only for me."

There was an unmistakable command in his voice, and it was so damn seductive.

I started to hum and dance and call out to the krewe as they approached. The costumes were phenomenal, and I wasn't jealous at all. I loved that there were others like me, keeping the tradition alive by making costumes.

Dancing this time felt different than at the bar, and even at the party. More intimate. Julian was right behind me, both hands on my waist, matching my rhythm. His hands felt red-hot even though I had a coat on.

He held his nose right above my ear. Every inhale and exhale sent ripples through me. I was looking at the floats, transfixed. The balcony was getting more and more crowded, yet Julian didn't leave my side. Even when others tried to engage in conversation, he brushed them off with a quick "later" or "not now." Then he turned back to dancing with me.

I applauded along with all the crowds below when the floats went past the balcony. Others on the balcony reluctantly started to clap too.

"You're making this a real Carnival party," Julian said into my ear, "and I like you even more for that."

"Even more, huh?"

I'd been dancing for what felt like two hours, although I was sure it was much less. I was slowly starting to lose steam.

"Yes," he whispered.

I turned around to face him, and he was much closer. Much, *much* closer than he'd been on the balcony at his bar.

"You need a break?"

"How did you know?"

"By the way you move. You've slowed down a bit." Holy shit, he was so in tune with my body. "Besides, your feet must be killing you. Just putting it on the table, but I'm up for giving you a foot massage if you need it."

I jerked my head back slightly and then brought my mouth to his ear. "It's an all-inclusive package with you, huh?"

"Sure, it comes with the fake boyfriend subscription," he added, and my previous elation instantly vanished.

"Ready to take me up on the offer?" His smile was even more seductive than before, but I was suddenly not in the mood anymore. I needed to be alone for a bit to get my bearings.

"It's not necessary, really." I stepped to the side, clearing my throat. "I'm going to the bathroom real quick. Besides, I think I've monopolized you long enough. I'm sure others want to catch up with the host."

He frowned but didn't say anything, just nodded.

I immediately darted to the restroom. I didn't need to go, but I wanted a bit of distance from him and everyone else.

The bathroom was all green stone. It felt very peaceful. Taking off the mask, I stood in front of the sink, looking in the mirror. Why was I out of sorts all of a sudden? This was the best Carnival event I'd attended. The motorized floats looked amazing from up here. And having Julian next to me was the cherry on top.

But that was the crux of the issue, wasn't it? Julian had the power to take me to elation and then complete sadness in an instant. I didn't like that at all. Damn it, I was a strong woman. I didn't just sway in the wind.

I rolled my shoulders back, still looking in the mirror.

Enjoy the party, Georgie. It's absolutely fantastic.

I took a deep breath, put the mask back on, and then returned to the main room, intent on keeping the promise I'd made to myself.

And I did. I thoroughly enjoyed the evening. I avoided Julian, but it wasn't hard because he was surrounded by guests all the time. I made small talk with some of them and chitchatted with a few of the ladies whose costumes I adored.

Around midnight, people started to filter out. I took it as a sign that it was time for me to go as well. I didn't want to leave without telling Julian goodbye, though. But that was proving to be difficult because all the guests had the same thought.

I stood by the door, chatting with everyone as they left. I didn't want to line up with everyone else. Besides, I was his fake girlfriend. That meant I had a pass to cut the line, right?

So, instead of doing the right thing and waiting my turn, I snuck up behind him and whispered in his ear, "Julian, I'm going. Just wanted to let you know."

I'd expected him to simply nod and return to the guest who was waiting to bid him goodbye, but to my astonishment, he grabbed my right hand and whispered, "Stay."

Chapter Seventeen

Georgie

I cleared my throat. "What?"

"Stay."

I wanted to ask him why, but it was truly impolite to hold up the line for any longer.

"Okay," I replied, taking a step back.

It had been a very thinly veiled command, but it also felt like a plea. How both things could be true at the same time, I had no clue.

The more I thought about it, the jitterier I became. To give myself something to do, I went to the buffet and poured myself a glass of champagne. Sometime in the past few hours, the waiters stopped circulating with trays. Instead, they'd put big buckets with ice on the buffet table. I took a large sip, and the bubbles did the job. I relaxed instantly.

Now that the room was emptier, I could take a good look at the decor. My God, it was exquisite. Very old money. Not quite historic, but classic. As a lover of old things, I was fascinated by the couches and the cushions. They seemed right out of a French museum.

I sat in an armchair, glancing outside. It was dark, of course, so I couldn't see much past the lights of the buildings on the opposite side of the boulevard. But for some reason, this soothed me.

After emptying my glass, I put it on a nearby table. Closing my eyes, I leaned my head on the backrest.

Oh, this is so comfortable. Not quite as perfect as my nana's armchair, but it was a very close second. I could snuggle up right here and sleep.

"Georgie," Julian whispered. "Georgie. Wake up."

I opened my eyes. "Holy shit. I fell asleep?" I immediately straightened up and then jumped out of the armchair. The room was completely empty.

Julian smiled at me.

"Everyone else is already gone?"

"Yep. The crew as well."

My body temperature instantly heightened. We were alone.

"Let me take off your mask."

"I can take it off myself," I said quickly, then reached behind my head, pulling at the bow. I must have pulled it wrong, though, because I only managed to fasten it tighter.

He grinned, then twirled his finger for me to turn around.

What choice did I have?

I felt him come up behind me, and his fingers fumbled in my hair. He tugged at the other end of the bow, but it wouldn't budge.

"This isn't going to work. I'll just cut it."

"Just pull it over my head."

"Some of your hair is stuck in it, and I don't want to hurt you."

"Okay."

Julian walked away, and I didn't dare move, for some reason. I was rooted to the spot, drawing in deep breaths.

He returned far quicker than I expected and immediately cut through the fastening at the back. He removed it carefully, still tugging a bit of my hair, but that was quite all right.

"You're free!" he exclaimed after a moment.

I turned around. "Thanks for... well, for everything tonight. It was a fantastic party."

His voice lowered. "Georgie. Why aren't you looking at me?"

I hadn't even realized I'd been averting my gaze, fixating on the streetlight outside like it was the most interesting thing happening at the moment.

"I'm just tired, I guess."

He touched my jaw lightly. I sucked in a deep breath. Ever so slowly, he nudged my chin, turning my head, meeting me halfway.

Leaning toward me, he said, "That's not it and you know it. What's wrong? Did I do something to upset you?"

Part of me couldn't believe he was actually asking that, as if he was a caring boyfriend. Not that I had a lot of experience with that, but still.

"It's been a long evening. Why did you want me to stay?" *That's it, shift the focus.*

"I did promise to take you dancing after the party."

"Oh, I completely forgot. But it's so late..."

"I know. That's not really why I asked you to stay. I wanted to clear things up. You've been avoiding me—you can't deny it."

I bit the inside of my cheek. I could just tell him. He wouldn't make a scene or berate me, I was sure of it.

"Today has been... confusing," I admitted. "One moment you were dancing with me, and the next you were saying it was all for show."

Julian looked at me intently for quite a long time. He glanced at my lips before making eye contact again. His hand was still at my jaw.

"It wasn't for show. None of it."

Aaaaaaaaaaand I could hear angels singing. My heart nearly burst out of my chest with joy. I'd gone from feeling moody to exhilarated in a fraction of a second.

"None of it?" I whispered.

"No."

"But then you said there were others here, that the foot massage was part of your 'fake boyfriend package.'"

He tilted closer. "I needed an excuse."

"For what?"

"For being close to you, touching you..."

"Julian," I whispered.

"I asked you here because I needed to see you."

"I thought it was because some of your guests would expect your girlfriend to—"

"It was all a damn ruse. I've wanted you since you showed up at my bar in your sparkling dress."

His words just wrapped around my heart, then traveled down below.

"That first kiss wasn't just because that moron was watching," he continued. "It was instinct, and I followed it."

"Do you regret it?"

"Hell no."

"Neither do I."

He kissed me, and I opened up without any restraint, without over-thinking. For the first time, I wasn't questioning why this was happening. And my God, it made such a difference. I felt everything much more intensely: his passion, his unbridled need to explore me.

He pulled my lower lip into his mouth, then licked the upper one. I instantly became wet. Then he kissed me again, and our tongues moved wildly. His hands were on my body, one over my ass, the other one at my hip, moving lower until his fingers brushed the hem of my dress and then my bare skin. A current of awareness traveled through me. He groaned against my mouth, and then he pushed my dress farther up. I grew even needier. Every cell in my body clamored for more of his touch. When he revealed my panties, he stopped touching me. I moaned, rolling my hips, trying to get him back.

Then I felt two of his fingers slip inside my panties, brushing my bare skin and my clit. I nearly broke out of my skin. The current of pleasure rocking me was so strong that my knees trembled.

"Fuck, Georgie, you're already so wet for me."

I dropped my head back, enjoying feeling his fingers on my body, touching me intimately, pleasuring me. He was moving them slowly up and down.

"Georgie, do you want to stay here with me tonight?" His voice was trembling lightly.

I knew what he was asking. "Yes, I want to be here with you. I want you, Julian, so damn badly. Please, just please..."

Chapter Eighteen

Julian

"Please, what?" I asked, keeping my hands still. I needed to know exactly what she wanted. "What do you want me to do to you tonight, Georgie?"

"Anything you want. Anything."

Carte blanche was more than I'd imagined, and I planned to put it to great use. I'd been fantasizing about having Georgie for far too long. It felt like years. Like a lifetime.

"Please touch me more," she begged.

The next second, I pushed her dress up, not even bothering to find the zipper. It was elastic at least, so I didn't rip it. I was about to explode.

Except for the panties, she was completely naked under her dress. No bra. Her breasts were exquisite, round and perky and begging for my attention. I licked one nipple. It was hard already. Her breath became more labored as I put one hand on her pussy. With the other, I was teasing her nipple. I needed to get her to the bedroom, though, so I took my hand away.

She gasped. "No!"

"Let's go to bed, Georgie."

"Where's the bedroom?"

I took her hand, leading her down a corridor. There were a ton of rooms in the presidential suite, but I opened the first door we came to. This room was huge.

Georgie tugged at my fingers, and I looked at her over my shoulder. Her eyes were fixed on the bed. She'd covered her breasts with one arm.

"Georgie?" I asked, pulling her toward me so we were facing each other. She was averting her gaze again. "Did you change your mind?"

She didn't reply.

"You can tell me anything."

If she said she wanted to leave, my dick would probably go on strike. I'd get blue balls for life. But it didn't matter. I wanted her to feel safe and comfortable, first and foremost.

"I'm just... I feel a bit self-conscious walking naked through the suite—"

I growled. "Self-conscious? Georgie, you're a beautiful woman. You don't have anything to be self-conscious about."

She finally looked at me, and I turned her around. The room was semi-dark, but there was enough light coming from the corridor so we could see each other in the mirror. It was huge, spanning the whole dresser.

"Every curve, every part of you," I whispered in her ear, "is absolutely gorgeous."

I ran both hands over her breasts, circling her nipples. She responded deliciously: gasping, jerking her hips slightly forward.

"Does this make you wet?"

She nodded.

"Good." I needed her completely ready for me.

I trailed both hands down, sliding one into her panties and pressing two fingers on her opening. I moved the other one behind her, gripping one ass cheek, then the other one.

"I love your panties."

I kissed her shoulder, and she closed her eyes. I wanted her to watch us, but this was probably her way of internalizing the sensations. And this was all about pleasing her, making sure this was the best night of her life.

I turned her around slowly. My hand was still in her panties, and she opened her eyes. I watched her intently while I slid one finger inside her. She moaned and then closed her eyes again. I kissed her deeply, exploring her mouth, running my other hand on the side of her body, feeling what I was already doing to her. Her skin was sensitive, her pulse racing.

She moaned louder than before, and I knew it was time to take her to the next level. She was ready and needed the release—the small tremor in her body told me as much. But I needed to get out of these clothes first.

She moaned again.

No, no time. I'll take them off later.

I wanted to take her over the edge. She needed it, and so did I. Watching her come apart because of me was going to be a damn honor.

I clamped one hand over her ass again, keeping her in place while I worked her pussy with my fingers. I kissed her even deeper than before, drawing circles with my tongue around hers. I could tell she loved it because she drenched my fingers.

That was it. She was so damn close. But now I needed to focus on her clit, so I moved my fingers, bringing them farther up. I pressed them hard on her sensitive spot, then relieved the pressure before pressing down again, turning her completely wild. Her ass cheeks tightened in response.

I kept my palm on her pelvis to increase the pressure and the pleasure. She came just like that in my arms. Her body was tense one moment, then soft the next as wave after wave of her climax rocked through her.

When she opened her eyes, they were completely unfocused. She put her hands on my shoulders like she needed me to help her stay upright.

"Julian. Oh, wow. This... I can't..."

"Just breathe. Deep breath in."

My hand was still on her pussy, my fingers moving in a slower rhythm now. I wanted her to completely come down from the wave before I took her back up again.

Slowly, I walked her to the bed. Only then did I take my hand out of her panties.

"I need to get a condom."

A strange look came over her. "You have one with you?"

"The hotel provides them. They inform me of that explicitly every year even though I always tell them it's not that kind of party and that most people will leave by midnight."

She laughed, and I could instantly see the tension leaving her body.

Fucking hell, what did she think? That I was prepared to sleep with anyone tonight? That wouldn't do. I wanted *only* her. And I was going to make sure she knew that.

"I'll be right back."

She simply nodded.

I hurried to the en suite bathroom. *Where the fuck are those condoms?* They told me they'd placed them in each room's bathroom, but—*ah, found them.* They were on the shelf next to the sink.

I grabbed one and went back to Georgie. She was lying on the bed on one side, watching me. I unceremoniously pushed my pants down and sheathed my cock. Then I shoved my pants and boxers all the way off, kicking them to the side.

"Sit up and spread your legs wide."

She immediately jumped up as if she wasn't expecting this command. Licking her lips, she parted her legs.

I kneeled between them, moving my hands up her inner thighs. I tilted my body at an angle so I could rub my cock along her pussy. I wasn't sliding it in, though—I just wanted this contact. I needed it.

"Julian..."

Her elbows trembled, and then her arms gave out. She fell on the pillow and covered her eyes with her palms. I grunted, moving my cock in precise strokes. I could make her come just like this.

"I like that you're so sensitive to me."

"Julian." Her voice was strangled. She was so damn close already. "This feels..." She couldn't even finish the sentence.

She moved her hands farther up. Her face was still covered by her arms, which I didn't like. She grabbed another pillow, digging her fingers into it. I breathed in through my nose, exhaling through my mouth, closing my eyes too. I needed to pace myself or I was liable to just sink inside her right now. I wanted her to climax again before that happened. With my eyes closed, I was even more aware of the way her pussy felt against my cock. If just this was so exquisite, being inside her was going to be my undoing.

"Julian," she cried out.

"Fuck," I exclaimed.

I was starting to come too. I had to stave it off at all costs. I couldn't believe that it was all it took. This woman.

She cried out again, and without my mouth covering hers, the sound filled the room. I loved it. I wanted to hear her all night long. She thrashed and moved her pelvis. I almost slipped inside her but caught myself in time, just rubbing my erection up and down her clit.

I only pulled back when her jerking movements slowed down and her body turned soft. It was exactly the breather I needed so I didn't explode. I leaned over her, kissing one nipple, then sucking at it. When I moved to the other one, Georgie put both hands on my chest.

"Your clothes. I want your shirt off," she mumbled, but there was no time.

I'd brought her over the edge twice and couldn't wait any longer. I simply couldn't.

I moved off her, resting on my knees on the bed. "I want you standing just like me. Grab the headboard."

Her eyes went from sleepy to wide in a second, and she immediately rose to her knees. She moved much faster than I thought she could, considering she'd been completely lost to the aftershocks of the orgasm just a few seconds ago. I kicked the pillows away from the headboard to make space for us.

"Grab the headboard tightly. You'll need it to brace yourself."

I positioned myself behind her at the perfect angle, then moved my hips forward and slipped inside her instantly. She was so ready and so soaked that she took me in all at once. I paused the last inch, wanting to make sure she was truly ready. But then she pushed her ass back, taking me in completely.

I dropped my head back. "Fuck! Georgie, babe, you feel amazing."

She just whimpered in reply.

I pulled back and slammed into her. She dug her fingers deeper into the headboard, scratching at the fabric covering it.

"The way your pussy feels around my cock... it's out of this world," I said into her ear.

She grew even tighter around me as her walls spasmed. She was rocking my world in a way I'd never expected. I touched her arms as I drove in and out of her, enjoying the way her muscles tightened. I moved one hand to her belly, alternating between touching her breasts and lowering it to nudge her clit. She moaned every time. Soon, she'd be close enough to get another climax. This time I was going to give in too.

When her skin turned clammy, I knew she was right there with me. I increased the pressure of my strokes on her clit.

"Julian, ohhhh." She shifted slightly, tilting forward. I didn't realize what she was doing until I noticed that she'd put her elbows on the headboard and rested her forehead on her arms. Seconds later, I climaxed.

Her pussy squeezed my cock tighter and tighter. Her sounds of pleasure were hard to hear because my own were even louder. The orgasm was almost brutal in its power. It fucking finished me. Every thrust took me higher, and Georgie too.

By the time I'd wrung every ounce of pleasure out us, we both fell backward, relaxing against the mattress. I was heaving like I couldn't possibly ever breathe normally again. I couldn't remember where we even were. But noticing the molding on the ceiling reminded me that we were in the hotel.

I turned my head to look at Georgie. She was staring at the ceiling too. I could clearly see her breasts rise up and down with her breaths. I moved my hand, squeezing hers, and she squeezed my fingers right back. But I couldn't speak. Not yet.

I was going to regain my wits any second now, I was sure.

But I didn't.

I simply fell asleep.

CHAPTER NINETEEN

JULIAN

I was prone to sleeping in, even during weekdays. It was a bit of a joke in the family, especially when my brothers and I planned meetings. However, the morning after the party, I woke up at eight o'clock. That hadn't happened in years, but I was full of energy.

Georgie was so buried in the sheets that I could barely see her, but she was here; I could feel the weight of her body pressing into the mattress. She'd put a pillow over her head, and the only part of her skin uncovered was her left elbow. I was tempted to lean in and kiss her, but I didn't want to wake her up. Instead, I carefully got out of bed, grabbed my clothes, and left the room.

I'd never actually spent the night here. Usually after the party was over, I went home. It was the first time I saw it the morning after. It looked decent. Then again, I always instructed the waiters to bring less alcohol out as the party came to close so people didn't get messy and start trashing the place.

I noticed a menu on the huge dining table and looked it over. I was famished. After showering, Georgie and I stayed up late, and I'd explored her body until the early hours in the morning. Yet I couldn't wait to do it to all over again.

They had decent options for breakfast. I wondered which ones Georgie would prefer.

Nah, this morning deserves something more special.

It was still early, and I was betting she wouldn't wake up anytime soon, so I had enough time to head over to Café Du Monde and grab beignets and coffee. Yeah, that was exactly what I was going to do.

I dressed quickly, putting on the crumpled shirt. It really did look like shit. Whatever. Without making any noise, I left the suite.

Taking the elevator, I was surprised when the doors opened to the lobby. The hotel was actually pretty crowded. People were probably checking out.

Outside, there were beads absolutely everywhere on St. Charles Avenue, but other than that, it was relatively empty. I was betting the Quarter would be even quieter than usual. Not for the first time, I was grateful that Café Du Monde was open 24/7. Usually I ran errands late in the evening for Bella's beignet fix. I couldn't remember the last time I was there in the morning. But I wanted to surprise Georgie and show her that last night was special.

She was mine, and I intended to keep her in my bed.

Well, not that one specifically.

The Quarter was just as full of beads and other paraphernalia as St. Charles Avenue. This was hands down my favorite place in the world. I traveled extensively for business, and no place could ever compare to the French Quarter.

The line at Café Du Monde was surprisingly short. It clearly paid off to be a morning person—something my brothers, and parents, and grandparents had touted repeatedly over the years.

I bought six beignets and two café au laits, then walked back at a very brisk pace. I didn't want the coffee to get cold.

Once I got inside the hotel, I went straight to the elevator. Obviously, there was no one working it like I'd hired specifically for my party last night, so it took a while. Apparently that whole crowd I'd seen before was checking in, not out.

An eternity later, I was on my floor, heading to the presidential suite. I opened the door with my elbow, listening intently. There were sounds coming from the bathroom, which meant Georgie had woken up. I put everything on the dining table, then headed that way. She was dressing fast, now clasping her shoes.

"Good morning," I said.

"Julian!" She straightened up, and her thick, gorgeous hair fell to one side. "You're back."

I frowned. "What do you mean?"

She looked around, and I realized she was nervous.

"Georgie?" I asked, slowly walking up to her, "what's going on?"

She bent down, putting on her shoes, and then rose to her feet smiling.

"Nothing. I just woke up and—"

"Thought I'd left," I said, realization dawning on me.

Her shoulders dropped. "You weren't anywhere, so—"

"Shit, I never even considered how that would look to you. I actually thought you'd still be asleep by the time I got back."

"Back from where?"

I took her hand, leading her to the dining table in the main room.

She gasped. "You went to Café Du Monde!"

I walked up behind her, kissing her bare shoulders and putting an arm around her waist. "Yeah. Wanted to wake you up with a surprise."

She softened against me. "Thanks. This is great."

I didn't like that she'd thought I'd left. It made sense, but I still didn't like it. I was going to bring that up later, though.

I pulled out a chair for her. "Sit down."

She immediately lowered herself onto it and opened the bag of beignets unceremoniously, making me laugh.

"Sorry. I'm like a bull in a china shop when I'm hungry."

"Go ahead, dig in."

She devoured her beignet. I ate two before stopping to breathe. Georgie was on her second one too. I liked watching her do mundane things like this. Was it insane? I wasn't exactly the guy who stopped to smell the flowers, so to speak. Sure, I took everything in stride, unlike Xander and even Chad to some extent. But this was different.

"Now I feel alive," Georgie said, taking a sip of coffee. She grimaced a little.

"Don't like the coffee?"

"It isn't my favorite in the Quarter."

"What a coincidence. Mine either, but I wanted to be quick. Let's finish the beignets, and then we can go grab some real coffee."

Her eyes lit up in surprise. "Great. I mean, I only have this outfit, but you know what? Who cares? We're still officially in Carnival season."

I nodded with a grin. "That's right."

"But let's finish the beignets first."

She ate the third one much slower than the previous ones.

"What are you thinking about?"

She put the beignet back down on the torn paper bag.

"That this is a bit surreal. I can't believe we're in this place. That you're here with me."

"Which part is harder to believe, that this is a presidential suite or that I didn't leave?"

She sighed, looking straight at me. "You really don't pull punches, huh?"

I rested my arms on the table. "No. I didn't want to push earlier because I didn't think it was the right time, but let's clear the air."

I shifted on the chair so I was facing her, and she did the same. I trapped her legs between mine, pressing my knees to her thighs. "Talk to me."

"Everything last evening was amazing, but unexpected. And I... I'm sorry. I know it's not fair to you to hold you to shitty standards."

I cleared my throat. "Technically speaking, it *would* be fair considering my... history. But you have to know this is different. It's been different from the very beginning. And believe one thing: I wouldn't just run out on you like that. Not in a million years. I wouldn't do anything to hurt you."

She nodded. "Thanks for saying that. But considering you woke up and went to Café Du Monde to bring beignets, that sort of cleared it up for me."

"Still, I wanted you to hear me say it."

"I appreciate it."

I pressed her legs closer together. She started to blush.

"What's that?" I asked, pointing at her cheeks.

"Nothing. I was remembering last night."

I tilted forward. "You know, we still have time. Checkout isn't until eleven."

"No, you did promise coffee, and I don't have that much time."

"You're working today?" I asked incredulously.

She scoffed. "Yes, of course, Hello, fellow business owner. Your bars are open seven days a week, too, right?"

"True." What could I say? That I had a team in place and told them I won't show my face today? That would sound pedantic. "How much time do you have?"

"We can grab a coffee and *chat* a bit more. Zelda is opening the store.
"

"Why did you say 'chat' like that?" I teased.

"So you don't get other ideas about what might happen after our coffee."

I burst out laughing. "Georgie, I've been getting the wrong idea for weeks now."

"Well, I'm glad it's settled," she said with an impish smile.

We rose to our feet and headed to the exit. Her coat was hanging by the entrance. I grabbed it, sliding it onto her arms.

"If I button this up, I won't look like I've just stumbled onto the street from a float." She giggled.

"Do you need to go home and change before work?"

"No, it's fine. I always keep some spare clothing there."

"How come?" I asked as we left a suite and headed down the lobby.

"Because I'm a klutz. I spill stuff over myself all the time. Once, I managed to rip my dress—don't ask me how—so I always have some things there. And sometimes I work so late, especially during the busy season, that I just spend the night and curl up on the recliner."

I stared at her. "Georgie!"

Her eyes widened. "What's with the judgy tone?"

"You can't work yourself to the bone like that."

"I'm not. It's only happened a few times over the years."

She avoided my gaze, so I assumed it was more than a few times. I liked her work ethic, but no one could work seven days a week straight forever and then put in extra hours during peak periods. It was a recipe for burnout. One of the reasons I was so laid-back was that I'd seen enough of my friends burn themselves into the ground over the years by overworking. I swore to never let that happen to me or any of my brothers. I didn't want it happening to Georgie either.

She looked around once we stepped out of the hotel, closing her eyes and holding her hands up. "Oh, New Orleans, how I love you. You can still smell the joy in the air."

I scrunched my nose. "Well, I can smell a lot of things, but it's not joy."

She opened her eyes, elbowing me lightly. "Hey, have a little bit of imagination."

"Yeah, that isn't going in the direction yours is either." I wiggled my eyebrows. "So, your coffee place or mine?"

She laughed. "Show me yours."

"Your wish is my command."

I took her hand as we crossed the avenue, completely ignoring that this wasn't a pedestrian crossing. There were barely any cars around, so it didn't matter. The morning was pleasant. I wouldn't describe it as warm, but I was comfortable even without a jacket.

"You like to break rules, huh?" she said once we were on the other side.

I winked at her. "Always."

"Oh no," she gasped suddenly. "We didn't take the masks from the suite."

"I'll tell my assistant to get them from the hotel tomorrow."

"Are you sure they won't just throw them away?"

"Positive."

We walked leisurely along Dauphine Street. Georgie kept looking around. "My, my. I do see my beads now and again."

She was bursting with pride—as she should.

"How can you tell they're yours?" I held her hand even tighter every time she stopped. It was ridiculous, but I wanted this contact.

"I can't explain it, but I always recognize my work."

"Fair enough."

"I can't believe I'm lucky enough to live in New Orleans and work in the French Quarter," she murmured as we continued our stroll.

"I was just thinking about that this morning. I've traveled a lot, and no other place compares to this."

"Really?"

"Yeah."

"I've always wondered if I'm not biased because I haven't been out-side Louisiana much. But between you and me, New Orleans is my favorite place in the state."

I laughed. "Oh, if those Charleston lovers could hear us now. I quite agree with you."

"A man after my own heart. I can't wait for the day when I'll live in the Quarter."

I wanted to make that happen for her. How crazy was that? I was thirty-eight. I hadn't had this thought about a woman ever.

"It's going to happen eventually."

"I love your optimism."

"Life is good," she said with a huge grin. "What's not to like?"

We turned right on Toulouse, and her smile fell. I immediately real-ized why.

"Is it on Bourbon?" she asked softly.

"Yes. I didn't think about it. Let's go to your coffee shop instead." Damn, why didn't I think about that? It bothered the hell out of me that her ex still had such a negative impact on her. I needed to change that.

We stopped on the corner of Toulouse and Bourbon. She rolled her shoulders, which I was starting to learn was her way of bracing herself.

"No. I'm not a chicken. I can't avoid Bourbon my whole life. For God's sake, I work in the Quarter."

"Sure, but we don't have to go there this morning." I pushed a strand of her blonde hair behind her ear. "You don't have to be strong all the time, Georgie. It's fine if you don't feel like it. Or if you'd rather avoid it for a while."

She looked at me strangely. "I never knew that not being strong was even an option."

"Well, it is. Especially when you're with me. So it's your call."

She stood up straight and nodded. "Let's go to your coffee shop. I want to taste something else, and... well, I'm not as brave as you think, but Kyle is never here in the mornings. Like, ever. The club only opens in the afternoon anyway."

"All right."

"I wasn't even aware that there were coffee places on Bourbon," she said as we strolled down the street. Probably the only place in the city where the stench of alcohol was acceptable... along with some other things.

"It's small, nowhere to sit down. More of a take-out place."

"Oh, I love those. I wish we had more."

"I think that's starting to change."

I'd noticed this trend in the Quarter. Every time a business went up for sale, it was replaced by three smaller ones. But it made sense. More square footage meant higher rent.

"All right, here it is," I said, pointing at a narrow door with a lopsided sign. "Maria's Coffee."

"This is so quaint. How did you find it?"

"Chad got me hooked on it," I explained as we stepped inside. Maria was standing behind the counter with her back to us.

"Good morning," I greeted her.

"Julian LeBlanc in person," Maria said, turning around. "Haven't seen you in a while. You usually send someone to get your coffee." She stopped talking when she noticed Georgie. "Hi."

"Hi, Maria," Georgie replied.

"What will you two have?" she asked in a polite tone.

That was very unlike her. Maria was a busybody. Belatedly, I realized that this was going to reach my family's ears sooner rather than later. Chad had gotten all of us hooked on Maria's coffee, and now it was sort of gossip central for the LeBlancs.

"I want coffee with milk."

"Same for me," I replied.

Maria looked at me expectantly, flashing me a knowing smile.

"To go," I added.

She frowned but turned around. Georgie gave me a curious look.

"Later," I mouthed, and she nodded, looking around at all the coffee blends Maria had.

She had shelves filled with coffee blends from the floor up to the ceiling, which was very high. That's what I loved about her shop—her focus was purely on coffee. She wasn't selling you mugs or memorabilia or any kitschy things that every other shop in the Quarter sold no matter what their actual business was.

"Are we supposed to choose a blend?" Georgie asked loudly.

"No. I give you what I think is best. Unless you're a longtime customer," Maria replied.

Georgie looked at me in surprise.

"I'm a longtime customer, Maria," I reminded her.

"Yep, but she's new. Cancels each other out."

Ah. That was her punishment because I hadn't even introduced Georgie by name. I was starting to like this game with Maria.

She handed us our coffees a few minutes later. "Have a great day," I told her after paying, and then Georgie and I stepped out onto Bourbon again.

She took a sip of coffee. "Oh, I might become a fan."

"I know. All it takes is one sip. Which way do you want to go?"

She bit the inside of her cheek, and it hollowed out. "We can walk down Bourbon."

"Or we can move on to Royal."

She immediately nodded. "Let's do that. I do like it far more than Bourbon anyway."

"Me too."

We turned right.

"The whole vibe couldn't be any more different," Georgie said.

"I agree."

The Quarter was waking up. The smell of food was thick in the air, a mix of gumbo and jambalaya, plus something sweet.

"So, what was that with Maria?" she asked.

I put a hand on her waist, leading her down Royal toward Books & Beads. "My entire family likes that coffee. And for some reason, she's very up-to-date with what's happening with everyone."

"Wait, what does that mean? You think—" She gasped loudly. "You think she realized we're doing the walk of shame?"

"I showed up at her shop in the morning wearing a crumpled shirt with a beautiful woman on my arm. Knowing my grandmothers and probably even my mom, they maybe let it slip about you. So I think we can assume she thought exactly that."

"But she seemed upset with you."

"Because I didn't introduce you. On purpose."

She smiled. "Sneaky. So I could just be anyone else."

"No, you couldn't." I leaned in close, kissing her forehead. "You really couldn't." She instantly softened but then pulled back, drinking her coffee. "There is no one else."

Georgie looked at me and sighed, then asked, "What exactly does your family know?"

I kept her close to me. Royal was getting more crowded, and I didn't want anyone slamming into her.

"That we've gone to a few events together and that I introduced you as my girlfriend."

"*Fake* girlfriend."

"Yes."

"What did they think about that? Oh, I'd hate to disappoint your grandmothers. They seemed so adorable when they came to my shop. What would they think if they knew what was really going on?"

"Georgie," I said seriously, "they'd be thrilled."

She immediately looked at me. "How come? They don't even know me."

"They gave you lilac."

"Oh... I remember you told me about that. It's supposed to have special powers." Her mouth twitched. She was clearly fighting laughter. "Your grandmothers are special."

"That's a good word."

"So, they're not... I mean, they weren't mad that you introduced me to their friends as your girlfriend?"

"They knew from Beckett before they came to your store. Clearly, they're not mad. Why would they be?"

"Because I'm not part of this world." Her hands drifted out like she was trying to show me something.

"Georgie, let's get one thing straight. Kyle Deveraux and his brother, they're not good people."

Georgie didn't reply. I stopped in place, and she did the same. I wanted her full attention for this.

"A lot of families in the city think like that," she replied eventually.

"Not mine."

She sighed heavily. "I hate that he made me feel so small. Before dating Kyle, I never, not once, thought I wasn't good enough. But he kept on with this status crap, and I just began to feel inferior. Stupid, I know."

"He's such a useless ass, and one of these days, I will kick him and his brother out of the Quarter. Swear to God, I will."

"Don't say things like that. "

"I mean it. They've gotten away with a lot of stuff for far too long."

"Well, whatever. You don't have to do that on my account."

"Trust me, Georgie, I'd be doing you and the entire Quarter a favor."

She laughed, but I could tell she was a bit wary.

"After things with him ended," she said quietly, "I swore to myself that I'd never date someone like him again."

My muscles stiffened. "I'm not like him."

"I wasn't implying that you are. He's an asshole, and you're the opposite. You're amazing."

I grinned. "Yeah. That's more like it, see? Keep thinking like that."

"What I meant is... from his world, the upper crust of New Orleans."

"Georgie, it isn't like that, not now. Sure, there's old money, and some in the older generation might feel superior, just like Kyle and his brother, but believe me, they're not. He made it seem like that because he loves feeling above everyone else. But all these invitations, all these parties, they're not my life. They're just something I do because it's good for business. It's not who I am."

She tilted her head, smiling. "I know that. God, I can't believe you're so different from my initial impression."

"Humor me. What was your first impression?"

"You sure you want to know?" She laughed, taking the last step as we turned onto Burgundy Street. The Quarter really was filling up quickly, and I knew she would prefer to be in her shop with her clients. "Arrogant. An asshole."

"Fucking hell, that was harsh. I understand arrogant, but why an asshole?"

"I couldn't believe that you would just brush me off on your employees."

"I thought everyone did that," I replied without thinking, which prompted her to burst out laughing. "I mean delegate."

"Ah, see? Big difference between you and me. I actually thought no one did that except if they wanted to be extra asshole-ish." We reached her store far too quickly. "Oh my God. How is it so full?" She tensed up as her front window came into view.

"People know where to go. That's a good thing."

"You are really buttering me up this morning. I wonder why."

"I just want you to have a good day."

She sighed. "Julian, thanks for everything. I had a great time at the party."

"And last night. Don't forget that," I pointed out.

"How could I forget? Wait, if I pretend to forget, will you remind me?"

"Fuck yes," I growled. "I can remind you right now, whenever you want me to. My house isn't far away."

"That's right. You live in the Quarter," she said.

"Exactly. So you know, anytime you're up for a reminder... call me." I wiggled my eyebrows.

"Will do." She laughed, throwing the empty coffee cup into the nearest trash can.

I watched her until she disappeared inside the shop, fighting the urge to throw her over my shoulder and carry her to my house. I wanted more time with this woman. I *needed* it.

And I would get it—just not today.

CHAPTER TWENTY

JULIAN

I purposely returned to Bourbon Street even though it was way out of my way. I wanted to pass by that moron's club. In fact, I was hoping he'd be there. I had the unquenchable urge to introduce his face to my fist.

I couldn't believe he'd made Georgie think she was inferior to him. That snake. She was such a confident woman. It was one of the things I loved about her. She was happy and proud of her life, as she should be. Georgie had a great business and was good at what she did. The only time she seemed down or out of sorts was when we spoke about that dickhead or when he was present. Then she sort of disappeared into herself.

The door to Deveraux's club was open, and I immediately stepped inside. There was just one person behind the counter, slicing lemons.

"Is Kyle here?" I asked him.

The guy looked up at me. "The boss? No. Who's asking?"

"Julian LeBlanc." My tone was authoritative enough to get his attention.

His eyes widened. Yeah, I was known around the Quarter.

"Want me to send him a message?" he asked. It hadn't occurred to me, but now that he asked, it did seem like a good idea.

"Tell him not to provoke me. He won't like my retaliation."

The guy stopped slicing lemons. "*That's* what you want me to tell my boss? I'm sorry, no can do. I thought you wanted to tell him something like 'Call me later.'"

I walked up to the bar and tipped him fifty dollars. "Give him the message."

"Dude, that's a fifty."

"I know."

"I guess I'll take my chances for a fifty. Let's hope he doesn't shoot the messenger."

With a nod, I headed out the door.

I felt much better after leaving the club. I'd never taken this thing with Kyle seriously. I knew he was an asshole back in school, but after that, we'd mostly avoided each other right up until we were bidding for the same building. But this business with Georgie was too much. No one should treat another person like that. Absolutely no one. And sleazebags like Kyle thought they could get away with everything. It was time someone told him he wouldn't.

I only needed about fifteen minutes to get home, where I quickly showered and changed into fresh clothes. But I still had too much energy. I didn't want to stay inside. Conversely, I didn't want to go to work either. Unlike Georgie, I could afford the luxury of taking a day off. I did that from time to time. It was a good way to recharge.

Usually, that day off also coincided with some of Bella's days off at school. She and I had spent many fun uncle-niece days in the city. But now those days were far and few between. Chad and Scarlett took turns whenever Bella had a random day off at school, and the occasional uncle fill-in was no longer needed.

I had half a mind to drop by Georgie's shop. And that thought had me stopping in my tracks. What had gotten into me? She had to work. I was a grown-ass man. I'd been with her the entire night. That should've been enough... but that impulse was growing stronger.

I decided to leave Georgie be and check up on my mom instead. On the way, I instructed my assistant to pick up the masks from the hotel next week. Mom's gallery wasn't far, and she was working today because she was receiving a big shipment from New York. I was certain she could use my muscles. She was always extra careful when it came to loading and unloading paintings because of her back issues. She usually called to ask if I had time to spare, and I wondered why she hadn't this time. She'd probably figured I'd be sleeping the whole day away after the party.

I bought her a coffee on the way, but not from Maria's. I couldn't dodge the woman's questions if I was alone.

There was a lot of commotion inside Mom's gallery when I arrived. A truck was in front with her delivery, and I whistled when I saw its contents. That was a lot of paintings they were unloading. I knew the layout of her gallery by heart, and I instantly knew she didn't have space to show all of them.

"Morning," I said, stopping next to her. She was on the sidewalk, coordinating the crew unloading the paintings.

"Oh my goodness! Julian, I didn't see you."

"I figured. Coffee?"

Mom immediately took the cup from me. "Thank you. I worked myself into such a frenzy this morning, I forgot to have one."

"I know. You always do when you have a delivery. Want me to jump in and help?"

"Actually, I'd prefer you here on the ground with me, keeping an eye on things."

"I'm at your service."

She looked at me intently, smiling even though she was clearly still anxious over all the commotion. "I thought you'd be sleeping in today."

"I had an early start. It surprised me too."

"That start took you by Maria's coffee shop?"

I jerked my head. "How would you know that? You said you didn't have coffee."

"No, but Chad went there to get coffee for himself and Scarlett. Maria told him you showed up with someone who looked a lot like Georgie."

"Chad told you that?"

"No, that was Isabeau. She also passed by the coffee shop."

I was laughing in earnest now. "I'm glad I didn't run into anyone while I was there with Georgie. That would've made things awkward."

Mom beamed. "Oh, honey. You know, none of us bought your story when Beckett told us."

"What do you mean?"

"About you and Georgie faking things."

"It wasn't a story. Our plan was—"

"I'm not questioning if that was your intention. But the way you spoke about her at brunch indicated that you already cared about her." I said nothing, and Mom nudged me. "I'm happy about it. Everyone is."

"Everyone?"

"Your brothers sort of probably know more than they let on. And your grandmothers gave Georgie a perfume with lilac, so clearly they're thrilled."

I sighed. "Aren't we all getting a bit too old to still believe that story?"

Mom gave me a full-on grin. "You say that, but it did work, didn't it?"

"It wasn't the... Ah, I give up." When Mom or the grandmothers started with the lilac, there was no stopping them. They believed it worked. Who was I to argue with them? Besides, this was New Orleans. Believing lilac had powers was the least of it.

She hesitated before adding in a lowered voice, "You've always been a bit of a loner. You're like me that way. *And* you have a mind of your own."

"Well, as you said, I take after you."

Mom had always been extremely strong-willed. Even though her family owned multiple businesses and she'd married into one who owned a truckload of other businesses, she did her own thing. So with me in tow, she'd opened this gallery when she was in her early twenties, and she'd been here ever since.

"Although, you're probably the most strong-willed of us all, opening the gallery and all that," I continued.

"I've always loved art, and New Orleans is a haven for finding new artists."

True, Mom was always on the lookout for local, undiscovered artists. Even so, she managed to constantly attract crowds.

"I admire you for it."

"Thank you. Anyway, a word of advice. I know you have a great life, and you like it."

"I do," I said in a measured tone.

"But if there is something there with Georgie, don't let it go to waste." I opened my mouth, but Mom shook her head. "Don't contradict me."

"I wasn't going to."

"Then you were going to placate me?" she suggested.

"Possibly."

"See, I know my sons well." She frowned as she looked at all the paintings that were already unloaded. "All right, I think we should divide and conquer. Each painting has a number, and I put Post-its on the wall to indicate what painting goes where."

"I'm on it."

"You need help?"

"You always ask me that. No."

"Well, not many people can hang up paintings single-handedly."

I winked at her. "I've had enough practice."

I immediately started with the painting numbered 1. The guys who unloaded them had already arranged them based on numbers, so all I had to do was unpackage and hang them.

As I got to work, Mom's words replayed in my mind. What was she trying to say? Mom was unlike Isabeau and Celine in that regard. Those two were always extremely direct—maybe too much so. But Mom was subtle. Even so, I understood her message. And I agreed with it.

I moved on to the second painting soon enough. It was of the bayou. Damn, this was good. I almost felt like I was there with my grandfathers, fishing. Mom truly had an eye for spotting talent.

She also had an eye for when her sons needed advice. Ever since I'd dropped Georgie at the shop, all I could think about was the next time I saw her.

But after chatting with Mom, an idea popped into my mind. The plan was crystallizing as I hung up painting after painting. Clearly, the motif was the bayou. Each painting was by a different artist, but they all formed a coherent story. Mom was a genius even when it came to arranging the paintings a certain way.

I finished setting them up two hours later. My right arm felt like it was about to fall off, and my left shoulder was sore as hell. I could do it all on my own, but it came at a price.

When I returned to the entrance hall, something smelled delicious.

"Just in time," Mom said. "Got a muffuletta for you."

"Thanks. I haven't had that in a while. Should drop by the Central Grocery more often. I forget how good it is."

"I agree."

I kept rotating my left shoulder as I ate a muffuletta. Perfect lunch. It was quick.

"What are you going to do today?" Mom asked.

"I'll drop by the office."

"And then the bar?"

"Nah, not tonight."

"You need an early evening after the fun yesterday." Mom successfully hid her smile behind her muffuletta, but I still heard it.

"You're behaving a bit odd today," I informed her.

It seemed I took more after Isabeau. I was far too direct when it came to family. But even in business, I rarely beat around the bush.

"It's not every day that I see the change in my eldest son that I always hoped to see."

My eyes bulged. "The change?"

"You had a light-bulb moment. I can tell."

"I'm not going to argue with that." I looked around. "Do you still need my help with anything? I don't *have* to go by the office."

"No, you've really done more than enough. I'm feeling guilty now. I think you might've strained your shoulder."

"It's just aching."

"You could drop by your grandmothers' shop. They have this divine new concoction cream that helps with muscle relaxation. I don't know where those two come up with the recipes, but they're always good."

"I don't doubt it, but the smell is usually too..."

"Feminine?" Mom asked, winking at me. "They're ahead of you with this one. They have it in two versions, for men and for women."

"Now I'm interested."

"But a word of warning. If you do visit them, you might get a lot of questions."

I chuckled. "Thanks for the heads-up."

On second thought, my shoulder was much better already. And I had more important things to do today—namely, figuring out my next steps in regard to Georgie.

CHAPTER TWENTY-ONE

GEORGIE

"You're in a great mood today," Zelda said as I bounced about the shop. That was an understatement. I was smiling constantly. "Is it because of that huge sale you just made?"

"Yeah, yeah, sure," I replied quickly, then turned around and arranged some of the new merchandise on the shelves. "How was the celebration yesterday?"

"Super crowded, but you know, the more the merrier. How was yours?"

"Fantastic."

"So *that*'s why you're in a good mood."

I looked at her over my shoulder. She was sporting a shit-eating grin. Clearly, she didn't believe my story about the sale.

"Hey, you're keeping secrets, but that's quite okay. We all do."

I turned around abruptly. "What do you mean, 'we all do'? What aren't you telling me?"

She put a hand on her hip. "Huh, so this isn't a two-way street, huh? I have to tell you everything, and you don't tell me anything?"

"I'm not sure exactly what to say," I admitted.

Because, well, Julian and I had a complicated thing going on. Everyone who'd been at the party believed we were dating. Now we'd spent a gorgeous night together, and I had no idea where that left us. The

Landry party was hanging over my head a bit even though it was quite a ways away. How were we going to play that out? What if he decided that things were too complicated, and we'd better just drop the whole thing altogether?

My heart gave a strange squeeze at the thought.

"You just totally deflated," Zelda said.

"It's just complicated."

"Okay, then I'll cheer you up with my story. I met the most amazing dude yesterday, and he asked me out."

"That's great! I already like the guy. He saw you, and he asked you out."

She grinned. "I do like a decisive man."

"When are you going out?"

"This weekend."

"Oh, I'll keep my fingers crossed for you. All right, I'm going to go into the back," I said. "I want to check on some admin stuff. I'll come if the bell rings too often."

I immediately went into the small office, which was more of a storage room with a desk. It was just big enough for my laptop, and I wanted to check my emails.

I'd sent some queries last week. I didn't know where I got the inspiration, but I'd sat down at the desk and thought, *Why not reach out to other businesses who might want to sponsor floats?* Worst case, they'd turn me down.

I didn't have high expectations. But every day when I checked and there were no replies, my stomach did drop a bit. Today, though, I had an unread message. My eyes bulged when I read the sender. It was from the Hensley Corporation. They were among the clients who'd dropped me, and I'd written to them months ago. Why were they replying now?

I opened it with trembling fingers even though I wasn't sure what I was afraid of. They couldn't drop me a second time, after all.

Dear Georgie,

I apologize for the quick manner in which we ended our business relationship a few months ago. I received a call from Calliope Tableau and Isabeau LeBlanc, and we'd be more than happy if you could work on our float again next year. Between you and me, the costumes and decorations you make are much more exquisite. Let me know if you're still interested and can fit us in.

Signed,

Meredith

Oh my God, she replied to me personally.

I couldn't believe Calliope and Isabeau had talked to her too. Of course I was interested.

My eyes got teary as I hit Reply.

Yes, of course. Let me know if I should send the contract to you or your legal team. I'm looking forward to reconciling our business relationship.

Yeah, that sounded professional enough. I signed my name before sending it.

Oh, I could dance for joy!

"Good things come to those who bust their ass and make things happen," my nana always said. And she was right.

After closing my laptop, I glanced at my phone. Holy shit, this day was getting even better. I had a message from Julian. I could practically feel my heart expand. I realized I'd been truly holding on to hope that he would contact me. A part of me had been afraid he wouldn't.

Julian: How's your afternoon?

It was a simple question, but it meant a lot to me.

Georgie: We're having a bit of a lull, but it's been a good day so far. How about you?

Julian: I helped Mom at the gallery, put up paintings. In exchange, she put some interesting ideas in my mind.

I liked that he helped out his mom. He could easily pay someone, but he went there and did it himself.

Georgie: What kind of ideas?

Julian: About you. Not that I didn't have enough ideas of my own anyway.

Georgie: Your mom knows I was at the party?

Julian: Of course. I think by now half the family knows.

God, I wasn't used to this. I mean, I had my friends, although I hadn't seen them in quite a while because I'd been in over my head since the flood. And I shared a lot with Zelda usually. But I wasn't used to other people knowing of my comings and goings. Then again, if they didn't, I probably wouldn't have gotten this client back, so I shouldn't complain.

Georgie: So, want to share those ideas with me?

Julian: The less you know, the better.

I rose to my feet, leaning against the desk, waiting for his next message with bated breath.

Julian: What are you doing this evening?

As I started to reply, he called me.

"Hey! What are you doing tonight?" he asked without further ado.

I was just about to say, *"Nothing. I'm yours completely to have your way with me,"* before realizing I did in fact have something to do.

Damn it. Pesky work, always getting in the way of fun.

"I have to do inventory and place orders. We've used a lot of stock that needs to be replenished. Unfortunately, I'll be here until late in the evening. Tomorrow too."

"How about Saturday?"

"I'm free Saturday." My heart was beating so fast that I almost felt nauseous. Did I suddenly have blood pressure issues or was I simply swooning? Yep, it was probably just the Julian LeBlanc effect.

"All right, then."

"All right, what?"

"Please reserve that evening for me."

"Reserve in what way? You want to, I don't know, talk about the Landry party?" I suggested.

"What?"

"I know it's a while away, but maybe we should be on the same page about it."

"Forget the Landry party. I just want to take you out."

I was definitely swooning. Thank God I had no blood pressure issues; otherwise, I'd be worrying about myself. But this was all good light-headedness. I even had some butterflies in my stomach.

"Yes, of course. Sure. What are we doing?"

"I'm still planning that. I wanted to lock down the evening first."

"You sound like Tarzan."

He started to laugh. "If you put it like that, 'Me, Tarzan, you, Jane' works perfectly."

I started to laugh, too, but I wanted to know exactly what this date was going to be. Should I bring out the big guns? Sexy or super-sexy lingerie?

"So is this a— " I cleared my throat. "—dinner, or—"

"It's a date, Georgie. It's a date."

All right, then. Super-sexy lingerie was on the menu.

"It's a date. I like that."

"You do?"

"Of course."

"Fuck yes," he growled. "Look, I know this started in a very unortho-
dox way."

"You could say that," I murmured.

"But you and I have something, Georgie. And I don't want to ignore
this thing between us. Which is unusual for me."

The last bit sounded strange. Almost like he wasn't even ready to
admit it to himself, let alone to me.

"Don't worry," I said in a serious voice. "I won't take advantage of
you."

"Thanks for the reassurance."

I was going out with Julian LeBlanc for real! I'd already started planning the outfit in my mind even though I had no idea what we were
doing.

The bell rang, and I figured Zelda could deal with whoever it was. But
then it rang ten times in a row, which told me a group had arrived.

"Listen, I think I have to go to the front and help Zelda."

"Sure. So, you're going to be staying up late tonight at the shop,
huh?"

"Oh yeah. Honestly, probably until ten or eleven or something."

"And then you'll leave the Quarter alone at that time?"

"Yes. But it's always full of people in the evening."

"A lot of drunkards, too, among those people."

"Julian, I've lived here my whole life, and this won't be the first time
I'll be leaving my shop very late. I can handle myself," I insisted.

"I can walk you to the bus."

"No, no, no, no."

"Why?"

I didn't know how to explain this without sounding completely silly,
but I had to try. "If I know you're waiting for me, I might not be able to
concentrate on my work."

After a few seconds of silence, Julian burst out laughing. "Georgie, you can't mean it."

"But I do."

"I don't like the thought of you being out in the Quarter at night."

It was endearing that he was so protective. "Look, I'm far from where the main bars are. I rarely run into drunks around here."

"Your station is next to the cathedral."

Of course he wouldn't be fooled that easily.

"Yes, but I steer clear of Bourbon anyway on principle. My route is safe."

"I have another proposition. You text me when you're done, and I'll come to the store and walk you to the bus station."

"But what if it's late and you're asleep?"

"I don't go to bed early. And my house is in the Quarter, so it's no bother."

I felt a strange pressure in my chest. "Okay. Thanks a lot, Julian."

"See you later, then. Now go. I don't want to keep you from your business."

Hell yes! I was going to see him much sooner than expected, and I was over the moon!

CHAPTER TWENTY-TWO
GEORGIE

Only after hanging up did I realize I forgot to tell him that his grand-mother and Calliope had convinced one of my former clients to hire me again. But then again, I was seeing that sexy man tonight, so I could tell him all about it.

Even though he was only going to walk me to the bus, guess who was unable to concentrate the whole day? Me. Not with clients, let alone doing inventory. I kept thinking about seeing him again. Julian was taking over all my thoughts.

Doubts started to creep in. Was this really a good idea? I liked Julian a lot, but there was a reason why I'd promised myself not to date anyone with so much influence and power again. I wasn't comparing him to Kyle because *that* was completely unfair. But what if things went south? Then I'd have to avoid even more streets in the Quarter.

I shook myself out of it. No, I was certain that no matter how things ended, Julian wouldn't behave the way Kyle had. He would be civil and respectful.

"Georgie, I think you filed that wrong," Zelda said.

Oh crap. I really had. We were sorting out boxes with beads and boxes with masks. They weren't even easy to mix up because they were different sizes, and I'd still managed to do it.

My phone beeped, and I glanced quickly at the screen.

Julian: How's inventory coming along?

Georgie: I'm starting to get tired. I might need some reinforce-ments even though I had dinner, but if I eat something now, I'll probably just fall asleep.

He didn't reply, which was just as well because I didn't want any sexy distractions, considering I was already mixing up beads and masks. Goodness, I was a goner.

"Yep, you're right. Sorry." I put it in the right box.

"Are you okay? I think you're a bit tired."

"It wasn't my greatest idea to do the inventory today, but there you go."

We worked side by side in silence for a while until there was the sound of someone knocking at the door. I frowned. I'd locked the door so customers knew we weren't open, so I couldn't imagine who it could be.

"You did turn the sign over that we're closed, right?" I asked Zelda.

"Yeah, I did. I'll go check."

I focused on the remaining boxes, keeping my ears peeled, but then I decided to join Zelda in the front. I might have put up a bravado with Julian, but there was a reason I didn't keep the store open until late into the evening. The Quarter *could* get a bit dangerous, especially during party season. But it sounded like Zelda was chatting in the doorway with someone. As far as I could tell, he was being perfectly polite and wasn't inebriated. Still, I wanted to make sure everything was all right.

After closing the door, she turned around and held out a box for me. Her smile was huge.

"Who was that?" I asked.

"Someone sent us pralines. They've got the LeBlanc & Broussard logo on them."

Ohhhh, the LeBlanc & Broussard pralines were famous in New Orleans. They were hands down the best ones around. They were also hard to get because they were only served at their restaurants or charity events.

"How did this even happen?"

"You tell me. Is there a possibility," she said, coming over to me and opening the box, "that a certain LeBlanc we both know has sent them?"

She put the open box on the cashier's desk, and I immediately took one and bit into it. This was filled with cherry liquor.

"How are they so good?" I mumbled.

"I know, right? I can't believe they don't sell them everywhere."

"I'd stock them." I figured every shop in the Quarter would. "So that was who, a delivery boy?"

"It was a kitchen boy, actually, from the LeBlanc & Broussard restaurant. Didn't give me many details, just that he was asked to bring us a box."

I was certain Julian had something to do with it. There was no other explanation.

"Now I'm starting to put two and two together," Zelda said, her smile fading a bit. "And also why you're not willing to share anything."

"It's not really a secret, just that—"

"Never mind. You don't have to give me any explanations."

She popped another praline into her mouth and then quickly said, "Right, I'm going back to work."

"I'll be there shortly."

"Take your time, boss."

She was clearly hiding a smile as she hurried to the back. I took my phone from my back pocket. Julian hadn't texted me anything, but I wanted to thank him for this. It was very thoughtful and exactly the pick-me-up I needed. Snapping a picture, I messaged it to him along with the caption **Perfect snack.**

He replied seconds later.

Julian: Glad you think so. Figured it would fit your requirements. Give you energy without making you drowsy.

Oh my God. I'd completely forgotten I'd told him that.

Georgie: These are my favorite pralines ever. I didn't think the restaurant would have any left.

Julian: They didn't have a lot. I had to fight for this box.

I wasn't sure if he really meant it, but either way, I appreciated it.

Georgie: Thanks. I'm going to call it a night in about an hour. Are we still on?

What if he said no? I'd hyped myself up all day for seeing him in the evening. He couldn't say no.

Julian: Of course. I'm a man of my word.

He kept repeating that, but it was true.

Julian: If you want, I can come even sooner and help you out.

I couldn't believe he was offering to help. He'd had a long night yesterday, and today he'd already helped his mom. Yet he still wanted to be here for me. This was completely unexpected.

I'd always wanted a relationship where we took care of each other. Having a family wasn't an urgent thing for me, but it was a long-term goal. Julian made me think things I shouldn't be thinking this early on, but I couldn't help it. He was so kind and thoughtful and everything I'd ever hoped for in a guy. Everything Kyle wasn't.

Georgie: No, we're good. I only need your muscle to protect me from possible wrongdoers on the way to the bus.

I liked to tease him, but I was feeling a bit more secure knowing he was going to come with me.

Julian: Then I'll see you in an hour.

Zelda left about forty minutes later. We were both tired, but we'd made a lot of progress.

After she left, I decided to relax until Julian arrived. I sat down in Nana's chair, but as I was about to pick a book, I saw a shadow move in front of the door.

Holy shit, Julian's already here.

I immediately jumped out of my armchair. I was feeling a bit drowsy before, but not anymore. I took the last remaining praline—I'd saved it for now—and shoved it into my mouth. That would make my kisses taste really good. I really hoped there would be some kissing involved this evening. After last night, I almost had withdrawals. I grabbed my bag and hurried to the door, opening it.

"You're early," I said, breathless.

"I was strolling around. Figured you might finish a bit earlier, and then I saw Zelda leave."

"We're both spent."

I was fiddling with my thumbs behind my back, biting the inside of my cheek. I couldn't explain why I was on edge.

"Ready to go?" he asked.

"Sure."

As we walked out the store, he turned to me and said, "I have a proposition for you."

A lot of possibilities were playing out in my mind. What if he wanted to lure me back to his home and have his sexy way with me? I would be totally on board with that.

"Okay," I said, locking the door and checking it twice.

"I can drive you home."

That was not what I'd expected.

"Why would you do that?" I asked him.

"Because it's more comfortable than you taking the bus."

I pushed a strand of hair behind my ear. "Julian, no. Our deal was that you were walking me to my bus, that's all."

"I know. That's why I didn't bring up the car earlier. I knew you would shut me down."

"Look, I don't want to seem rude or like I don't appreciate your offer, but just walk me to my bus, okay? I really don't mind riding it home. It helps me cool down after work, and really, the deal was that—"

"I know what it was. It's fine. I don't want to overstep any boundaries, just wanted to make it more comfortable for you."

"Thanks."

"When does the bus leave?" he asked.

"Well, if we hurry, I can actually catch an earlier one."

He looked to his right and then to his left as we proceeded down Burgundy Street.

"You're really taking this vigilante role seriously, huh?" I teased.

"It's second nature to me. I'm out and about in the Quarter often during the evening. I've seen a lot of shit going down. It all looks so quaint and cozy during the day but at night, it's different."

"You go into your other locations as well?" I guessed.

"Correct. I mostly stay in one bar, the one you came to, but I do want to be seen in the others too. You know, to check with the team if all is good. Want to show me your route?"

"Of course. Thank you again for the pralines," I said, just as he touched my back.

Oh, that's it. That's what was missing. He wasn't touching me. God, why was I craving this so much?

I simply leaned into him, needing more, and more, and more. I was insatiable, especially after last night.

He kissed the side of my head. "Figured I'd surprise you."

Then he brought his mouth to my ear. "I wanted to deliver them in person, but you explicitly forbade that."

My skin turned to goose bumps, his hot breath on my ear taking me right back to our night together.

"See what you do to me?" I pointed at my arms.

He pushed my sleeve farther up, kissing that spot. I felt that as if he'd kissed straight between my legs. Holy shit, we were in the Quarter, and he was turning me on by doing nothing more than whispering sweet nothings—not even sexy things—in my ear and kissing my forearm. I didn't even recognize myself.

He'd looked up from my hand before straightening, amusement clear in his eyes. He knew what he was doing and how good he was at it.

"So, what are we doing on Saturday?"

He was holding my hand, interlacing our fingers. My first instinct was to ask myself if this was all for show, but there was no one to show off for. It seemed like an incredibly romantic thing for two grown-ass adults to do. I vividly remembered him telling me that he didn't do relationships, so this handholding thing had to be as new to him as it was to me.

"There's a restaurant I really like around here. I've made some special arrangements for us. It's best if you dress a bit warm."

That was interesting, but perhaps we were in one of those inner courtyards that I loved so much.

"Got it."

We arrived in Jackson Square sooner than I'd wanted to.

"Where's the station?" he asked.

I burst out laughing.

"Hey, don't judge me. I've never used it."

"You don't use public transportation at all?" I asked.

"Streetcar sometimes, but that's it."

"Across the park," I told him.

We walked straight through the park. It looked lovely at this time of night with the lampposts lightly covered in fog and St. Louis Church beautifully lit up.

"This area is so romantic at night. I like when it gets this foggy."

"We can gallivant through the Quarter after our dinner," Julian said.

"Oh, yes, yes, yes. That's an amazing idea."

He grinned at me. "You're fascinating."

We both stopped suddenly, and he turned to me.

"How do you mean that?"

"I don't know. The way you live life, the way you honor your nana with the shop, the passion you put in everything you do, the way you celebrate everything, even the tiniest of things."

"Why shouldn't I? My nana always said that things should be celebrated as they come, no matter how small. She was very wise. I tend to do a lot of the things she told me."

"You miss her," he stated matter-of-factly.

"Every day." My voice broke a bit.

She'd been gone for a long time, but I still remembered everything about her as if it was yesterday. Her perfume—she always used lavender oil in her hair, and it smelled amazing—the way she dressed herself, always just a bit more elegant than necessary.

I sighed. My eyes were filling up with tears. "Sorry, I'm being silly."

"Not at all. You just experience everything deeply: joy and sorrow. That's amazing."

He wiped away the tear sliding down to the corner of my mouth, then kissed my cheek there. Oh yeah, I was getting that kiss I was so hoping for, I was sure of it. But then he straightened up. I frowned, tugging at his T-shirt, pulling him farther down.

"Why did you stop? You were about to kiss me."

"That won't happen tonight."

I gasped. "Why not?"

"Because I need to kiss you very thoroughly, deeply, until I make you mine. And I can't do that right here in front of the church and the whole town."

"Good to know you do have some shame," I teased.

"Nah. One thing you should know about me, Georgie, is that I'm completely shameless. This was more for your benefit."

"Then I take it back. You don't have shame, but you are thoughtful. It's still a win."

"Are you sure you need to be at home?" he asked me.

My heart was beating faster. He was asking me over to his place, huh? Hell yes! But then I remembered that I didn't have another change of clothes at the store. The corners of my mouth dropped.

"Yeah, I do."

He took in a deep breath, looking down toward my shoulder. I felt his fingers press harder on my rib cage as if he needed to brace himself. For what? Then he dropped his hands and took a step back.

Oh, he needed to brace himself to let me go. I liked that a lot.

The fact that I could turn this man on so much made me happy. Our chemistry was mutual and intense. I hoped we could give this a chance, find out what it all meant... but then I remembered Julian wasn't one for relationships.

"Then we should probably hurry, or you'll miss your bus."

"Oh my God, that's right. You made me forget my head."

I couldn't help but laugh when he grinned.

"Apparently not enough to forget you need to go home, so job only half done."

I gave him a sheepish smile as we walked toward the bus station. There were quite a few people waiting. Julian looked around us and then scoffed.

"What's wrong?" I asked him.

"Thought I could give you *one* kiss, but it's impossible with so many people around us."

I moved closer to him, putting a hand on his chest and running the other one through his hair. "I see. So, your kisses have now evolved to being too hot for the public?"

"Something like that." He brought his mouth to my ear. "I can't start kissing you without wanting to devour you. I can't stop myself. It's bigger and more powerful than me."

I couldn't believe I was standing here in this bus station with Julian LeBlanc whispering sweet nothings in my ear. Well, hot nothings, but still.

The bus came just then, and passengers disembarked.

"I need to go." Then, because I liked to tease him, I rose on my toes and pressed my lips to his. No tongue, just a quick, chaste kiss. Even so, Julian growled. I felt like the most powerful woman on the planet.

"You did that on purpose," he said when I pulled back.

I turned around quickly and glanced at him over my shoulder as I went up the bus stairs. "Of course I did."

CHAPTER TWENTY-THREE
GEORGIE

On Saturday evening at 7:00 p.m. on the dot, I turned the sign to Closed and then hurried to the back. Everyone had already left, and I had twenty minutes to get ready before Julian was picking me up for our dinner. It was a good thing he'd told me that I had to put on warm clothes so I wasn't tempted to forgo comfort for sexiness. I did have super-sexy lingerie underneath my jeans and sweater, though. My sweater was hanging off one shoulder, but it was wool, so I was certain that it would keep me warm enough. I also had an office-style suit jacket that I could put on in case it became too chilly.

Since I couldn't wash my hair at the store, I couldn't really style it the way I wanted, so I just ran my hands through it before brushing it. My curls were loose, and I liked the way they fell over my shoulders. I applied minimal makeup, only foundation and some blush. My pièce de résistance lately had been the perfume. I loved it so much, and I couldn't explain it. I'd never been a big fan of fragrances—I typically bought one and had it for years because I kept forgetting to use it—but if I continued at this rate, I'd run out of this one soon.

Even though I thought I'd changed quickly, I must have procrastinated a lot, because there was knock at the front door before I'd even finished putting on my blush. Julian was already here.

I took one last look at myself, put my small makeup set in my bag, and hurried toward the front door. I forgot that I'd locked it, too, as I'd only meant to turn the sign around.

I immediately unlocked it, seeing my man, and said, "We can go. I'm ready."

Julian took a step back, looking me up and down. "Nah, we have a few minutes. Let's go inside first."

"Why?" I asked, baffled.

"Because I need to kiss you."

"Oh, in that case, by all means, come in." I gestured for him to step inside the store.

The next second, he grabbed my hand, leading me to the back room.

"You know, with the lights off, no one can see us from the street, I think." I couldn't be totally sure.

"It's better in the back."

His voice was completely uneven, making my entire body tingle. We didn't make it too far before he plastered me against the back wall and immediately covered my mouth. I sighed against him. The kiss was deep and so damn desperate that it only fueled my own desire more.

I felt his hand at the waistband of my jeans and then moving farther up, onto my bare skin. I hiked a leg up him on instinct. He grabbed it, pressing my thigh into him. Groaning, he trailed his mouth down my neck, inhaling deeply at the nook where I'd applied my perfume.

"Georgie..."

He skimmed his fingers farther and farther up my torso until they brushed my bra. Then, just as abruptly, he let them drop and straightened up.

"Why did you stop?"

"That's the only way."

It was too dark back here for me to see his expression and determine what he meant by that. But from the way he sounded, I felt that he was very close to tearing off my clothes.

He grabbed one hand, interlacing our fingers. I liked that a lot. It felt more intimate than kissing, somehow.

"Let's go. Dinner is waiting for us."

"You're right."

I thought he might try to kiss me again or something, but nope, he just led me to the front door.

"Where's the restaurant?" I asked after locking up.

"Toulouse Street."

"Hmm. I'm trying to guess which one it is..." But I wasn't such a restaurant connoisseur that I knew all the places in the Quarter, and there were a lot of them. "Does it belong to your family?" I asked.

He turned to me, grinning. "Of course. I know most people love LeBlanc & Broussard, but I like this one more. It's more intimate."

"I can't wait to see it."

Music resounded through the streets, along with the sound of chatter. It was surprisingly warm, and the air wasn't as humid as usual. Even the weather wanted us to have a great date.

"Spring is in the air," I murmured.

Julian squeezed my fingers. I loved that he wasn't letting go.

"What makes you say that?"

"I get this feeling when the air changes slightly. I'm usually not wrong."

"It is a very pleasant evening," he agreed as we arrived in front of The Apothecary.

I blinked a few times, then glanced through the window again to make sure I wasn't having vision problems.

"This is a restaurant?"

Julian nodded. "Yeah. It used to be an apothecary. When my family took over the lease on the building two generations ago, they decided to keep the name. It had been an apothecary for five hundred years, and I think it's fair to honor that."

"Your family is big on tradition, huh?"

"We usually try to keep the name of the places we acquire. And there's even an entire wall dedicated to the family who owned it."

"Do they still have heirs?"

"No. That's how my family ended up snapping up this place. They wanted to close it down. Couldn't find anyone to continue their business. Ready to go in?"

"Sure."

Julian opened the door for me, and I looked around in wonder when we stepped inside. The tables were generously spaced out, and even though half of them were occupied, it was still pretty quiet. Jazz music played in the background.

I immediately noticed the ode to the apothecary in the decorations. They had shelves filled with all sorts of bottles on every wall.

"Julian, hi," an elderly man said.

"Good evening, Oliver. May I introduce you to Georgie," Julian said, then asked, "Is everything ready?"

"Yes, sir, follow me."

He was taking us to the back—maybe to the inner courtyard?

Nope, we walked up a staircase, where there was nothing except for some boxes and other supplies on the next level. But then we went up another flight, and Oliver opened a door to the rooftop.

I instantly smiled. There were two big trees in huge pots that were completely leafless now. But they looked absolutely romantic with twinkle lights entwined among the branches.

A table for two was set in the middle of the space, and there was an ice bucket next to it. We were completely alone up here.

"I've taken the liberty of bringing you a bottle of white wine." Oliver pointed at the bucket. "The red is on the table."

"Thank you," I said as Julian held the chair for me. It was a bit chillier up here, and I was glad I had my jacket on underneath my coat. I did take off the coat but kept the jacket on.

After we sat down, Oliver asked, "Would you like me to serve you some wine?"

"I would like the red," I said, looking at Julian. "I don't even care if it pairs well with what I order. I always prefer red."

"What the lady wants, the lady gets," Julian said, and I shimmied in my seat for no reason. "And you can pour me some too."

"Right away." Oliver opened the bottle quickly and poured us a very generous amount. I'd have to make sure I didn't drink it too fast. He then pointed at the table. "These are the menus, and bread's in the basket."

I immediately grabbed some, as did Julian. I saw a hint of a smile on his lips.

After taking a bite of the roll, I glanced at the menu.

"This all looks so good." I turned to Oliver. "What's your favorite entrée?"

"I might be biased, but I think we make the best jambalaya in the Quarter." He looked at Julian. "My apologies to the chef of LeBlanc & Broussard."

Julian laughed. "Don't worry, Oliver. My lips are sealed. I won't give you away."

I smiled. "If you're such a fan, then I'll order just that."

"And what would you like for appetizers?" he asked.

I looked at Julian, who deferred again to Oliver. "Surprise us."

"All right. I'm starting to like this evening. It's good to see you," he told Julian. "It's been a while."

After Oliver left, I grinned at Julian. "I love this place. I love, love, love it. All these twinkle lights."

"I had a feeling you'd like them."

"So, what did they do with the other tables?"

Julian frowned. "What do you mean?"

"I assume this is usually open to the public, right?"

"No, there's no rooftop service except specifically for us." He pointed. "Including the twinkle lights."

"Wow. This is so romantic."

"I wanted you all to myself. I like the restaurant downstairs, too, but this feels better. Like exactly what I need." He reached for my hand over the table. "I'm very happy to be here with you tonight."

"So am I."

He was looking at me intently, and I was melting inside. I couldn't keep his gaze for fear that I might say something stupid, so I glanced at the two candles sitting on the table. The jars that held them were very intricately painted.

"I know that this all started... Well, I guess that's always going to be a good story to tell," I said.

He chuckled, and that made me relax, so I finally glanced up at him. "That's true. But the more time I spent with you, the more I realized I wanted you. I didn't care about pretending."

Sweet heavens. I loved where this conversation was going.

I moved my legs under the table, feeling a bit jittery. Julian somehow seemed to know, because he immediately put his legs on the outside of mine, rocking them lightly from one side to the other.

"I've wanted you for a very long time, Georgie. Actually, from the first time I saw you. Everything after that was more or less an excuse."

"That can't possibly be true."

"I swear. You think I couldn't have sent that moron Kyle flying out of my bar any other way? But I thought, 'Hey, here's an opportunity to kiss her.' And before I could think about any pros and cons, I went ahead. My brothers had such a field day with it."

"What exactly do they know?"

"Almost everything. Probably what happened at the Marriott too."

"What? How?" My stomach lurched. Embarrassment crawled up my throat.

"Mom knows. The grandmothers know. But they usually don't share everything with my brothers, so I guess time will tell."

"Goodness. How are you so blasé about this?"

He chuckled. "I've been dealing with my family for a long time. I've learned that it's easier to just roll with the punches. I can't say I mind them getting into my business because I'm also in everyone's business too."

"I like that you aren't pretentious. I mean, you don't hold yourself to different standards than everyone else. And you could because your family made this town, but you... I don't know. I guess I'm rambling..." *Good God, Georgie, what are you saying?*

Julian smiled. "I hate people who do that. Think they're better than the next guy."

Oliver came through the metal door then, holding a tray with what looked like mussels with baked cheese on top.

"Yum, that looks good," I exclaimed.

"It's our specialty. And we got some excellent cheese in today's delivery. I'm certain you'll enjoy it. If you want seconds, call me."

"I think we're good," Julian said, and I could only nod.

There were two dozen. No way would we need another round.

"I'll check back later. You want me to pour more wine?" Oliver offered.

"I'm good." I'd barely taken a few sips.

Julian also shook his head, so Oliver left us alone.

"This looks delicious," I said.

"I forgot they serve mussels. I usually only come here for a quick lunch, so I never order appetizers."

"How often do you come here?"

He shrugged as we each reached for a mussel. "Not too often. I try to stop by every establishment we own in the Quarter once a month."

"Why?"

"It's just a habit I started and kept. I like feeling the pulse of the Quarter, so to speak, and to people watch. I want people to be happy in our establishments."

"So, you mostly go as a client." Understanding dawned on me. "That's so smart."

"It also gives me a chance to catch up with my brothers if they're there. I mean, Xander never is. He's got an office in the finance district. He's my polar opposite. He can get a sense for how a business is doing just by looking at the numbers. But I need more than that. I need to be in the middle of things."

"Do all of your brothers have offices at one of the locations?"

"Most of them, yeah. And somehow we all ended up in the Quarter, so it's easy to run into one another." He leaned closer. "It's also very difficult to keep secrets."

"Apparently so." I moaned in delight. "These are divine." I realized with shock that I'd already eaten four. "Wow. I thought I was going to feel full after a few."

"Nah. I mean, there's more cheese than actual mussel in it, but I still don't think we're going to need seconds. I wouldn't recommend it. The main courses are big enough, especially the jambalaya."

"So..." I tried to gather my courage to ask what I couldn't when he'd first asked me out, but my words fizzled. I was very nervous all of a sudden.

I took a bigger sip of wine and then ate another mussel, checking to see if my courage had returned. Nope. So I took a few more sips of wine. That seemed to help more than the mussels.

"Georgie?" Julian asked.

I nearly choked when I looked at him. He was staring at me so intently, it made me wonder if he'd been doing that for a while.

"You're hesitating. What?"

"How do you know?" I was miffed.

"You started to say something and then cut yourself off. And you've gone from relaxed to very jittery in a span of seconds."

Right. There was no more prolonging this. Maybe it was for the best.

I bit the inside of my cheek. "I was wondering what this all meant... this evening."

He tilted his head slightly, eyes still fixed in me. "I already told you it's a date, Georgie. "

"So, you and I are dating, as in actively?"

CHAPTER TWENTY-FOUR

GEORGIE

I sounded ridiculous even to my own ears, but I needed to know.

He straightened up and flashed me a huge smile. "Yes, we are."

I felt as if someone had taken a huge weight off my chest. My shoulders seemed lighter too.

"Sorry for sounding so..."

"Georgie, tell me what's on your mind. Tell me what you're afraid of."

"I don't know. I'm not sure if I'm afraid of something per se," I replied slowly. But yet another knot in my chest unfurled. It was easy to talk to him. No need to keep my guard up.

"If you're ever ready, just tell me."

And he wasn't pressuring me to open up either.

"You said this isn't your MO"—I waved my hand between us—"that you never brought a date to any event. I surmised that means you just don't date."

Julian cleared his throat. "That's a very correct assessment."

Shit. My stomach constricted again.

"But that doesn't mean things can't change," he continued.

Having his blue eyes trained on me was truly unnerving. I wasn't used to having such open conversations with a man, let alone one where we held eye contact the entire time.

"How so?"

"Most people resist change. Not me. I've always been open to reconsidering my ideas and beliefs."

He reached both hands over the table, putting them palm up, and I knew what he meant. I sat on the edge of the chair and put my hands in his.

"I met you and decided some of my beliefs needed to be reconsidered."

"I can't believe you'd just openly say that."

He squeezed my hands, then let go because it was a bit awkward talking like this over the table. I immediately missed his touch.

"Why not? I like calling things like they are."

I went back to eating my remaining mussels. Funny, they tasted even better after our conversation. I hadn't realized I was carrying this fear around.

"Anything else on your mind?" Julian asked between gulping mussels down.

Ah, that was a very efficient way of eating. But I preferred to savor each one slowly. Besides, if I ate them with a fork, I could scoop up all that cheesy goodness.

"I don't know. I don't think so. Do you have anything you want to talk about?"

"No, I just want to enjoy you. That's it. That's my plan. Away from any party and anyone watching us."

Warmth filled my limbs. "It's a nice change. Okay, last mussel." I rubbed my palms together, glancing down at it.

Julian smiled. He'd already eaten all of his.

"If you want, we can order more," he offered.

"No, it's fine. I want to be able to enjoy the jambalaya. And you were right, that cheese sort of does fill your stomach quickly. It's one of the best things I've ever eaten."

"I can have them bring these to you every day at the store if you want."

My eyes bulged, and then I laughed.

"I mean it."

"You would...?" My words faded. "That's very generous of you."

That was an understatement. Wow! He wanted to have this brought to me just because I enjoyed them?

I focused on the mussel, scooping up every last bit of the filling and then chewing slowly, closing my eyes while enjoying its flavor. I took in a deep breath and swallowed before opening them again. Julian was still looking at me intently.

"Fucking hell, woman. The way you savor things is giving me ideas."

I winked at him. "Keep them all for later."

Oliver practically burst through the door the second I put down the empty shell. He was holding a huge tray with two big plates. Was there a camera in here? How else could he tell when we were done? Maybe he spied on our conversation from the door... Nah, that wasn't possible.

He put down the tray and moved with excellent dexterity, immediately taking away the empty plates and placing the jambalaya in front of us. I drew in a deep breath. It smelled absolutely amazing.

"Thank you, Oliver," Julian said, and I realized that the man was standing still, looking at me expectantly.

He reluctantly took up the tray and nodded at us before leaving.

"What was that?" I asked Julian.

"He was waiting for your verdict."

I started to laugh. "But he's not the chef, is he?"

"No, but he's been with us for a very long time. He's very attached to the restaurant."

That spoke volumes about the way the family treated everyone working in their establishments. If people had so much loyalty, it meant they truly loved what they did.

"Just a word of warning: whatever you think, tell Oliver it's the best you've ever had." He winked. "But you can tell me the truth. Always."

I had a hunch that he wasn't simply talking about the jambalaya. And I also instinctively felt that he meant it, that whatever I told him would not be met with judgment or disdain, and that was so refreshing.

I immediately dug my fork into the jambalaya and held it up, making a whole show out of smelling it. I closed my eyes again, breathing in a few times. I was doing it for Julian's sake mostly, but also because having my eyes closed allowed me to take in aromas in a different way. Then I shoved the forkful into my mouth. My eyes flew open.

I chewed it quickly and didn't even manage to swallow before saying, "This is fantastic."

"But is it the best?" he teased.

"Hmm. I still have to think about it." But something interesting was happening. The more I ate, the more I liked it. "This is addictive."

Julian watched me with a playful smile.

"Why do you look like you know something I don't?"

"It's a common reaction. I think you feel the flavors more intensely after a few mouthfuls. There was a huge debate going on in the family for years about which restaurant served the best jambalaya."

"Oh, because Isabeau and Celine were the chefs at LeBlanc & Broussard."

"Bingo," Julian said.

"And they agreed that this one was the best?"

He burst out laughing. "No chance in hell of that. Isabeau is still convinced hers is the best in New Orleans."

"What's your opinion?"

"I'll only say it if you promise not to tell a soul."

His voice was playful. God, I liked this side of him.

"I promise. And Isabeau sounds like a hoot."

"I think she's hands down the most stubborn person in the family. This is my favorite."

"So, you lie to your grandmother to her face?" I asked with a grin.

"Not at all. Isabeau always assumes everyone prefers her jambalaya. She doesn't even ask."

Oh, I hoped to be that self-confident one day.

"You were right about not ordering anything else. I'm already full and haven't even finished."

"I told you. It's huge."

"I need a break, though," I said after a few more forkfuls.

"Sure. We're not in a hurry."

"Aren't we?" I said in a very sassy tone. "It seemed different back at the store."

His eyes flashed. "Georgie, don't remind me. Fuck, the way you tasted..." He drew in a deep breath, looking at the table as if it was suddenly ten times more interesting. That I could heat him up that quickly made me happy. It showed me how much Julian was into me. "You know, we've talked about me, but not about you."

"What do you mean?"

"Before Kyle, were you in other long-term relationships?"

"I wouldn't quite call Kyle long term. It was just a few months, but they certainly made a lasting impression. Before that, I mostly dated. My last long-term relationship ended when I took over the store from Mom."

"How come?"

"Because I was working a lot. I'd stupidly assumed that since I'd already been working there for years, it would be more of the same.

But being in charge of everything takes up a lot more time. My then-boyfriend didn't really like that."

"What a fucking imbecile. Of course it takes a lot of work to manage a business. I'm sorry for that."

"It is what it is," I said honestly. "It was a few years ago, so I'm not really hanging on to that. Was it difficult for you in the beginning, when you first took over the bar businesses?"

He nodded. "Some aspects. Like you, I'd assume that because I'd been in the business world forever, it couldn't be that hard. I'd interned for a long time, but I learned the ropes quickly, and I wouldn't trade it for anything else."

I resumed eating my jambalaya as I was listening to Julian. He was almost done with his plate. How did he eat so fast? I thought I ate quickly, but he bested me.

Suddenly, I was very eager for us to finish our dinner. It was lovely up here, but I wanted to move to the next part of the evening.

"Why are you eating so fast?" Julian asked as he lazily took his last forkful.

"Well, you're already done, and I didn't want to hold us up."

I realized how weird that sounded, but judging by Julian's smirk, he understood exactly what I meant.

"I see. You're in a hurry to go somewhere. Where exactly?"

I glared at him. "Julian, you know. Don't make me say it out loud."

"Why not?"

"Because I might burst into flames."

His smirk was more pronounced. "Fine, then I won't. I take it you're not in the mood for dessert?"

"I can't believe I'm saying this, but I'm too full, and I still want to be able to... you know. Take advantage of you. You wouldn't let me at the store, if I remember correctly."

Julian growled. "Georgie, if I'd done everything I wanted to you at the store, we would've spent the whole night there."

"That doesn't sound half bad."

"The only comfortable piece of furniture you have in there is that armchair."

I gasped. "No, we're not going to defile that." But he did have a point.

"We can go if you're finished. Want more wine?"

"No, I'm done. But don't we need to pay?"

He shook his head. "All taken care of. Tip included."

I smiled. "Okay, then we're ready to go, I guess. Do you think anyone will know why we're in such a hurry?"

"Nah," Julian said, then leaned over quickly, kissing my cheek. "Leave it to me."

"I fully trust you."

We walked to the first floor with quick steps.

Oliver immediately noticed us. "Leaving so soon? You didn't even have dessert."

"No. Georgie here is in the mood for Café Du Monde." I barely hid a gasp. Oliver seemed downright affronted, but Julian continued with "Nothing can beat those beignets. You know that."

Oliver cocked a brow but didn't reply. I had a feeling it was only because Julian was a LeBlanc.

"Oliver, the jambalaya truly was the best I've ever had." It was an attempt to salvage this poor man's evening, and I succeeded.

He flashed a huge smile. "Thank you. I'll pass the compliments to the chef. Let me get your coat."

He stepped into a side room for a few moments, returning with my coat. Julian helped me put it on right away.

"See you around, Oliver," Julian said as he took my hand and led me out of The Apothecary. The restaurant was completely full now.

Once we were outside, I told him, "I'm never trusting you again. Why did you tell the poor man we're having beignets?"

"I know Oliver. If we told him that we ate too much, he would insist on us having at least a small dessert. Next thing you know, he'd bring us a selection of everything. It's happened to me several times. I learned not to fall for his tricks."

I giggled. "Oliver sounds a lot like my nana. She never understood when people told her that they were too full. She seemed to take it as a big compliment, so she just piled on more."

The street was a bit more crowded than when we came to the restaurant.

"So, about that stroll...," he said, eyes glinting.

It had seemed like a good idea while he walked me to the bus station. I couldn't for the life of me figure out why I even thought I'd want to *now*, but oh well.

"Yes, of course. What direction do you have in mind?"

He tilted his head, looking at me playfully. "At the end of it, I was going to invite you for a nightcap at my house."

"Is that so? So you could—how did I phrase it before?—take advantage of me?"

"That might be my plan, yes." His blue eyes seemed to pop even more against the dark, the only light coming from the windows and the occasional lamppost.

"Where is your house?"

"Right at the very edge of the French Quarter, three blocks away from the bar. I didn't want to be too close to the hustle and bustle."

I nodded. "That makes sense."

"So, my suggestion is to stroll toward my place and explore what's on the way."

I threw my head back, laughing. "I see. As opposed to what? Doing a sprint toward your house?"

He chuckled. "That is the only other remaining option."

"I'm totally on board. Besides, in all of these years, I haven't even explored the quieter part of the French Quarter."

"Then we have a deal."

He stepped closer, and we walked arm in arm down the street.

"You want to stop by the bar too?" I asked him. "You always go on Saturday evenings, right?"

"Nah, this night is for us. I want you all for me."

I grinned. "Okay."

We strolled down the cobblestone street at a lazy pace... right until Julian straightened up and groaned. I didn't realize why until he reached out his hand.

"Robert, good evening."

I immediately tensed too. I felt as if we'd been caught doing something wrong, which was ridiculous.

"Hey! I can't believe I'm running into you two," Robert said. "How's it going?"

Julian immediately interlaced our fingers, bringing the back of my hand to his mouth and kissing it.

Was this for Robert's benefit? Or was this a way of reassuring me? "We're good. It's date night."

"It's good that you youngsters call this a date even after being together for some time."

My muscles went on lockdown even more. Shit, we should probably have talked about this. I didn't know how to react. I mean, we were dating now, but were we still faking the relationship part? If that even made sense to anyone but me.

"I like to spoil my woman," Julian replied.

"I'll see you two at the Landry party," Robert said.

"Of course you will."

"Good. I look forward to chatting with you." He shook Julian's hand again before bidding us goodbye.

Once he left, Julian glanced at me. "You okay?"

"That felt a bit bizarre."

"For me too. Not really sure why."

"We should talk about the Landry party now, don't you think?" I bit the inside of my cheek.

"Don't fret over that, Georgie, okay? It'll all work out."

"You're right." I shook myself out of my thoughts. I didn't have to think about any of that tonight. "Please, be my tour guide from here until we reach your home."

"Since we're in the neighborhood *anyway*, do you want beignets?"

"Usually, I don't turn them down, but right now, I really am truly too full."

"All right, then. Let's avoid the corner of Decatur and Ursulines, then."

"Good plan."

As we walked, Julian kept pointing out several buildings where his family either had business or were points of interest for them. His house was on Marais Street near Governor Nicholls Street. I didn't remember the last time I'd been around here, though I'd probably passed it on the way to Esplanade Avenue a few times. It was relatively quiet. The houses were quaint, and one in particular looked as if it had been renovated recently. The coat of paint was near perfect.

He pointed at the very same building. "This is my home." The facade was light blue, and the balcony railing was painted either dark blue or black. It had two stories, with three windows on each. It was exactly the kind of house I wanted to own one day.

Once inside, I was stunned by the mix of modern and traditional. The kitchen was ultramodern with marble countertops. The TV area looked like something out of a futuristic movie as well, with a sliding panel that could be pushed out of the way when no one was watching. The corridor paid tribute to the age of the house with a huge crystal chandelier and exposed brick walls with a staircase that led to the upper level. He took off his suit jacket, then helped me out of my coat, putting them on a rack by the entrance. We took off our shoes too.

"This place is absolutely stunning. Did you move in here recently?" I asked.

"No. I've been here ten years, but I renovated the facade last year."

"Do you have a courtyard as well?"

"A small one."

He led me to a door with an old-fashioned window on the other end of the living room, and we peeked outside. It was rather dark, but I could spot a bench in the courtyard. It was all paved with stones.

Julian came behind me and whispered in my ear, "Want us to take the nightcap outside?"

"Oh, I forgot about the nightcap." I turned around to face him. "No, let's keep the party here. What did you have in mind?"

"I've got an excellent rum I just scouted for the bars. Would you like a shot?"

My eyes bulged. "I didn't know you could drink rum in a shot."

"Most times you don't, but this one is exquisite."

I nodded. "Sure."

We walked to the kitchen island, and he took a bottle out from under it, along with two shot glasses.

"You weren't joking about that nightcap," I teased.

"It was a spontaneous idea to lure you here."

He gave me the shot, and I sniffed it.

"I'll chug it, but you can sip it if you prefer."

"Oh, that'll get me good and drunk."

I did take a sip, though, because I wasn't sure if I could drink it quickly. I was never a shot drinker. "Delicious."

"I told you."

"It's soft and aromatic."

Julian immediately downed his, and I followed suit. It didn't even really burn my throat, which was perfect. It allowed me to savor the flavors more.

"I feel my feet melting already," I said in earnest, walking up to him. "A great nightcap. But just so you know, it wasn't really necessary. You could've just lured me here with this." I fondled his right bicep. "Or this." I moved on to his left one. "Or this." I placed my palms over his pecs. "I really wouldn't mind which. I would've fallen hook, line, and sinker anyway."

Julian laughed, but his eyes flashed and then darkened as his pupils dilated. He took our two empty shot glasses and put them on the counter, moving with so much precision that you'd think he was performing surgery.

He turned to me, and I practically saw the moment his control slipped completely away and instinct took over. A thrill coiled through me, and then Julian kissed me even hotter than at the store, and far deeper. And yet I couldn't get enough.

CHAPTER TWENTY-FIVE

JULIAN

I had no idea how I'd managed to keep myself in check all evening, but I could no longer do it. I needed this woman—her mouth, her skin, her body. I wanted all her sounds of pleasure and her release.

I kept an arm around her back. With the other one, I pressed her into me, flattening my palm over her ass. I wanted her to feel that I was already hard.

"Julian," she murmured, then put her lips around my Adam's apple, sucking at it.

Fucking hell.

I walked her away from the kitchen counter. I had to get her upstairs quickly. My cock twitched, and I lowered my head to capture her mouth again, tangling our tongues. I wanted this woman so damn badly. I needed her naked right now. I reached for the fly of her jeans before we approached the staircase.

I wanted to get rid of the barrier and quickly unzipped them, pushing her pants past her ass. She was wearing a thong, leaving her practically bare. Her skin was soft, and I couldn't stop fondling her.

Abruptly, I stepped back a few inches, turning her around and lowering myself onto my haunches. She was already two steps above me, which was perfect because her ass was right in my face. I moved my lips and tongue over each globe.

"Julian!" Her voice shook.

When I put two fingers between her thighs, pressing them against her panties, her knees gave in momentarily. I immediately grabbed her left thigh to keep her stable as I teased her ass cheeks while I moved my fingers back and forth, back and forth. She was already drenched, and my erection was so hard that I couldn't stand the pressure of the zipper anymore, so I immediately opened the button and yanked down my zipper. As she got wetter and wetter, I reached inside my boxers and grabbed my cock, squeezing it long and hard, trying to stave off my release.

Georgie looked over her shoulder and then turned slightly, glancing down at me.

"Oh my God, Julian."

Her lips were red from how much she'd bitten into them. I was going to make her come right here on the staircase. I slipped my fingers under the fabric of her panties, caressing her bare skin. Her shoulders buckled forward as she pushed her ass right into my face, nearly knocking me over. Then she straightened up abruptly.

"Julian, oh my God! I'm so sorry. I didn't mean to bump into you."

"Babe, you can put that gorgeous ass on my face anytime. I don't mind. In fact, I love it."

I touched her clit, squeezing it between my fingers. Once again, she buckled forward, gripping the banister. Then she started a rhythmic move with her hips, back and forth, back and forth, rubbing herself against my fingers even more. She was so damn exquisite that I risked blowing in my pants, so I let go of my cock even though I needed the pressure now more than ever. But I couldn't touch myself and focus on her at the same time. I needed to give her more.

While I kept pinching her clit between my forefinger and middle finger, I pushed my thumb inside her pussy. I curved it, knowing it would brush her G-spot. Georgie was overwhelmed right away.

"Julian," she cried out, bending at the waist.

I didn't realize what she was doing until I saw her reach for the staircase. She kneeled with her knees on an upper step, putting both her hands five stairs higher. Fuck yes, she was bracing herself for the orgasm. It was exquisite to watch her on all fours like this. I worked her with my thumb and fingers, positioning myself so I could still reach the upper part of her buttocks with my mouth. She arched her back and then squeezed my thumb until she pushed it out completely.

She was already climaxing, so I pressed hard on her clit, and she came spectacularly, crying out loud. The sound ricocheted throughout the open hallway. I removed my hand from between her legs, keeping her steady; her body was spasming, and I didn't want her to accidentally hurt herself. Eventually, her breathing calmed down. She looked at me over her shoulder, completely red in the face.

"Julian," she murmured, then glanced between her thighs. "My God, I still have my jeans on."

I grinned. "Yeah, I'm going to rectify that right now."

Careful not to destabilize her, I pushed them and her thong past her knees, then pulled them off and dropped them behind us on the staircase.

She rose to her feet, and I did the same. She looked even more delicious like this, naked from the waist down.

Her sweater was fucking sexy hanging off one shoulder, but I wanted her without anything at all. I groaned as I slipped it off, as she was wearing no bra. I turned her around and frowned at her breasts.

"Whoops. I've got on those self-adhesive cups."

She immediately took them off, and her nipples perked up. She put them down on the staircase, too, then rose with a grin.

"I'm ready to be thoroughly fucked."

Groaning, I took her up in my arms, her legs hanging at my sides. I kissed and kissed her until we were both out of breath while I walked up the staircase. If I didn't hurry, I was going to fuck her right here. I liked that she was the perfect size for me, her petite frame quite comfortable for me to carry.

The master bedroom and en suite bathroom took up the entire second floor. I barely had enough self-restraint to make it to the bed.

"Will you look at that?" she murmured when I put her down. "The bedroom. I thought you were going to have me on the stairs."

"Still so sassy. You need a few more orgasms, don't you?"

She nodded. "Oh yeah. We're in complete agreement about that. But first, I want this."

Before I managed to even ask what she was talking about, she reached right into my pants and squeezed my cock.

I dropped my head back. "Georgie!" Then I yanked my shirt over my head after only undoing the first two buttons. I didn't have any patience to do this slowly.

At the same time, I felt Georgie push down my pants. I kicked them off, and she kneeled in front of me, looking up with hooded eyelids.

I needed to be inside her. But then she put her lips around my crown, and I was a goner. *Her mouth... fucking hell.* She took in more and more of me. When she had all she could, she bobbed back and forth. I grabbed her hair with one hand because I wanted to see her better, to see her shoulders move, her neck undulate, to see my dick plunging in and out of her gorgeous mouth.

I could come just like this, and it would be fucking spectacular. But I needed more. I needed her pussy. I needed to fill her up until she cried out for me.

"Georgie, I need to be inside you."

She groaned, looking up at me. The vibrations against my cock were almost too much. Energy shot from my balls right to my tip. I was close. Too damn close.

"Open up for me, beautiful. I want to pull out."

She stopped moving and relaxed her lips, and I slowly removed myself from her mouth, but my dick was protesting. Then I helped her to her feet and kissed her slowly. I wanted to explore her at a different pace now. But she reached between us, squeezing my cock, and just like that, the slow kiss wasn't enough anymore.

I moved her backward until we were right at the edge of the bed, and we tumbled onto it. I was on all fours, and she was lying flat under me with her elbows bent, hands near her head. Her knees were still bent, and I grabbed her left leg, putting it up on my shoulder. "I want to open you up good, Georgie. I'm going to go in so damn deep."

"Yes. Yes, please."

I looked between us, and the sight just put me even more on edge. "Fuck, I forgot a condom."

"I'm on birth control anyway," she stated. "Last time too. I just didn't tell you because—"

"You don't owe me an explanation," I assured her. Swallowing hard, I added, "I'm clean."

She nodded feverishly. "So am I. All my tests are good."

"I need to be inside you right now."

I rubbed the head of my erection against her clit, then farther down. She was so wet from her orgasm that I slipped in right away, and I had to make a concerted effort to slow down. I almost didn't move at all. I wanted her to be comfortable and take me in as well as she could.

"Fucking hell." When there was just one inch left, I pushed in all the way, and she threw her head back, moaning.

Watching her succumb to me and feeling our skin-on-skin contact was better than anything in the world.

She squeezed me good with her inner muscles. I groaned as a spasm rocked my body. My back straightened up and then curved. I paced myself, watching her reactions. Every time I came too close to release, I stilled and only moved enough so I could kiss her shoulders.

A thin sheen of sweat covered her. I turned on the light. That night at the Marriott, I hadn't been able to see her the way I wanted to, and right now I wanted to observe every reaction.

When I felt my pulse quickening, I commanded, "Touch yourself. Touch your clit. Show me what you like."

"But you found it all by yourself earlier," she muttered.

"Touch yourself," I repeated.

She immediately slid a hand between us. I followed it with my gaze, looking at her, but I instantly realized it was a mistake. I was going to come even faster watching her. So instead, I focused on her beautiful face as I kept thrusting and pushing, snapping my hips faster.

"Julian!" She rolled her head backward, jutting out her chin, stretching out her neck. I went in, kissing the exposed skin. I felt her fingers slide on the side of my cock as she pressed her palm to her clit.

The next few seconds were a complete blur. My senses were on fire as pleasure rippled through me. I came so damn hard that I couldn't even move any longer; I just thrust deep and then stilled, crying out her name. All I felt was her squeeze me even tighter.

Her face was crumpled, mouth opening and closing. No sound came out at first, and then it did, a guttural sound that somehow intensified my own pleasure.

I stayed like that, buried inside her, until we were both spent and satisfied.

This night is absolutely spectacular.

CHAPTER TWENTY-SIX

GEORGIE

The next morning, my head was pounding. I opened my eyes, but the broad daylight hurt them, so I closed them again. I moved my head to the other side and felt a wave of nausea rise up my throat.

What's going on? I didn't have that much to drink last night. And I felt as if my entire body was surrounded with hot coals.

"Okay, she's waking up. Let me know how soon. Thanks."

That was Julian's voice. It sounded as if he was super far away, but that couldn't be. The room was big, but it wasn't huge.

I opened my eyes again and struggled against the light. I couldn't see him anywhere, though. Then I pushed myself up on my elbows and fell back again.

"Don't get up." Julian sounded closer now. I felt the mattress cave in next to me, and he came into focus as his shape obscured the window behind him.

"What's going on?"

"You woke up with a fever. You threw up last night."

"I don't even remember that."

Julian pressed his lips together. He was more serious than I was used to. "You seemed pretty out of it."

I cleared my throat. "But I didn't make it to the toilet and back a-alone?"

"Why does it matter? I took care of you."

"Please tell me you didn't watch me throw up."

"Babe, I took care of you."

I wanted to disappear under the covers.

"I think something last night didn't agree with your stomach."

"Have you been sick?" I asked him.

He shook his head. "No."

"Then I don't think it was the restaurant food. I ate some cheese I had in the fridge at the store yesterday afternoon. It tasted a bit off, but I figured it was still okay. You really saw me throw up? At least tell me you didn't have to hold my hair." He fixed me with his gaze. He was still serious. "Oh no, you did," I groaned.

"You want me to lie to you?"

"You know what? Yeah, try it."

"Then no, I was fast asleep, didn't even hear a thing. You just told me what happened when you came to bed."

"Nah, it's not working." I took a good look at him now that my eyes were accustomed to the light. "Did I keep you up all night? You look like you haven't slept much."

"I've been up for a while. You had a fever, and I was worried. I kept calling the family doctor, and he finally answered. He's coming right away."

"Julian, I'm sure I just need some water."

"That's the thing. I've tried to give you water all night, after each time you threw up. You just got sick again."

I stilled. "So, I did throw up multiple times."

"Why are you so caught up in that?" he inquired, and I could tell he was genuinely baffled.

"We just started dating. I don't want you to see me puking."

"Georgie, stop that. There is no reason for you to feel uncomfortable. You were sick. I looked after you as best as I could. And I'm going to do that for the rest of the day."

I groaned, lying back. "What time is it?" I pushed myself up again and was hit with a fresh wave of nausea.

Right, brisk movements aren't good.

"Eleven o'clock."

I gasped. "Oh my God, Zelda must be freaking out. I need to call her."

"She called a few hours ago. I answered the phone and told her what's going on. She assured me that she'll take care of the store until you're back on your feet. I offered to send some reinforcements in case she needs it."

I felt a strange pressure in my chest. "Who would you even send?"

"Probably one of my brothers."

I laughed. "As if they don't have anything better to do on the weekend."

"They'd do it as a favor to me if I asked them. Not sure how much use they'd be in the actual store, but they'd do it."

"Oh, Julian."

"The doctor suggested you have some toast. I'm going downstairs to bring you some."

"Thanks."

Now that he mentioned it, my stomach *was* rumbling. Though I didn't know if it was with hunger or with another bout of vomit—fingers crossed that it was the former.

After Julian left, I stared at the ceiling, realizing it was a full-blown painting. It looked almost as old as the house and was absolutely breathtaking. It wasn't a pattern, simply swirls of color, sage and light brown and nature hues. I could look at it endlessly; it was so relaxing. I took in a deep breath, breathing out slowly.

Julian returned in no time at all, holding a plate with two slices of toast and a glass of water.

He put them on the nightstand, but when I tried to push myself up, he said, "Stop. I'll help you. Here."

He slid a hand between my back and the mattress, then pushed me up. God, this side of him was beyond anything I'd expected. He was so gentle with me. I straightened up and didn't get nauseous this time. He propped the pillow against the headrest, and I settled against it.

"How are you feeling?"

"No nausea."

"That's good."

He held the plate of toast for me, and I reached for a slice, munching on it with very small bites. I chewed it carefully before swallowing.

"I think I can eat this," I said after a few moments.

"That's good."

I took two more bites before taking a break.

"This is good. It hasn't made me feel like puking."

I was feeling a bit more optimistic as I moved on to the second slice.

"Don't eat it too fast," Julian cautioned.

"You're right."

"Want to try and drink some water?"

I eyed the glass. Somehow, I felt like that might not work. "Do I have to?"

Julian laughed, and I knew I sounded like a kid. "The doctor said that if you can't keep down liquids, he'll have to give you an IV."

I raised a brow. "That's a bit much, isn't it?"

"No. He asked me exactly how many times you threw up last night. When I told him, he got concerned. That's why he agreed to come."

"Then I'll try a few sips."

I was even more cautious than with the toast. Julian was holding the glass as if he feared I didn't have enough strength to do that myself. It was endearing.

I took a few very small sips and said, "I think I can keep this down, but I don't want to overdo it."

"All right. My instructions are to get you to drink half of this glass before he shows up."

"Which is when?"

"Half an hour, give or take."

"Bossy doctor," I complained. "And you're bossy too. I'm sick. Aren't you supposed to be nice to me?"

Julian cocked a brow but didn't reply.

Over the next half hour, I dutifully drank while also eating my toast. It all stayed in my stomach, thank goodness.

The doctor arrived on time. Dr. Charles was an elderly man who appeared to be in his seventies. His beard and mustache were white as snow, but his hair was still gray. He even had strands of black in between.

"All right," he said gently. "Julian gave me the rundown of what happened last night. Tell me exactly how you feel."

He looked at my glass of water suspiciously. I tried to describe how I felt as best as possible.

"I'd like to get out of bed, though," I finished.

"I'm afraid I can't approve that today."

"At all?" I was shocked.

"You can move around the house." He looked at Julian. "But I would try and keep her well rested."

"Even though you don't remember last night, you were up a lot," Julian said.

"It's not just that," the doctor said. "You're severely dehydrated. People think doctors joke when we say, 'You need to drink water,' but having an imbalance of electrolytes is extremely dangerous. Since you managed to drink that amount within half an hour and keep it down, I'm positively optimistic that you should be able to get the liquids you need on your own." He turned to Julian again. "You need to be very strict with her. She needs to drink eight ounces every hour. I usually recommend my patients consume a minimum of seventy ounces a day."

Even though his voice was very severe, his eyes were kind.

"I'll do that."

"Get one of those sport drinks for her, like Gatorade. That will help her hydrate even better." The doctor then turned to me, saying, "See if you can stomach the taste. If you do, it's going to help. Don't overdo it, though. One bottle is enough."

"Gatorade it is," Julian said.

"That's all. Please keep me updated. If you start throwing up again or you can't take in any more fluids, we'll need to give you an IV."

I groaned. "I hate hospitals."

"You don't need to go to a hospital for that. I'd arrange for you to have everything you need here."

I tried to contain my shock. I didn't even know that was possible.

"All right, then. I promised the missus I'd take her for brunch, and I don't want to be late. But I'm on call anytime you need," he told me and then looked at Julian.

I swear to God, I hoped we wouldn't have to call him. I was embarrassed enough that we had to drag this poor guy down here on a Sunday morning.

While Julian walked him downstairs, I eyed my glass again and then took another a few sips. I listened intently for Julian to come back up after I heard the front door close. To my intense surprise, it was completely silent. Maybe he'd decided to walk a few feet with the doctor. I was the only one who had to stay indoors and lie around doing nothing, after all. He was free to move around.

Julian returned a short while later, and he sprinted up the staircase.

"Hey, where have you been?" I asked.

He held up a bottle with a fluorescent blue liquid inside. "Got you Gatorade."

My heart gave a mighty squeeze. "That's why you went out?"

"Yes. The doctor said you need it. Far be it from me to disagree."

"I thought you always played things by ear," I teased as he came over to me.

"Not when it comes to a doctor's instructions." He began to uncap it, then looked at my glass and smiled. "You drank all of it."

My God, he sounded so proud, like I'd just finished a marathon or something. "Yes, I did."

"Okay." He put the cap back on. "Then you'll have this later. Don't think it's good to have too much at once."

"I don't think I could keep it down, honestly."

"What do you want to do?" he asked me.

"I'll order an Uber."

He stared at me. "What are you talking about?"

"To go home. I like the bus, but even so, I couldn't possibly take it right now."

"Georgie, what are you talking about? You're not going anywhere."

"But the doctor said I should rest."

"Yes, and you will. Here. You'll alternate with the couch downstairs, and you're not leaving this house."

"You don't want to spend your entire day indoors."

He sat down on the edge of the bed, touching my face. "I want to spend the day with you. Besides, I want to keep an eye on you so I'll know if I should call the doctor again."

Oh goodness, this didn't feel like we were simply dating. It felt like a relationship.

"Are you sure?"

"Yes, I'm fucking sure. In fact, if you try to leave, I might just tie you to that bed."

Now *that* sounded interesting.

Julian looked at my cheeks and then started to laugh. "Your mind just went to sex, didn't it?"

"Hell yes."

He grinned. "Then I guess you're starting to recover."

Chapter Twenty-Seven

Julian

Georgie slept on and off for the rest of the day. I didn't like that she was so drowsy. I kept checking her temperature and making sure she drank at the intervals the doctor suggested. I hated that I had no medical knowledge—I was not a fan of things being outside my control.

Toward the evening, she started to be much more alert and could even keep down a full meal. The doctor assured me that there was no need for another checkup.

She slept like a rock through the night, which I took as a good sign, because that meant she'd managed to keep down dinner, which was no small thing.

The next morning, I woke up at nine o'clock as usual. She was still sleeping, so I decided to prepare breakfast for both of us. Yesterday, she took a look at the fridge and pointed out that she would've loved some honey on her toast, so that was what I was making for her this morning. I didn't butter it because Dr. Charles said fat could be problematic after she'd had such a rough time, and instead I paired it with some green tea and put everything on a tray. I wanted to spoil my woman with some beignets, but the doctor had been strict about her diet, emphasizing bland foods for now. Yeah, I'd asked.

I carried the tray upstairs, and to my astonishment, she came out of the master bathroom.

"I feel alive again. What's that?" She looked at the tray.

"Breakfast in bed."

She grinned and dropped her towel, jumping on the bed completely naked.

"Take it easy."

"Nope. I feel good, and I intend to use every ounce of my energy. Honey on toast," she murmured as she noticed the contents.

"Like you wanted yesterday."

"I actually woke up thinking about it."

"I figured you might."

Seeing her naked body in my bed was exquisite. It was all I wanted. But she was still recovering.

"I have another idea," I told her. "Do you want to go out on the patio for breakfast?"

"I love that patio. But wait, why? Julian, why aren't you looking at me?"

"You're completely naked, and you look fucking fantastic. Babe, I'm trying not to jump you."

"Oh, I see where this is going. Far be it from me to tempt you. Let me just take a bite, and then I'll put on clothes."

"I'll wait for you downstairs on the patio and set everything up."

She snorted. "You really have no self-restraint, huh?"

"Not at all," I assured her as I looked at her from the corner of my eye. She was standing next to the bed, feet planted wide, hands on her hips. Her breasts were on full display.

Fucking hell, she was doing this on purpose. Her grin told me as much.

She giggled, and I took in a deep breath. "Woman."

"Okay, I got it. I got it. I'll dress quickly."

"Good."

I went downstairs and got the patio ready; I didn't use it nearly as much as I should, but I could see why Georgie liked it. I made a coffee for myself, but by the time I returned, she was already sitting outside, eyes closed, chin tilted up. The sun was shining on her face. I wanted to frame this moment. She fit so damn well here in my house.

She opened her eyes, glancing at me. "I love this morning."

I loved having her here more than I could explain. I wanted to *keep* her here. How insane was that?

I sat down on the other chair, drinking my coffee.

"No breakfast for you?" she asked.

"I'm not hungry."

She'd already eaten half of her toast.

"Do you want more?"

She shook her head. "No, let's not push it."

I sipped my coffee again, and then my phone vibrated. The family group had quite a few messages. I'd put it on silent yesterday, so I just scrolled through all of them and grinned.

"What is it?" Georgie asked.

I looked up at her. "Right, I forgot. My family is having brunch today at the mansion."

She blinked. "When do you have to be there?"

I stared at her. "We. I'd like you to come with me, Georgie."

"The mansion is one of your restaurants?"

"No, that's the house where they all live."

She suddenly straightened up on the chair, pushing her shoulders back. "Wow. Sure, why not? I'd love to see your grandmothers again and meet everyone."

"It's a pretty big group, but it helps that you already know some of them."

"And you can just bring someone on such short notice?"

"This is my family. Everything is short notice. And yes, I can. If I told them that I was showing up with an entire party, they wouldn't even bat an eye."

Georgie started to laugh. "Sounds like a lot of fun. But I don't think I'll be able to eat much."

I figured that would be the case, but I liked that she was like me. Fun, spontaneous. Why hadn't I realized before that we were so much alike?

"When do we have to leave?" she asked.

"About five minutes."

She looked down at herself. "Good thing I'm wearing casual clothes. Except, wait..." She glanced at me and bit the inside of her cheek. "Is this like an event? Am I supposed to dress up?"

"No, it's just brunch. Don't worry about anything."

She laughed, but it sounded more nervous than usual.

I rounded the table and went up to her. "What is it, Georgie? We don't have to go if you don't want to. We can spend the day here or venture out in the city."

"The store—"

"Zelda's got it covered."

"I know, she texted me that things are fine. But..."

"I'm still keeping an eye on you. That's part of the reason I want to take you with me." I used it as my excuse and stepped closer, brushing my lips on her forehead.

"What's the other part?" she whispered.

"I just want you there," I confessed and looked down at her. Her breasts were pressing against me. I could feel her heartbeat accelerating. "Let's go."

The Sunday brunches at the LeBlanc-Broussard mansion were always a bit erratic. My grandmothers prepared food, and everyone could show up at the time they wanted. There wasn't an official sit-down.

The food was laid out on the dining table, but everyone was gathered on the couches in the living room, just going back and forth back to fill their plates. There were already quite a few LeBlancs present. My grandmothers were nowhere in sight, but my grandfathers, Felix and David, were sitting on the couches with their plates. Mom and Dad were chatting with Bella. Chad, Xander, and Zachary were here too. Anthony and Beckett were the only ones missing, but they were typically even later than me. I could always count on my youngest brothers to make me look good.

Georgie hadn't said a word since we came in. She kept looking around, surprise etched on her face.

Maybe I should've eased her into this and told her how to tackle each of us. Then again, sometimes the best way to tackle the LeBlancs was to just go with the flow. That was what I did. But I did have thirty-eight years of experience.

"Hello, everyone. This is Georgie."

The room's reaction was almost comical. Mom and Dad practically jumped to their feet. My grandfathers were a bit slower, but they stood as well. They truly were Southern gentlemen through and through.

Bella clapped her hands. "Nana, you were right. Uncle Julian does have a girlfriend."

That essentially broke the ice, as the entire room burst out laughing.

I immediately looked at Georgie. She seemed stunned. Her face had gotten a bit pink.

I tilted toward her, whispering in her ear, "Sorry about that. My family can be a bit much."

Georgie made a small sound at the back of her throat but didn't utter a word. That was understandable. If this had been someone's reaction the first time they saw me, I'd probably be too stunned to speak too.

Mom came right to us, looking at me apologetically. "I'm so sorry about Bella's outburst," she whispered. "She... well, she and I were talking, and I think she might have jumped to conclusions. Georgie, it's so nice to meet you. I've heard so much about you. I believe you've met most of my sons already, but why don't we make the rounds?"

As I introduced Georgie to everyone, I kept my eyes firmly on her, looking for any sign that it was too much.

Then my grandmothers came in. Both of them had huge grins. "We heard Georgie's here," Celine said.

"Hi, Isabeau. Hi, Celine," Georgie said, looking at my grandmothers like they were her saviors. Little did she know, they were just going to pile on more. In fact, maybe I'd been too quick to judge Mom over the "girlfriend" incident. I could imagine Celine and Isabeau, especially the latter, filling Bella's head with stories about their lilac perfume and giving me and Georgie as an example.

"Georgie, darling, it's good to see you," Isabeau said.

"I wanted to thank you for talking to one of my clients. She contacted me and reinstated our contract."

Isabeau beamed. "Good for her!"

My grandmothers didn't say more and moved right on to the brunch offerings.

"Now, we've made some of our specialties. You're welcome to taste all of them, of course, and give us your opinion," Celine said.

"I'm going to take it easy on the food. I was sick yesterday evening," Georgie replied.

Celine straightened up, and Isabeau's eyes went cold.

"You were sick after you went to The Apothecary?" Isabeau said, then turned to Celine. "We must pay a visit to that kitchen."

I was so shocked that they knew about our date that I didn't reply quick enough.

Georgie's mouth was simply open.

"How would you even know about that?" I finally asked sharply.

Georgie seemed to want to disappear into the floor. I really should've prepped her better.

"Oliver called to brag that he'd gotten yet another LeBlanc to agree that The Apothecary's jambalaya was better than mine," Isabeau said. "And I was suspicious because as far as I knew, all the LeBlancs had already been there. He didn't really volunteer the information, but I put two and two together."

"Oh!" Georgie exclaimed, but she was still red in the face.

"Way to put someone on the spot, Isabeau," Anthony said, walking into the living room from behind her. Beckett was with him too.

"I believe you've already met these two," I said to Georgie.

"Oh yes, we did." Beckett narrowed his eyes at me. "It seems I've missed an episode or two. When did this become real?"

Anthony groaned. "Dude, you're worse than the grandmothers."

"The details don't matter," I said vaguely, and I could feel Georgie relaxing beneath my touch. Good. Because this *was* real, and my girl needed to know that.

Zachary had gone toward the couch after the introductions, but he hurried back over as Isabeau and Celine ganged up on us.

"You need my intervention? Calming spirits and all that?" he asked me without further ado.

Georgie started to laugh. Zachary had this unique power of putting people at ease. I called him our problem solver.

"Dude, I would've needed your intervention a few minutes ago. Now it's too late."

Zachary looked at Georgie. "Truly sorry. I was too busy discussing with Bella if... never mind."

Beckett glanced at me and said, "I was about to pile on, but I think you've had enough teasing for today."

"Mark my words," I told Georgie. "He usually doesn't let me off the hook so easily. It's all because of you."

"I'm pleased," she said, some of her sass coming back. She was slowly getting used to this, which was fantastic because it was only going to get more intense. They were simply warming up. We'd taken them by surprise.

"I could eat something, though," Georgie said. "My stomach is rumbling."

"Babe, you only had toast with honey this morning. Of course you're hungry."

As we turned around to the table, I caught Beckett and Anthony staring at us with open mouths. Zachary, on the other hand, gave me an appreciative nod and thumbs-up. I could perfectly understand my youngest brothers' reactions. Ever since they were kids, they'd heard me say that couple-hood wasn't for me. And this sounded very much like couple-hood. But I didn't regret it one bit.

I led her straight to the dining table. "Just take what you want."

"This is so fancy," Georgie said. "It's almost looks like a restaurant setting."

"Once a chef, always a chef," Chad said, joining us. "The grandmothers like to say that they might not be able to run a restaurant anymore, but they do everything professionally whenever they can."

He moved closer so only we could hear him. "By the way, I'm really sorry about Bella sort of outing you," he said. "I had no idea anyone even spoke to her about you two."

"Brother, this is the disadvantage of having a village around you to raise kids."

Chad laughed. "It's all good. I mean, it's obviously unfair to you, but I don't mind. So, how's business going, Georgie?"

I liked that he was inquiring about Books & Beads and taking an interest in her.

"We ended up having a great Carnival season. Much better than I was fearing before Christmas. And I might even have gotten inspiration for one or two additional business lines, so to speak."

I couldn't help but beam at my woman. Her business savvy was unique. Georgie honored their family legacy but kept up with the market's needs simultaneously.

"That's fantastic," Chad said as we all headed back to the living room with our plates.

Everyone spoke with Georgie at one time or another. I was damn proud of the whole clan for making her feel welcome. Even though this was only supposed to be brunch, it lasted the whole day.

In the evening, Georgie asked me to take her home. I was tempted to convince her to come by my house again because I wanted to keep an eye on her, but she did need fresh clothes.

"Want to come in?" she asked me after we'd parked.

"Of course. What did you think about today?"

She beamed. "I had so much fun. When you first suggested it, I wondered if I'd feel out of place, but that wasn't the case at all." She opened the door to the house. "Welcome to my kingdom."

CHAPTER TWENTY-EIGHT

JULIAN

As we stepped inside the house, I kissed the back of her neck, holding her hair up with one hand.

"Oh, now I see why you wanted to come in," she teased. "Hmm, let's see. My bedroom is right there." She pointed and then walked toward the door off the living room.

Her bedroom was a decent size. When she entered, she looked like a vision. It was semi-dark, but there was a full moon tonight, and she had stepped right into its light.

"Could you help me undress?" she asked.

"Sure. In fact, it's going to be my pleasure." I stepped right behind her. "Your neck has tempted me the entire day," I confessed in her ear. Before moving my mouth to the back of her neck, I pushed her head forward, exposing it even more.

"Really? Why didn't you try anything?"

"You know me, Georgie. There is no trying. I would've pulled you into the corner and had you right there."

She shivered, the skin on her back turning to goose bumps. After taking off her sweater, I kissed along her right shoulder blade. Even though I'd wanted her all day, I wasn't in a hurry right now. Everything around us was happening at such a fast pace, but this moment here was different. I moved over to her left shoulder blade as I touched her spine, and she shivered again. Interesting place for a sensitive spot. I planned to return to it later. Then I pushed down her jeans, leaving her in only her bra and panties.

"You're magnificent," I told her. "I couldn't take my eyes off you all day. I like that the sweater isn't revealing so no one can see what's mine."

She laughed softly, her entire rib cage vibrating against me. "A bit territorial tonight, huh?"

"*A lot.*"

Her breath caught. I turned her around so I was facing her and immediately took off her bra.

"You taste so damn good."

I moved my mouth from her clavicle in a straight line to her nipple and sucked it into my mouth. Her back went ramrod straight. No doubt she thought I'd ease into it, and I'd planned to. But the sight of her breasts in my face tempted me too damn much.

I gave her right nipple an entirely different treatment. I didn't take it into my mouth, just cupped her breast in my palm, teasing the tight part between my fingers. She groaned and started to move back and forth, from her heels to her tiptoes. She was slowly coming exactly to the point where I wanted her—where I'd been all day. My need for her took over every other thought.

I then moved straight to her navel. Grabbing her panties, I yanked them down. She gasped, stumbling forward a bit when I was past her knees. She buckled forward, putting both hands on my shoulders, and laughed.

"Again. Last time I nearly face-planted with my ass in your face."

"And now your pussy," I said with a grin. "I don't mind, babe. Anytime."

I tilted forward, swiping my tongue right over her pussy.

"Julian!" Her voice broke toward the end, and she swayed slightly but didn't lose her balance.

Now that I'd had a taste of her, I wanted more. I wanted her up here, level with my face, which gave me an idea. Instead of putting her on the bed, I looked at the desk she had by the window and walked her backward toward it.

"Sit on your desk," I commanded. "Spread your thighs."

"How wide?"

I loved that she asked for more instructions.

"As far as you can. Open up that pussy for me so I can have all the access I want to it."

I pulled back the chair she had under it, then got a better idea. I sat on it. *Fuck yes, I'm a genius.* Now I truly had her pussy in my face.

I planted both her feet on my thighs, pushing her knees farther apart. She positioned herself right at the edge of the desk. The window was behind her, which gave me yet another idea.

"Put your back against the window."

The glass was going to be cool but not cold. I paid attention to the motion of her moving backward and swiped my tongue over her clit the second she leaned against the window. She gasped, pressing her feet into my thighs as her ass hitched right off the desk. That was better, actually. I slipped my hands under her ass, keeping her a few inches in the air. This way I could also tilt her pelvis the way I wanted it. The downside was that I couldn't use my fingers to pleasure her, but my lips and tongue were all I needed. I pushed my tongue inside her, and her glutes squeezed tight, then even tighter, along with her inner muscles.

I pulled my head back and moved my tongue in huge circles around her pussy. Moving up to her clit, I pressed the flat of my tongue against it. Georgie went feral as she pushed her pelvis up. I gave her a few moments of reprieve before pulling her back down. Then I feasted on her clit earnestly, nipping with my lips before circling again with my tongue.

"You taste so damn good. I can't get enough of you."

She gasped in response. She'd moved away from the window, but that was okay. Of course she couldn't keep the position when I was making her this wild.

I proceeded to nudge her clit with the tip of my nose as I pushed my tongue inside her. The combination turned her even wilder. Once again, her entire body arched upward. With her ass hanging in the air, she started to move back and forth, fucking my face.

I instantly turned painfully hard. This was so damn sexy that I wanted to push down my pants and fuck her right here on this desk. But there was no space, and I wanted to make her come once before then. It was my guilty pleasure to give to her as many orgasms as possible, and she deserved them.

But I needed my fingers, too, so I only held her ass in the air with one hand. Then I gave her two fingers at once. She was more than ready for them. She dropped her head back, groaning more powerfully than I'd ever heard her before. The sight of it was enough to bring me to my knees: Georgie spread out over this desk and the moon shining down on her, highlighting her delicious shapes.

I didn't give her much reprieve, moving my hand at the same rhythm I'd be moving my cock. I leaned in from time to time, nipping at her clit as well, working her up slowly and then very fast. When the muscles in her legs clenched, I knew it was only a matter of minutes.

I'd been wrong. It was seconds. I moved two fingers in a curling motion and sucked her clit between my lips as hard as I could. The orgasm took over her entire body instantly. Her shoulders spasmed backward, pushing her chest up, her breasts bouncing with the movement. Her rib cage expanded, she drew in her stomach, and her legs fell sideways.

One of her feet slid down from my thigh, but I was keeping her safely up in the air. I pressed one hand on her pussy until her moans turned to winces and she finally could breathe. Then I put her ass back on the table.

She leaned back against the window again, panting, eyes blazing. I wanted to memorize the way she was looking at me.

I immediately undid my shirt, practically tearing it open. A few buttons seemed to pop, but I couldn't care less.

"Hmm. Destructive striptease," she mumbled. "I like this."

She sat up straight and worked at my belt and then my pants while I took off my shirt. She immediately pushed them down, and then I moved my boxers past my ass, where they fell in a lump at my feet.

She gasped at the sight I'd revealed. "You've been hard like this all along?"

"Georgie, I've been hard for you for hours. Everything about you makes me want you. All the damn time."

I realized a split second later that I couldn't wait until I took her to the bed. Her bare pussy was far too tempting, and she was at the perfect height for this.

I put the length of my cock along her entrance without sliding in. She shuddered, and I knew why. She was still sensitive, and the flesh-on-flesh contact was delicious. I tilted over her, kissing her mouth while I rubbed my cock back and forth, slowly, teasingly. It was more torture than pleasure, but somehow, I also relished the contact. I was savoring our connection in a whole different way.

Georgie moaned against my mouth. I felt her body start changing again, tensing up. Then she whimpered. I knew what that meant—I was going to make her come just by doing this. Heat spiraled through every cell at the realization that I held the key to this woman's pleasure.

But making her come was costing me all my willpower. With every rub, I felt the need to slide inside her more and more until it was like I was about to break out of my skin.

She was so close, her whimpers becoming more high-pitched. She put one hand on my bicep, clasping it tight, digging her nails into my skin. Then she unhitched her lips from mine, throwing her head back. The groan that erupted from her filled the entire room. Hell, the whole of New Orleans, probably. It was the most delicious sound I'd ever heard.

As she climaxed, I slid my cock inside her pussy. She was so drenched that she took all of me in at once.

"Georgie!" My voice was hoarse, I didn't even think she'd understood that I was calling her name. Being inside her after wanting her all day was the best reward. So much need and pleasure. She was pulsing around my cock, and I was already so on edge that I knew if I wanted to, I could probably come just like this.

But hell no.

I started to move, controlling the strokes, at least in the beginning. I kissed her while I thrust in and out. No matter how close we were, how much of her I was touching, kissing, or fucking, it simply wasn't enough.

I shifted her legs so they were wrapped around me and I could push as freely as I wanted. Then I leaned slightly over her, putting my palms on the desk. I needed more of this angle.

As Georgie began to moan again, she pulled her legs up, resting her knees against my rib cage.

"Fuck," I exclaimed. "Georgie, babe... This is amazing. You're amazing."

On every thrust, I alternated between kissing her mouth and her neck. I liked hearing her sounds too much to cover them, yet capturing her mouth while I was balls deep inside her really heightened everything.

Her third orgasm took me by complete surprise. Or maybe I was too lost in my own desire to notice the signs. When she cried out, my own release mingled with hers. I let go of all self-control and self-restraint. I didn't need them anymore. I was giving everything up for Georgie. My pleasure was all hers. *I* was all hers.

I thrust and thrust until I suddenly couldn't move any more. All I could do then was sustain my weight by resting on my forearms, still buried deep inside her, making sure I didn't press her too hard into the desk.

"Are you okay, beautiful?" I murmured in her ear.

In response, she simply tugged on my earlobe, but it was answer enough.

Chapter Twenty-Nine
Georgie

The day of the Landry party came much sooner than I expected. It had seemed so far away, like it would only happen in months, but then it snuck up quickly enough. With the Carnival season over, my business was back to focusing on books. We were already working on the designs for next year's floats but weren't in a rush.

"You were right," I said, taking in a deep breath and smiling at the crowd gathered in the garden at the Landrys' home. This was right up my alley. Everyone was laughing and holding a drink, but they weren't champagne flutes. The guests all had either a cocktail glass or a beer, some even drinking from the bottle. I was wearing a dress again, but it was very casual, as Julian had instructed. And I was in flats because I wasn't risking another ankle incident. It was already seven in the evening and dark, but there were plenty of lights around the yard—and heaters, thankfully.

"Let's say hi to the Landrys," Julian suggested.

"Sure."

He took my arm and led me across the yard to a couple who were probably the same age as Calliope and Bo.

"Julian, how good to see you. And this is the famous Georgie," Mr. Landry said.

How did he even know my name? Oh, from the RSVP, probably.

"Yes, it is," Julian replied.

"Thank you so much for having us," I said wholeheartedly. "I'm already enjoying the festivities."

"That's what this is all about. We were very lucky to have such great weather, but if it changes, we're ready to take the party inside."

"It's usually not outside?" I inquired.

"No," Mrs. Landry replied. "It depends on how long the Carnival season is. We always wait until after Mardi Gras to have the party, but it usually doesn't end so late in the year." She waved to someone off to the side and then smiled at us. "I hope you have fun. Maybe we'll catch up later."

"Of course," Julian replied.

Once we stepped away, he kissed the side of my head again. I loved when he did that. "You okay?"

"Sure." Even though I knew Kyle was attending, I was remarkably relaxed. Honestly, I didn't really much care about him anymore. I was strong now. I wasn't sure when that had changed, when he'd lost the power to hurt me, but I knew Julian had a lot to do with it. I'd changed since he came into my life. And I couldn't be happier about that.

"Should we find Robert?" I asked.

Julian nodded. "I already spotted him."

Robert was near the long table where there were a lot of different dishes. This truly was a party after my own heart. I even spotted a band at the side of the yard. I couldn't wait for some dancing.

He was picking up a bottle of beer. Clearly, he liked the casual atmosphere too.

"Hello, Robert," Julian said.

He glanced up from the table. "Hey." He shook Julian's hand and then mine. "Nice seeing you two here. I think I'll come back for food later. Want to walk with me for a bit?"

"Sure." Julian took my hand. I liked being completely glued to him. I craved every touch, and his nearness in general.

"Have you given my offer more thought?" Julian asked.

"Jumping right into business, huh?"

Julian didn't reply, but I knew he was getting impatient. It wasn't as if this was the first time he'd wanted to seal the deal.

"We're here to relax," Robert said, and Julian shook his head.

"Look, Robert, I'll be honest. This has been dragging on for far too long. I'm going to take it as you're not interested. No hard feelings, but I need to move on and find someplace else."

Robert's face fell, and I felt a small amount of satisfaction. My man had some sweet negotiation techniques.

"Damn, you LeBlancs are always in a hurry. I've been thinking about this a lot. I've actually been doing some digging about you and Kyle too. I'd much rather you buy my buildings."

I swear I could feel Julian's rib cage expanding in pride. I wanted to jump up and down with joy. *Yes, yes, yes.* I was extremely happy for my man and also ecstatic that Kyle was out of the running. It was nothing less than he deserved.

"That's great news indeed," Julian said. "How fast can we move forward? I can have my team draft up some contracts for tomorrow."

Robert chuckled. "I don't usually move that fast, but if your team does, and all I have to do is ask mine to double-check it, go ahead. Terms are the same as discussed, what you gave me on the proposal sheet. And between you and me, I do need to get rid of those buildings fast. They're just eating up money since there are no businesses in them."

"I'm happy to take it off your hands," Julian said smoothly.

"So, how are you two doing?" Robert asked, looking from me to him. He genuinely seemed interested.

"We're good," Julian replied.

"Any plans for the future? Just saying that if there's a LeBlanc wedding, I wouldn't mind getting an invitation."

I stiffened. Julian simply laughed.

"Way to put on the pressure," he said. "No plans for now, though we are looking at buying a huge-ass place with a big yard, white picket fence, all that."

My entire body warmed up. Even though I loved the idea of living in the Quarter, the house Julian just painted popped into my head in complete detail.

"Now that sounds like a plan. Keep it up," Robert said. "Ah, speak of the devil."

I glanced over my shoulder. Kyle was heading our way, already frowning at me and Julian.

Oh, this is going to be so good.

"I see LeBlanc got to you first, Robert. Hope you didn't seal the deal already," Kyle said.

"As a matter of fact," Robert said, "we did. Sorry, Kyle. Some things I found out about you weren't to my liking at all."

For the first time ever, I saw Kyle completely bewildered. He jerked his head back. "Whatever lies you found, Robert, I can prove that they are not true. And LeBlanc doesn't exactly have my best interest at heart."

"I didn't say a thing," Julian said, clearly enjoying this.

"Don't insult me. I do my own research, boy," Robert said in a somewhat cutting tone. "And the buildings go to Julian. Now, if you'll excuse us, we still have to discuss some details."

Kyle looked even more bewildered than before. We moved away from him because he clearly wasn't going anywhere.

Robert shook his head. "He certainly didn't take that well. Very unprofessional of him."

"Thank you for your trust," Julian said.

"You know what? Let's hammer out some details after all," Robert replied. "Since we're here anyway, let's not postpone this any longer."

"Gladly!"

"I'm going to look around a bit," I said, wanting to give Julian some privacy.

"Sure, babe. Let me know if you need me."

I was still swooning at his description of the house we'd buy. Was it possible that Julian was envisioning a future for us? Because goodness, I definitely was. He and I hadn't been together that long, but my entire heart belonged to this man. For the first time since the fiasco with Kyle, I dared to think about entrusting Julian with my future too.

I glanced at the buffet, eyeing a jambalaya I really wanted to try. Ever since our night at The Apothecary, I kept wanting to taste every jambalaya I could get my hands on. But I wasn't very hungry yet, so I moved toward where the band was getting set up.

"What the hell was that?" Kyle's voice came from behind me as I looked at the musicians' instruments.

I turned to look at my ex lazily. There were quite a few people around us, and he wasn't bothering to keep his voice down.

"What are you talking about?"

"That business with Robert and LeBlanc. I don't buy that LeBlanc had nothing to do with it."

"Funnily enough, Kyle, he didn't. But you know what happens when you're being a scumbag? Word travels."

"You take that back," he growled. "What do you know about business anyway?"

"Honestly, nothing at all about your business. And news flash: I don't even care. Never have. But you're a jackass overall. *That* I can attest to."

I realized that several other people were watching, but who cared? They *should* hear this. I had nothing to hide.

"You weren't even man enough to break up with me. You asked your new girlfriend to do it." I raised my voice so everyone close could hear. "That's right. I went to his club to see him, and he actually sent his *girlfriend* to break up with me."

Kyle took a step back, looking around. "Take that back."

"It's the truth!"

He was getting red in the face. Kyle loved appearances more than anything else. And this made him look really bad.

Movement out of the corner of my eye caught my attention. Julian was walking up to us.

"Problem?" he asked.

"You two are fucking unbelievable!" Kyle exclaimed. I thought he might push more, but apparently the public humiliation was enough for him, as he turned on his heel and left.

Julian looked down at me, concern etched on his features. "Babe, are you okay? Sorry, I didn't even realize he'd come up to you."

"I'm perfect, actually. It feels so good to get things off my chest."

His face transformed into a smile. "You were spectacular."

I gasped. "You heard me?"

"The entire party heard you, but that's okay. That jackass fully deserves it. I think people are starting to get the picture of what Kyle and Beau Deveraux are all about."

"I think so too. And you know what? His presence didn't bother me one bit."

"You mean that?" Julian asked, caressing my jaw.

"I nodded. "Yeah, I truly do. And I have you to thank for that."

"No, babe. You're always strong. He just made you forget that."

"Anyway, I want to repay you."

"How?"

"With some dancing and then later... oh. Nothing later, because I need to get to bed early tonight. I've got an early morning tomorrow. I'm getting a delivery."

"We'll negotiate later," Julian said, taking my hand and leading me over to where the band had set up.

He hadn't exaggerated. The music was truly exquisite at the Landry party. They played jazz, but also a lot of other genres. It was always rhythmic, always perfect for dancing, and I congratulated myself for wearing flat shoes.

By the time Julian drove me home, it was truly late in the evening. I was almost asleep when we arrived at my house.

"Are you sure you don't want me to stay?" he asked.

"No, because I've got a super early morning, and you tend to keep me up all night."

He grinned. "I can be on my best behavior."

I narrowed my eyes at him playfully. "Nah, I don't trust you to keep that promise."

He shrugged. "Just as well. I don't really trust myself either, to be honest." He interlaced our fingers and kissed the back of my hand. "I had fun today."

"Yeah, me too. I have to say, you were really good with that whole 'big house, white picket fence' description." I felt my heart grow just remembering it.

Julian barked out a laugh. "I can't even believe that myself. I managed to make that up on the spot."

My heart shrank instantly.

"It was bizarre," he continued. "I never think about the future in the first place."

Crap, why had I thought he'd meant it? And why was I feeling so disappointed that it had all been make-believe?

Probably because I'd loved what he'd described. I could see myself at his side forever.

But clearly, he didn't.

"Wait, I'll walk you," he said as I opened the car door.

I waved my hand. "Not necessary."

"I can be on my best behavior if I don't get inside the house."

"Somehow I don't believe that either," I murmured. I suddenly wanted to be alone.

"All right, then. I'll stay here and ogle you until you get inside."

I laughed before I got out of the car, darting toward my entrance with quick steps. I could feel him watching me. Once I unlocked the door and pushed it open, I glanced over my shoulder.

"My offer still stands," he called out.

"No chance," I replied before ducking in and leaning against the door.

Oh goodness, the evening had been a doozy. The only good part of it had been Julian so enthusiastically describing our hypothetical future house.

The bad part was that none of it had been real.

CHAPTER THIRTY

JULIAN

The next morning, I felt like I was on top of the world. I headed into the Quarter, where the LeBlanc-Broussard building was located. Our legal team was there, and I wanted them to immediately start working on the contracts with Robert and officially make him the offer so he wouldn't be tempted to pull back.

As soon as I went up, my phone pinged. It was my assistant. Just as well, as I wanted to tell her I wasn't coming into my office above the bar today.

"Good morning," I said as I stepped into the office I used here. Since I wasn't here all that often, it didn't really feel like mine. "Listen, I meant to tell you, I won't be coming in today. I'm at the LeBlanc-Broussard headquarters."

"Right. So, um, what happened at the Landry party?"

I blinked, leaning against my desk and looking out the window, frowning. "What are you talking about?" I wasn't even aware that I'd specifically told her I went to the Landry party. "Aside from the fact that I convinced Robert to sell to me?"

"That's great. Congrats."

"But that's not what you were referring to," I surmised from her surprise.

"No, it's just that we've had a call this morning from the Tableau family. They're asking if we've actually had any issues with Georgie and her work."

"Excuse me?"

"I was shocked. They said that Kyle Deveraux had told them that some of her clients had complained. I guess they were trying to find out what clients those were. Honestly, it was a bit bizarre. I don't know what's going on."

"I think I do," I replied through gritted teeth. Kyle was starting a smear campaign against Georgie. *That motherfucker.* "Thank you for telling me this. I'll take care of it."

"What do I tell the Tableaus?"

"That Deveraux is a fucking liar. He's trying to spread these rumors because he doesn't like that Georgie put him on the spot in front of everyone at the Landry party."

"Good for her. I've never liked him. Thank goodness someone's finally taking him down a peg."

"And I will do the rest," I assured her.

"I'll call them back immediately and let them know, but in a more polite manner."

"Yes, of course." We had to remain professional, after all. But my thoughts were anything but.

After hanging up, I stared out the window some more. I wasn't prone to gazing off and being unproductive, and even less so when I was preparing to make an acquisition. I made a quick call to our legal department, letting them know about the next steps, but that was the most I could focus on. Deveraux was still front and center in my mind.

The guy needed to be taught a lesson, because he wasn't going to stop. He hated losing, and he'd lost Robert's buildings and, to top it off, was humiliated by Georgie at the Landry party.

There was only one thing to do—call Xander. This was one of those times that I wished he had an office here too. It would make things easier, but he answered after the first ring.

"Hey," he greeted.

"Hi, Xander. Thanks for picking up."

"You're early today," he replied. "Is it because you got Robert's property?"

"News travels fast," I said.

"The important news does, yes. "

"That's not what I'm calling."

"Then why?"

"How much do you know about the swindling Kyle Deveraux did last year?"

"A lot. I've researched that in detail because I wanted to make sure we weren't caught up in it."

"Do you have any documentation to prove it?"

"What do you have in mind?" Xander asked.

"I'll need that documentation."

"That's not how I work, brother. I need the details."

"This is not the time for it." I wasn't in the mood for a lengthy conversation.

"You're asking me to hand you confidential information. Of course I need to know what you want to do with it."

When he put it like that... "I want to make everyone aware of Kyle's swindling. Absolutely everyone."

Xander whistled loudly. "Damn, you truly don't like him. Is it because of Georgie?"

"Fuck yes, it is. He's trying to make her lose clients again by spreading lies that some of them are unhappy with her work."

"What the hell?" I was proud of my brother's indignation on behalf of my woman. "That fucker."

"My thoughts exactly." I paced the office, already forming a plan in my mind.

"Some people will be pissed off about this. No one likes to look the fool, even if Deveraux swindled them."

"We can do this carefully. We don't have to reveal names. We can simply track his funds, see where all that money went."

"I'm starting to like this. I need more details."

"Xander!" I was infuriated now. "I don't have them. I'm making them up as I go."

"See, that's not how this will work. I need a solid plan."

"You want to create a PowerPoint out of it?"

"That wouldn't be a bad idea."

I groaned. "I was joking."

"I know. But I think there's a way we can do this. I'm sure Anthony, Beckett, and Zachary can help."

"You've lost me. How, exactly? What do we even need their help with if you have the documentation?"

"Our younger brothers have skills we don't," Xander said.

"I'm going to sound like you now, but care to expand on that?"

"They'll know how to find out exactly where Kyle transferred the money. And also how to let people know without revealing that the information came from us."

"You sound like you're in a James Bond movie," I countered. I wanted to tease him some more, but I knew he was right.

"All right," Xander said. "I'm going to talk to our brothers. Do you need me to look at the documentation for your acquisition of Robert's bar?"

"If you have time, sure."

"This is family business. Of course I have time."

"Thanks, brother." I trusted our legal and finance team, of course, but Xander was simply better at everything. "We'll stay in touch."

After hanging up, I felt so full of energy that it was insane. I had half a mind to talk to my brothers right now. But since Xander wanted to do it, there was no point.

I checked my emails for news from the legal team. They wanted to meet in the afternoon. I grinned—served me right. Why would I assume they'd just be able to do this at the drop of a hat? I was impulsive, and I'd trained the people working directly with me on a day-to-day basis to accommodate that. But the legal team was handling everything for the entire Orleans Conglomerate, not just my stuff.

It made no sense for me to stay here until the afternoon, so I called Georgie as I walked down the stairs to the ground floor. It wasn't anywhere near noon, but I could drop by for coffee.

"Hey!" I greeted. "You busy right now?

"Not that much. I have a bit of a lull, so I'm working on checking in the next batch of book boxes."

I was so proud of my woman. She had a very solid business mind.

"Listen, I'm not sure if you heard, but Kyle is—"

"Spreading some rumors."

"So you know."

She sighed. "Yes. I got a call from Calliope today. I had a lengthy conversation with her. When I told her everything that went down between me and Kyle, she quickly understood his incentive to spread lies."

"Don't worry. Soon everyone will know what a scumbag he is."

"How do you mean?"

"Xander and I will show everyone that he's a stealing bastard."

"Julian, you don't have to do that on my behalf."

"It's not just on your behalf, though it'll ensure that he never bothers you again. He's a menace to everyone. And it's time someone made it known what they're dealing with. Want me to drop by with a coffee?"

"Um... no."

"You sound off. Something wrong?" I asked as I reached the foot of the staircase and took the employee exit toward the back. The narrow side street was relatively empty at this time of day.

"I don't know."

I was confused. She stayed silent. "Georgie, talk to me." I was certain something was wrong. I just didn't know what. "Georgie, you're worrying me. You can tell me anything. You know that, right?"

She cleared her throat but still didn't say anything.

"I'm coming to the store."

"No, no. Maybe it's easier to say this on the phone."

I stopped in my tracks just as I was about to step onto Royal and leaned against a brick wall. It sounded serious. "I'm listening."

"It's just that... yesterday at the party, when you told Robert all those things about the future and our house..." *Why is she bringing that up?* "It all felt so real."

That was a bad thing? It was supposed to sound real.

"I guess I got my hopes up," she said quietly.

I was starting to understand what she meant. "Georgie—"

"No, just please let me finish. Otherwise, I might lose my nerve."

"Sure. Sorry. Go ahead."

"And then, when you said that you just made it all up and you're not envisioning anything close to that in the future, I realized that... well, if our visions of the future differ so much, maybe I should reevaluate some things. You, too, I guess."

I swallowed hard. To my intense dismay, I was speechless. I'd never had a raw conversation like this my whole life.

I was so out of my depth that I had no idea what to say. Not even how to reassure her. Ultimately, I went with "Georgie, it was not my intention to hurt you. I'm sorry."

"I know. You've been nothing short of amazing to me, but this isn't just about what we're doing now. I mean, it's great, but if I keep falling for you and getting my hopes up, it's not... I can't let my heart be broken again."

"Fuck this. I'm coming to the store. We need to talk about this."

"No! I wouldn't know what to tell you," she said hurriedly. "I'm sorry. I don't have things clear in my mind either. I'm just telling you how I feel."

"Thanks for being honest. You can always share what weighs on you with me," I reassured her. I was of half a mind to go to her store anyway, but she'd explicitly asked me not to, and I needed to respect that.

"Listen, I have some customers." I'd heard the bell chime a few times, so I knew she wasn't making up an excuse. "We'll talk later, all right?"

"Sure."

I groaned as the line disconnected. *Damn! Talk about a fuckup.* I wasn't even sure what just happened.

I stumbled down onto Royal, needing a coffee, so I headed to Maria's shop. I was still deep in thought, mulling over Georgie's words. I couldn't believe I'd hurt her and hadn't even realized it. I needed to fix it.

There were already a few customers inside the coffee shop when I stepped in, and I patiently waited my turn.

Maria kept throwing me suspicious looks as she took care of the other customers. Then when my turn came, she asked, "Two coffees to go?"

"Just one."

"Hmm, don't want to surprise the Mrs. this morning?"

"Just one."

"Actually, do you mind taking two coffees over to your grandmothers' store? They called and said they'd love some coffee but will drop by later. They're very busy." Maria spoke quickly, averting her gaze.

Strange.

"Sure, I'll take their coffees to them, then."

I wasn't feeling like going into the office at all, so it gave me a good excuse to postpone. I needed to be out and about, to think over this matter with Georgie.

I was expecting Maria to prod me with some more questions. Maybe she even knew about the Landry party. But she didn't say anything at all.

"All right, here you go," she said as soon as she put all three in a cupholder. "I'll call them to let them know you're on your way."

"I don't think that's necessary."

She darted her eyes away from me with a noncommittal hum.

She was definitely acting strange, but I didn't have the brainpower to focus on it because I needed to focus on Georgie.

I wanted to understand what was happening and how I could fix it. This woman's happiness was everything to me, and I couldn't believe that she was unhappy right now because of me.

I arrived on Dumaine quickly. There wasn't much foot traffic at this time, which made me wonder if my grandmothers had a group of tourists. Why else would they be so busy that they couldn't grab a coffee?

Their store was completely empty when I arrived. Isabeau was in the doorway. "Come in, dear boy. Maria told us you were stopping by."

"She asked me to bring your coffees."

I put the holder on the counter. Both Celine and I grabbed a cup.

"She actually said you didn't have time because you were busy. I assumed you had a group."

Celine looked at Isabeau. "Yeah, about that. Maria made it up."

I nearly spit out my coffee. "What?" I glanced at Isabeau, who'd shut the door and actually put the sign to Closed.

What is going on?

"I think Maria's exact words were 'I know what someone who is in *very deep love troubles* looks like,'" Isabeau said.

I jerked my head back. "She actually said that?"

"Yes. She also figured that you might need us."

How is everyone such a busybody? I took another sip of coffee, steeling myself for this conversation.

Isabeau walked from the door to join us, leaning against the counter. "Dear boy, I've always lived by a certain rule. Troubles seem smaller when you share them with others."

"Oh, Isabeau," Celine chastised. "Maybe Maria was overreacting."

Isabeau looked at me intently. "No, she wasn't."

Celine sighed, drinking her coffee. "I'm sorry, my poor boy. I tried. But if you don't want to share anything with us, that's perfectly fine too."

I nearly laughed at Isabeau's expression. Her eyebrows were in the middle of her forehead. Clearly, she disagreed with that.

I took yet another sip of coffee. I wasn't really pissed off. In fact, if there was ever a moment when I needed a sounding board, it was right now. I was never too proud to admit that I was out of my depth.

"Georgie and I started this, our relationship, as a ruse," I said slowly.

Isabeau smiled sardonically. "That's debatable. I'm not sure we ever thought that."

"Most people thought we were a couple before we actually became one, including Robert."

"We heard you bought his buildings, by the way. Congratulations."

I had to tell Xander that he didn't need to worry about spreading the news about Kyle. The French Quarter would do its thing one way or another.

"During the conversation with Robert, he assumed Georgie and I were already making plans for the future. I made a big deal about how we had envisioned a huge house with a white picket fence and everything."

Isabeau frowned. "But that doesn't sound bad at all."

I swallowed hard.

Celine closed her eyes. She was a bit like Mom—they both had strong intuitions.

"Yeah, but that's the thing. I didn't really mean it, which I told Georgie last night before dropping her off at home." Now that I'd said it out loud, the conversation came back to me. Replaying it bit by bit, I realized how cold that sounded.

"Oh, Julian," Celine said.

Isabeau just pressed her lips together, which was a sure sign that she thought I'd completely fucked up.

"She's upset." I didn't want to give them more details.

"I can understand that," Isabeau said finally.

"She also said that she needs to reevaluate things because she might be falling for me and doesn't want to get hurt."

"What did you say?" Celine asked.

"Not much," I admitted.

Isabeau put a hand on her chest. "Julian, I thought you cared for this girl."

"I do! A lot."

"When a woman goes out on a limb to tell you how she feels, she usually hopes you're going to reassure her and reciprocate," Celine said quietly.

"Fuck," I exclaimed. Neither of them even winced at my use of profanity, something they always chastised us about.

"That sums it up."

"I was so shocked by the whole turn of the conversation that I wasn't thinking straight," I said.

"Sounds about right," Celine said. "So, you do reciprocate?"

"I care about her so fucking much. I didn't realize she was... How the hell did I miss it?"

"Word has it that you were planning how to expose Kyle Deveraux. There are only so many things people can focus on at once, I suppose."

"You spoke to Xander?" I asked.

"Briefly, but let's talk about you and Georgie," Isabeau replied.

"Yeah, let's not." I looked from one to the other, already making a plan.

Oh, screw this. I was never good at making plans.

"How quickly can you make custom fragrances?"

Both of them straightened up, rolling their shoulders. "Very fast. Why? What do you need?" Isabeau asked.

"I need something that says, 'I'm sorry. I love you, and I want you to be mine forever.' How fast can you do that?"

Chapter Thirty-One

Georgie

I was starting to love the offseason. I'd missed selling books. Something strange happened during the Carnival season. People seemed to forget the books part of the store. Truth be told, so did I, because almost no one walked in to buy them. Everyone was too focused on the beads and other Carnival items.

But I'd gotten a new delivery today. My "Surprise Book Boxes" had been a success in the past, so I thought I'd try them again.

Customers came in, told me what they usually read, and also what kind of TV shows they usually watched, and I made a box with twelve books pertaining to their interests. So far, I had a perfect track record—zero complaints. Before starting it, I'd been terrified that I would get too many returns, but that hadn't been the case. Today, I'd sold a record number of thirteen boxes. I was over the moon.

If only my heart weren't so heavy. I'd kind of hoped that Julian would call me again sometime in the afternoon, but he hadn't. I'd probably been too honest and scared him away, but I didn't want to hide anything from him. I realized now that I'd been hoping deep down that he would tell me it had just been a figure of speech, and of course he saw a future together for us. But that hadn't happened.

Then again, it was unfair of me to hold him to that. He and I had been so caught up living in the moment that we never even discussed the future.

Georgie, always count your blessings, I reminded myself. I had a man who spoiled me rotten. At least I hoped I still had him. And if not, I had some really, really good memories to look back on.

My store was doing a lot better than I'd expected for the lull after Mardi Gras. My clients trusted me enough to actually call me when they heard the nasty things Kyle was spreading about me. Everything was going perfectly. I had many things to be grateful for.

I was about to go in the back when the front door opened and the bells chimed.

"We're closed," I yelled, then turned around. "Oh! Hi, Julian."

"Hey." He flashed me his trademark lazy smile. Was I imagining it, or was it a bit more reserved than usual?

"I was about to lock up," I said nervously.

He stood by the doorway for a bit before taking a few steps inside the store. "I've wanted to come here quite a few times today."

My heart grew a bit lighter at his words. "You did?"

He came even closer. I wanted to round the corner and meet him in the middle just to feel him near.

"But you specifically said not to, and I figured waiting was better. Now we get the place all to ourselves."

I stayed put, taking a deep breath. I exhaled in relief when Julian walked up to me.

"I apologize for the way I reacted this morning. I apologize for last night too. I didn't realize how callous I sounded."

I shrugged, looking down at my feet. "It wasn't callous, just not what I wanted to hear."

He touched my jaw with the back of his fingers. "What was it that you wanted to hear?"

I shook my head. "I don't know," I whispered. The truth was that I simply wasn't ready to open up my heart like that again. I already felt far too vulnerable.

"Then I'm going to tell you what I should've said. How I really feel. I love you, Georgie."

I glanced up so quickly that he had to pull back. I'd been millimeters away from bumping my forehead into his nose.

"I love you so fucking much. I should've told you that a while ago, but..."

"Things have been moving too fast," I finished for him. I was smiling with my entire face.

And would you look at that? My heart was no longer heavy.

"When you were at my house, I realized how strongly I feel about you. I simply didn't want to let you go."

"Watching me puke made you reach that conclusion?" I giggled.

"I liked taking care of you, Georgie. I want to do it forever. I liked having you there: in my bed, in my house, on the patio, you smiling in the sun. All I could think about after you left was how to lure you back in. This isn't my forte. It has never been. I honestly never thought I'd want to be in a relationship. But now I'm thinking my grandmothers were right. That I simply hadn't met *you*. And now that I've found you, Georgie, no way in hell am I letting you go."

I narrowed my brows. "Wait, your grandmothers know? What do they have to do with us?"

"Long story. I don't want to get into it right now. Let's just say that they did give great advice. And," he said, reaching into the pocket of his pants, "I also brought you this."

I immediately took the bottle from him. "Is this a refill? I've been meaning to ask for one." I uncapped the little dark red container and sniffed it. It wasn't my perfume, but it was the most delicious thing I'd ever come across. This one was light and seductive at the same time. It was fresh but also had a certain gravitas that I loved.

"This is heavenly."

I opened my eyes. Julian was looking at me intently. He took the bottle, put it on the counter, and then grabbed my hands, bringing them to his mouth.

"It's supposed to say, 'I love you, and I want you to be mine forever.'"

I swallowed hard, my eyes burning a little. I couldn't start crying when this man was declaring himself so beautifully. "It definitely, definitely says that."

"Good."

Then he lowered my hands and kissed one corner of my mouth. Heat shot between my thighs. He kissed the other corner of my mouth, and now the tips of my breasts were on fire. I was extra susceptible to this sexy man right now.

I sighed and Julian groaned. He put a hand at the small of my back, pulling me against him. And then he kissed me so hard that I couldn't restrain myself and moaned against his lips.

I pulled my head back slightly. "Julian, " I whispered. "People can see from the streets."

"Then let's go in the back," he said between growls.

I had absolutely nothing against that.

The way my body was acting, there was no way we could make it out of the store. But I couldn't even make it to the back. Instead, I rose on my tiptoes and literally attacked my man right here in my store for the whole street to see. He took me in his arms, hands gripping my ass, and headed with me to the back.

I clicked off one of the light switches on the way so the front of the store was pitch-black.

───────────

Julian

We moved into one of the rooms in the back where there wasn't much except a mirror, some chairs, and a table. Boxes were stacked in one corner. There was a thick carpet in front of the mirror.

Georgie's skin was exquisitely soft to the touch. I stroked her arms with the back of my fingers, moving my hands up and down slowly. Her skin turned to goose bumps. I was savoring every reaction, every huff of breath, every sharp inhale.

This moment right here was more special than any time we'd been together before. I felt closer to her now than I ever had. When she stilled, I knew she was ready for more. I tilted forward, kissing a line from her earlobe to the corner of her mouth. She parted her lips slightly, but I didn't kiss her. Instead, I moved my lips to the other corner of her mouth and then traced up a line to her earlobe.

"I want you so much, you have no idea."

I lowered my mouth to her neck. She tilted her head backward on instinct, making it easier for me to explore her.

"I'm going to keep you right here forever so I can do all the things I want to you."

"I'm not complaining," she whispered.

But now I needed to feel even closer. I straightened up after reaching her clavicle and captured her mouth. She was resting her forearms on my chest, and I could feel the moment she went from taut to relaxed in my grasp. She was so on edge that even a simple kiss provided her relief. I grabbed her dress by the middle, tugging it upward. It went easily, thank fuck, because I was already so desperate to explore her that I couldn't pay attention to what I was doing. I was acting on instinct.

I paused the kiss, stepping back.

She held up her arms, and I immediately pushed the dress higher. It got caught on her bra, but I freed it easily enough.

Once it was over her head, I found she was staring at my own shirt. It was easier to get rid of that. The fucking pants were always more work, and I didn't want to pause touching or kissing her for that long. So I placed my mouth on her shoulder, teasing it by drawing small circles with my tongue while I took care of my belt and zipper. I dropped my pants and boxers and kicked them off as soon as possible.

"This is a record," she whispered as I lowered myself to my knees so I could kiss down her body. "You got completely naked faster than me."

"I wanted nothing between us," I groaned against her skin. "Don't worry. I'll take everything off you too."

I stopped shortly above the hem of her slip, moving my mouth lazily as I'd done on her shoulder from one side to the other. I gave her my tongue, too, and felt the way her abs contracted more.

"Julian," she whispered.

My name in her mouth was a plea. I pushed her panties to one side. Fuck me, she was so damn slick. I knew she was wet but had never imagined she was so drenched.

She was looking down intently, trying to anticipate my next move. Maintaining eye contact, I pushed two fingers inside her. She jerked her hips backward and then forward while crying out, her eyes wide and unfocused.

Fuck. Watching her come undone fueled my need even more. I grabbed my cock, pumping up and down. Her eyes widened even more.

I motioned to the mirror. "Look there."

Watching her profile in the mirror while I worked my own cock was almost too much for me. It definitely *was* too much for her, because she coated my fingers even more.

"Watching turns you on, doesn't it?"

"Yes," she whispered.

My woman was naughty, and I liked that a lot.

I could pleasure her with her panties moved to one side like this, but I always wanted to be able to put my mouth on her clit too.

Taking out my hand, I commanded, "Take them off now. Quickly."

"Julian," she whimpered.

"I know you need my fingers, gorgeous. I'll give them to you right away. I'll give you everything. Everything that pussy needs, it will get."

She gasped as she stepped out of the panties and then resumed her position. I pressed my fingers on her opening before sliding them inside her again, and she moaned.

I squeezed my cock even tighter at the sound.

"Look in the mirror," I commanded.

She was already trembling lightly, but she turned her head.

"Look at me putting my mouth on you while you feel my fingers inside you."

"You're touching yourself," she whispered. "That's so sexy."

When I swiped my fingers over her clit, she gasped and jerked her chest forward, clenching around my fingers so tight that I couldn't move them anymore. Then the tightness released a bit, but that was okay. I didn't need to move my fingers to make her come. I curled them slightly while I started to suck on her breast.

"Julian... Julian..."

Every time she called my name, I squeezed my cock tighter. Fuck, I wanted her mouth on me. I needed it just as much as I needed my next breath. And I wanted that right now.

So I pulled her down on the carpet. "You are fucking gorgeous. Take my cock in your mouth."

She moved fast, and that turned me on even more. I positioned us so I was lying on the carpet and she was on top of me.

This was perfect. Her clit was right over my mouth *and* I could move my hand freely inside her.

Then I felt her tongue on the tip of my cock. She pressed the flat of it against me, licking while holding one hand at the base. I momentarily lost all sense of myself. But then I moved my tongue against her clit the exact same way she licked my cock, and she groaned loudly. This was turning both of us on even more than I'd anticipated. When she lowered her mouth on my cock, I knew it was time for her to come.

I curled my fingers once more. I knew her body well enough, what she needed. She didn't need me to nip at her clit right now, no. While I curled my fingers, touching her G-spot, I circled her clit with the tip of my tongue. She came with my cock in her mouth. The experience was absolutely surreal. Because her body was over mine, I felt every vibration coursing through her, starting from her center and traveling up her belly and breasts. I felt it through her mouth, too, forming a cycle of tension and release. I relentlessly licked her clit and curled my fingers inside her until she was trembling in earnest. Then she slowly started to calm down, though her muscles were still spasming. With my free hand, I grabbed her ass.

"Julian." She let go of my cock, taking in a deep breath. "Julian, oh!"

I sucked her clit into my mouth, and her body convulsed once again. Her ass cheeks tightened. Then she went completely limp.

"Turn around, Georgie."

Even though she'd seemed spent a few seconds earlier, I felt her body tense up once more. She needed my cock.

She moved on all fours around me until her face was level with mine. She had a huge smile.

I motioned with my head to the left. "You can watch us in the mirror."

Licking her lips, she turned her head slightly and frowned. "Why do I like this so much?"

"Enjoy it, babe."

I grabbed her ass with both hands, lowering her onto my cock. After having her mouth on me, I was already on fire. I watched her in the mirror as she closed her eyes and moved her shoulders in a jerking manner. Then she dropped her head back. A groan reverberated through her whole body once more as I buried myself balls deep inside her.

Every time we were together, everything felt more intense. But nothing, *nothing* compared to this. I felt the pleasure take over every cell of my body. She started rolling her hips with her head still tilted backward. She looked like a vision, and I couldn't get enough of her. But I also wanted far more friction, so I started to move too. I grabbed her hips and shifted her on top of me while I also rolled mine under her. I was pressing my pelvis against her clit every time, but I knew she would need more than that to come again.

"Touch your clit with one hand and your breast with the other. Circle your nipple and your clit the same way."

"Now?" she whispered. "I'm going to explode if I do that."

"That's exactly what I want, beautiful. To watch you explode while my cock is buried deep inside you."

She tentatively put one hand on her breast and the other on her pussy. She moved her fingers in a circling motion over her clit right away, but it took her a few seconds to do the same on her nipple.

It had precisely the effect I wanted. Her eyes shot wide open, and she squeezed me so tight that if I were in any other position except under her, she would've pushed me out. My woman was coming, and I could watch her all I wanted by looking straight at her and in the mirror.

Her mouth formed a huge O, but no sound came out. The rest of her body was like a live wire. She undulated on top of me. She took her hand off her clit, crying out, and grabbed her other breast as well.

I briefly glanced at her in the mirror. Fuck yes, her back was arched. But then I watched her directly because I wanted to look at her face. She was always beautiful, but even more so when she was overwhelmed by the sensations I was giving her.

The tension inside me spiraled. Pleasure moved over me in a tidal wave, gripping me completely. I shut my eyelids to process everything. But even as my own groans filled the room, I was still aware of her, the way she felt on top of me, the furious way in which she moved, and the delicious sounds she made. I drank everything in.

When I knew she'd ridden out her orgasm, I pulled her lightly to me so she was lying on my chest, my cock still deep inside her. I turned my head sideways, watching us in the mirror.

I'd please her just like this every single day—multiple times a day, if I could.

Forever.

Chapter Thirty-Two

Georgie

Four months later

I closed my eyes in the morning sunlight, enjoying the way the rays felt on my skin. The sun was still strong at the end of summer, but mornings like this were absolutely perfect. It was completely silent in Julian's inner courtyard except for a few birds chirping. I'd been spending most of my evenings here at his house.

"I don't think I'll ever tire of watching you enjoy mornings."

I opened one eye and glanced sideways to where Julian was. "It's my favorite part of the day," I admitted.

"Mine too."

"But you never join me here."

"No, but I like watching you."

Oh goodness, he's watched me every morning? How did I not catch on to that?

Julian came up to me with a smile, which was when I realized he was holding something behind his back. I tried to look past him, but he kept moving around so I couldn't. "What are you hiding?"

"A surprise." Then he put a beautiful blue box on the table. It had no logo, nothing to hint at what it was.

I immediately took off the lid. There was a key inside with a bow. My entire body tingled. I knew it was a key to the house.

He towered over me when he gathered me from behind, putting a hand on my waist and kissing my earlobe. "I wanted to make it official that we live together."

"Oh, Julian," I whispered, "are you sure?"

"Yes. Fuck yes. I've wanted you here ever since you spent that first night with me."

I laughed because honestly, I was just trying to block that first night out of my memory. He kept bringing it up like it had been super romantic, but I knew it had been anything but. "Thank you. I'd love to officially move in here with you." This house was hands down my favorite place to be except perhaps Books & Beads.

When I tugged at the key, I realized the bow was tied to the bottom of the box, which came up a bit. "Oh no, I think I'm ruining the box."

"Or there's something else under the bottom."

I pulled at the key, and indeed the bottom of the box came off, revealing something gorgeous. I gasped, then felt Julian move around me as I straightened up on the chair.

There was a ring inside.

Glancing to my right, I saw that Julian was already down on one knee, watching me with an enormous smile. I licked my lips and opened them to speak, yet no words came out.

"Georgie, I love you with everything I have and everything I am. You mean the world to me. What we have together is..." His voice shook, but he interlaced the fingers of my left hand with the ones of his right. "It's the most beautiful thing that has ever happened to me."

He took the ring out of the box and held it in front of my left ring finger.

"I'd love for you to be with me forever. To be my wife, the mother of my children, to build a life with me. Would you do me the honor?"

I took in a deep breath and opened my mouth again, hoping I could reply this time. No such luck, so I simply nodded as eagerly as I could.

Then Julian slid on the ring. "Fuck, is it the right hand or the left one?"

I burst out laughing. "I don't know." Tears were streaming down my face.

He pulled me up from the chair at the same time that he rose to his feet. Then he lifted me onto the small table. I placed my arms on his shoulders, and he kissed me deeply. I swear my entire body vibrated. I felt this immense love he had for me like a physical force.

I kissed him back feverishly, moving my hands from his shoulders down to his chest, then even farther down to his abs, until I reached his belt. Then I slid my fingers under his shirt, touching his delicious muscles, tracing his abs until he groaned.

I looked down at my ring and then glanced sideways on the table at where the key was. This was the best day ever, hands down.

He brought his mouth to my ear. "I want us to stay right here at the house all day."

"What a coincidence. So do I."

"I want to do so many things to you."

"Then what are you waiting for?"

My heart gave a mighty sigh as he smiled down at me. My team was handling the store this Sunday morning. I'd intended to drop by in the afternoon, but if my sexy man had sexy plans for me, I was more than happy to forgo my own.

I was surprised we weren't meeting his family today. They called us to the mansion most weekends. These past few months had been so amazing, not only with Julian but getting to know his family as well. I liked all of the LeBlanc brothers, but Xander was probably my favorite. He'd played a big role in taking Kyle down after he started trying to

sabotage me with my clients. When Julian first told me that he'd em-
bezzled money from clients, I'd thought he might be blowing things out
of proportion. Turned out, he wasn't. Xander was a very good financial
detective. Then again, the whole thing had been a group effort between
the brothers. Kyle had somehow narrowly escaped prosecution, frus-
tratingly, but he and his brother skipped town without a penny. His
father took over the company, selling off some of the assets.

And of course, Julian snapped up his location on Bourbon. I was
extremely proud of my man for that. And I was so grateful to him.
Feeling that he had my back was absolutely amazing. In fact, the feeling
that all of the LeBlancs supported me in one way or another was more
than I could ever have hoped for.

My whole life, it had been just Mom, Nana, and me. We didn't have
an extended family. And now we did. My mom had attended a few
family events, and she'd enjoyed herself quite a bit. I'd been feeling a
little guilty for not telling her about my relationship with Julian from
the get-go, but she assured me that she knew exactly where this was
going from the short talk she'd had with him before the first party we
attended.

Julian took me in his arms, making me laugh. I immediately put an
arm around his shoulders and relaxed against him.

"You do like carrying me, huh?"

"Hell yes, babe." He brought his mouth to my ear. "I've liked it since
that evening when I carried you into the house. I wanted to take you in
my arms even at the party from the second you hurt your ankle."

"Damn, you're always wanting to feel me up, huh?"

"And I make no apologies for that."

He continued to speak in my ear as he went up the staircase to the
master bedroom. Feeling the tip of his nose on my neck made the hair
on my nape stand on end.

"I knew I wanted you to be mine, Georgie. Only mine."

"That first kiss was that good, huh?" I teased as we reached the upper level.

He took me straight to the bed, laying me on it. All the windows were open, and jazz music was filtering in from the Quarter. Usually there was a cacophony of sounds because more than one artist played at any one time except in the early mornings. Then you had just an odd one here and there. This one was playing something very slow and romantic. I didn't know the name of it, but I loved it, and it fit this moment perfectly.

Julian put a knee on the bed, leaning in slightly and touching my jaw with the backs of his fingers.

"That kiss. It changed everything." His eyes flashed.

"Is that so?"

"Yes. I felt it in a way I couldn't explain." He laughed, shrugging. "I can't even explain it now, but it was one of those moments that sort of splits everything in two—before that kiss and after it. I thought that if I kissed you, it would be enough, but it was exactly the opposite. I simply wanted more."

He pushed me even farther to the center of the bed—and then someone whistled from down the street, which startled us both.

"Yeah, maybe you should close the window. Judging by that hot look in your eyes, I can guess the plans you've got, and... well, I might be loud," I sassed.

He didn't take his eyes off me as he went to the window, closing it and then returning with quick steps.

This time, when he lay over me on the bed, I didn't stop him. I just pulled him even closer.

Epilogue

Georgie

*O*ne month later

I loved September in New Orleans. Then again, I loved every season, but there was always something magical about September. The kids were back in school, everyone was back from vacation, the hot summer days were behind us, and the time came again to stay indoors, snuggled up with a good book. It was a very good sales month for my books. My team and I were busy bees again, already preparing merchandise for the floats for the next Carnival season.

"We should get going," I said as Julian kissed my neck. We were meeting the entire family for lunch at LeBlanc & Broussard, and I didn't want to be late.

"I've changed my mind. I should tell my family to stop planning stuff on weekends when I have other plans for us."

I giggled because his breath tickled me. "We'll come back from brunch eventually," I teased. "Just keep all those ideas for later."

He growled in my ear, and a tingle went through me. "Right. Now let's go before I lose myself in you completely."

"By the way, do you want us to tell the family today that we set a date?" I asked him.

"Yeah, I think that will make them very happy."

He opened the door, and we stepped out onto the street.

There was already some commotion. Then again, it was almost eleven o'clock.

"Hey, you two!" Xander's voice came from somewhere behind as we turned onto Royal Street.

"Hey," I greeted.

"What are you doing around here?" Julian asked him.

Xander held up a bag from Café Du Monde. "I bought beignets for Bella."

Julian threw his head back, laughing. "You're good, I'll give you that. I didn't even think about it."

"Won't there be a ton of food at the restaurant anyway?" I asked.

Xander grinned at me. "Beignets are her favorite."

These LeBlanc brothers were something else entirely.

"You look tired," I said. "Working overtime again?"

"Babe," Julian said, "he always works overtime."

"I was at the office until eight yesterday."

My eyes bulged. "On a Friday? Sweet heavens."

"I've been running some of the financials of the Orleans Conglomerate. We're spread too thin in some areas. We should shut down some things, or at least properly finance them."

"Like what?" Julian asked.

"Like the pralines confectionery."

I gasped. "No!" I exclaimed. "Xander, they're the best pralines in the city."

"The whole operation is just bleeding money, though."

"Dude, word of warning," Julian said. "Don't even think about it. And whatever you do, don't mention it to the grandmothers. You know it's one of their pet projects."

Xander shrugged. "I wasn't going to bring it up today. But I will eventually."

"I don't think everything in the conglomerate needs to be profitable. And I know Bailey and her sister, Avery. They've come to the mansion a few times during the Christmas season at the open house event. They're really great." Julian had told me before that they managed that end of the business.

Xander shrugged again. "That's neither here nor there, really."

I looked at Julian pleadingly. "Please tell me this won't happen. I don't think the city can survive without LeBlanc & Broussard pralines."

He laughed, pulling me closer and kissing the side of my head as we arrived at the restaurant. "I make no promises. Xander has a mind of his own, and he's usually unstoppable."

"Damn right I am," Xander replied.

Hmm, our financial guru is a bit of a Grinch.

We entered the restaurant and headed straight to the huge table in the opposite corner from the entrance. The place was filling up nicely already even though it only opened two minutes ago.

The entire family was at the table. Bella noticed us first. Well, she noticed Xander and his bag of beignets. Her little face lit up, and it was the most adorable thing I'd ever seen.

"You're very good," I told him.

"I know," Xander replied as Bella came running to him.

"Are those for me?" she asked innocently, batting her eyelashes.

"Of course they are."

"Thank you, Uncle Xander." She took her bag, keeping it to her chest as if it was a prized possession. Then she headed back to the table.

As we all sat down, Julian cleared his throat. "By the way, we have some news. We want the wedding to be next June."

"Oh my goodness," Isabeau exclaimed. "Congratulations!"

"I can't believe another one of our grandsons is getting married," Celine added. She looked at me with so much affection that it warmed my heart. "We're so happy for the two of you."

"Thank you," Julian said.

I just nodded, too much emotion clogging my throat to reply.

"You were right," Bella told Isabeau. "When can I have the lilac perfume?"

The entire table burst out laughing.

Felix put a hand on her lower back and said, "Let's see how you get out of that one, darling. I told you that bragging about the lilac too much would come to bite you eventually."

"Nonsense," Isabeau said to him, then turned to her great-granddaughter. "Bella, darling, not until you're of age."

"Excuse me?" Chad said. "Shouldn't you consult with me whenever you do that?"

Bella turned to him, and by her expression, I knew she was going to give him a sassy reply. "No, she doesn't have to, Dad. Once I'm eighteen, I'm an adult. I won't need your permission."

The laughter around the table intensified, but Chad simply shook his head.

"What's the whole story behind the lilac in perfumes?" I asked, looking from Celine to Isabeau, who both seemed extremely glad that I was interested.

"Celine should tell it," Isabeau said. "After all, she's the one who started it all."

Celine rolled back her shoulders, smiling at me. "My Adele was upset before her prom that she didn't have anyone to go with."

Adele shook her head down the table from us. "I really didn't."

Julian just smiled in reply.

"I'd always dabbled in making fragrances," Celine continued. "I believe herbs and flowers have powers and that their scents encapsulate said powers. So I made her a custom perfume and included lilac."

"And guess who took her to prom," Remy said, putting an arm around his wife's shoulders. "It was love at first sight." He looked at his mother-in-law. "And I'm sorry, Celine, but I don't think it was your perfume."

Celine immediately frowned, crossing her arms over her chest. "You take that back, young man."

I barely stifled my laughter. It was truly comical to hear anyone call Remy "young man."

Scarlett leaned forward. "I'm sorry to say, Remy, but I do agree with Celine and Isabeau. I wholeheartedly believe that their perfumes have magic powers, not just the lilac but... the other one you made for me too."

A ripple of excitement went around the table. Bella looked like she was about to burst at the seams—and then she did. "I'm going to have a baby sister or brother!"

Chad started to laugh, as did Scarlett. Clearly, this was not how they'd planned to announce the pregnancy, but it was very cute nonetheless.

"Oh goodness. We're so happy!" Isabelle exclaimed. "This is such a fantastic day."

After everyone congratulated Chad, Scarlett, and Bella, I asked, "So, wait, what does your perfume have to do with it?"

"They made a special one for me last Christmas with ingredients that are known to boost fertility," Scarlett explained.

"Oh, that sounds so technical," Isabelle said. "But, well, it is the gist of it."

"Well, damn, the family's getting big fast," Xander said.

Zachary nodded. Anthony and Beckett were in deep talks with Bella, who was instructing them that even though there was going to be a baby in the family now, she still wanted to be spoiled. The guys were listening to her so intently, you'd think she was throwing a business pitch.

"Anyone else have such happy news?" Isabeau asked. She looked pointedly at Xander.

He squirmed in his chair. "Not exactly, but I do have news of another type."

Julian threw him a warning look, but Xander didn't heed it.

"I'm thinking of making some changes at the confectionery."

Isabelle blinked "Changes? How come?"

"I don't have a plan, but I'll share as soon as I do."

"Dude, why would you change anything? Avery and Bailey are doing such a great job," Zachary said.

"Does everyone know the sisters except me?" Xander asked.

There was a chorus of yeses around the table.

"We don't know them *well*," Anthony said, "but they're sassy."

"Yes," Beckett continued. "I wonder who's going to give Xander a harder time. My money's on Bailey."

The brothers went back and forth with guesses. Even Chad and Julian joined them. Xander was clearly not amused.

Oh, this man is a true grump.

Isabeau and Celine were having a different conversation altogether. I was close enough to know they were talking about their perfumes. And though I couldn't hear everything, they did mention both "Xander" and "lilac" in the same sentence.

Oh my, these next few months are going to be fun...

Dear Reader, this is the end of the book. For a full list of Layla Hagen's books, please visit laylahagen.com

Printed in Great Britain
by Amazon